DARK
MOTHER
EARTH

DARK MOTHER EARTH

KRISTIAN NOVAK

TRANSLATED BY ELLEN ELIAS-BURSAC

AMAZON **CROSSING**

Text copyright © 2013 by Kristian Novak
Translation copyright © 2020 by Ellen Elias-Bursac
All rights reserved.

Previously published as *Črna mati zemla* by Algoritam in Croatia in 2013. Translated from Croatian by Ellen Elias-Bursac. First published in English by Amazon Crossing in 2020.

Published by Amazon Crossing, Seattle

www.apub.com

Amazon, the Amazon logo, and Amazon Crossing are trademarks of Amazon.com, Inc., or its affiliates.

ISBN-13: 9781542016100 (hardcover)
ISBN-10: 154201610X (hardcover)
ISBN-13: 9781542093569 (paperback)
ISBN-10: 1542093562 (paperback)

Cover design by Kimberly Glyder

Printed in the United States of America

First edition

For my father

FOREWORD

There were eight suicides reported between mid-May and late June of 1991 in one Međimurje village on the south bank of the Mura. According to the official records and police reports, there was no hint of a link among the suicides. The 1991 census reported a total of twenty-one suicides in all of Međimurje (population 119,966)—one of the lowest regional rates anywhere in Croatia. The six-month death rate in the municipality of 2,500 residents wasn't significantly different from earlier or later rates, and so the series of suicides attracted little attention in the local and national media. The public was focused, of course, on the outbreak of war in Yugoslavia. It was becoming clear that the previously sporadic bursts of violence and mounting tensions would lead to clashes of far greater proportions, so something out on the farthest periphery of the country was unlikely to draw attention from the press. In addition, these events stayed out of public awareness because the people living in the affected village, though terrified (later statements suggest phenomena bordering on collective paranoia), were reluctant to share information about the mysterious events. The suicides were mentioned only twice in the news beyond brief death notices in the local paper, and even these appeared many months apart: in January 1997 during an episode of the talk show *Latinica*, about depression among war veterans; and, a year later, in the segment *A Little About Health* on Radio Sljeme's afternoon show. Both times the cluster of suicides was referred to as a statistical anomaly by psychologist Mario Torjanec, affiliated with the Zagreb Police Academy. In a scholarly article published in 2002 in the journal *Društvena istraživanja*, psychologist Darija Benci criticizes Torjanec's determination that this case was one of collective, or mass, suicide. Benci points out that the suicides were asynchronous, and there are no indications of the shared motive usually found in collective suicides, such as the People's Temple of 1978, when 918 members of an American religious cult died en masse after ingesting cyanide and other poisons.

Of the eight suicide victims, five were males between the ages of 24 and 54 (Mario Brezovec, 1967–1991; Zdravko Tenodi, 1957–1991; Mladen Krajčić, 1949–1991, Imbra Perčić, 1939–1991; Zvonko Horvat, 1937–1991), two were women, one aged 83 (Terezija Kunčec, 1908–1991) and one aged 29 (Milica Horvat, 1962–1991), and one was a boy who was not quite ten (Franjo Klanz, 1981–1991). Six of the suicides were by hanging, one by drowning, and one by slit wrists. Only one farewell note was found, from Zvonko Horvat, suggesting the terminal phase of a serious illness as a possible motive. The other suicides remain unexplained; none of the victims had a history of psychopathological behavior.

In July 2010, this series became the subject of a research project. Dr. Tena Miholjek-Lazanin from the Institute for Anthropological Research in Zagreb and Dr. Dubravka Perković from the Sociology Department of the Faculty of Humanities and Social Sciences at the University of Zagreb began collecting material as part of a ComRem (Community in Retrospective Laymen Explanatory Models) project along with twenty other institutions in Europe. The principal goal was to describe the collective aspects of the mechanisms of memory and how we explain phenomena to ourselves. Miholjek-Lazanin and Perković investigated how the people living in the village had created meaningful ways of explaining these inexplicable occurrences. The suicide cluster was well suited for this project because it had had a significant impact on every member of the community but had not undergone a significant recontextualization through public media, which might have distorted the community's formation of explanatory patterns. And furthermore, as the researchers noted, this community was, at the time of these strange events, functioning in "remarkable isolation."

By May 2011, 108 village residents across three generations had been interviewed: 37 third and fourth graders, 28 high school seniors, and 43 persons who had been between the ages of 27 and 35 at the time of the events. Only 5 of the subjects stated that the events had no impact on them, while 72 reported a notable degree of anxiety arising in their closest circle as a result of the suicides. Thirteen of the subjects mentioned "communal terror" in the village, or "collective paranoia," and 58 spoke of the "confusion" and "odd behavior" of many people in the village, especially after the last two suicides.

There was additional fear stemming from the fact that no one had a sense of when the suicides would stop. One subject said:

> To me, it seemed like we were all of us stricken, but nobody knew . . . nobody had any idea who would be taken by the disease, something would just snap inside and . . . they'd end it all. When one person took their life, the disease was theirs alone. When four people took their lives, the whole village was afflicted.

As many as thirty-five of the subjects invoked a similar model of infectious disease causing the afflicted person's mind to unhinge.

Research shows that there were six different ways, according to the subjects, that people in the community explained the suicides. In addition to rational, usually psychological, social, and physiological explanations, most of the subjects included elements of the supernatural. However, they ascribed the beliefs in supernatural causes to elderly residents of the village and generally distanced themselves from these beliefs.

In the subjects' narratives, the following explanations, which could be considered rational, were recorded by the researchers:

1. As many as eighty-four subjects say that sporadic acute melancholy and depression are characteristic of people living in upper Medimurje. Based on what the subjects say, this could be attributed to two things. First, they believed that depression and suicidal behavior occur more frequently in the areas between two rivers where groundwater pools and that during periods of heavy rain or drought this pooling may have a serious impact on mood. However, global research to date into the epidemiology of suicide has found no substantiation of this. The other possible cause the subjects offered is the fog off the Mura River on autumn and spring mornings, which lingers in the village sometimes through the afternoon during inclement weather. According to some village residents, this can cause behavioral changes.

2. The suicide victims were overcome by depression after workers were laid off from jobs in Slovenia. According to this explanation, the residents of the village feared further layoffs, unemployment, and problems arising from this. At the time, 176 village residents had been employed by Slovenian businesses, and three months before the suicides, twenty had been laid off. However, only one of the victims had been employed by a Slovenian company, and no one knew whether they were likely to be fired. The larger wave of layoffs of Croatian employees from Slovenian firms came later, in 1993, but it's possible fears had already been sparked by the worsening economic situation in the village.

3. Many of the subjects blame alcoholism for a number of problems, such as serious depression, and problematic behaviors. But none of the victims were described as consuming alcohol in excess.

4. A stranger, or even a village resident, went from one resident to another in secrecy and convinced them to kill themselves, or perhaps killed them and then arranged the scene so that it appeared as if the victims had killed themselves.

5. All the suicide victims were members of the Black Rose sect, a satanic cult that, during the 1980s, attracted an unknown number of followers in northern Croatia. When a cult member received a black rose in the mail, that person was obliged to commit suicide. Village residents may have come across this idea in the popular press, but there is no indication that these individuals were followers of this or any other sect.

6. Nineteen of the subjects say that after the second suicide, people wondered if there had been a homosexual relationship between the two deceased men and if they had made some sort of suicide pact. There is no indication of such a relationship between the first and second victims, Mario Brezovec and Zdravko Tenodi.

The next three explanatory models refer to supernatural elements.

1. The suicides were the work of ogres and fiends believed by older members of the community to dwell in the forests above the village. There is a legend about the undead

bodies of forest dwellers who were killed by the villagers in an ancient mythical battle. These ogres are condemned to languish in the woods until the end of time, and in return they curse the village. Seven of the subjects say this same explanation had been given for every major problem to beset the village, such as epidemics among livestock, a 1970s outbreak of downy mildew on the grapevines, and the great floods of 1962, 1983, and 1985.

2. Only Mario Brezovec, the first victim, had a "tangible" reason for suicide (nine subjects mention an unhappy love affair with a married woman as a possible motive), while the other suicides were caused by a spell Brezovec cast from the realm of the dead. There was a belief in the village that when someone takes their life they are relegated to a special part of hell, and from there they are able to compel the living to follow them. The only remedy is the burial of the suicide victims outside the graveyard or at a crossroads, as dictated by centuries-old custom. All eight victims were buried at the graveyard but without funeral rites, per the Code of Canon Law of the Catholic Church.

3. Eighty-six subjects mention a supposition that all eight suicides were caused, mysteriously, by M. D., a boy who was seven years old at the time. This belief sprang from the odd coincidence that the boy was associated with each of the eight victims in some way shortly before they took their lives. All subjects who offer this explanation say that the boy had begun manifesting troublesome behavior several years earlier, after the death of his father, and even attracted the attention of local people and social services. Most of the subjects remark that even being in

the presence of the boy made many villagers uneasy. After the last suicide, the boy's mother decided to move with her two children to Zagreb.

In early June 2011, a sizable manuscript arrived at the workplace of Dr. Dubravka Perković, signed by M. D. himself, describing the events that happened during his childhood. How he learned of the research project is not known, because, as he himself put it, he had severed all contact with his native village.

In the manuscript, he described in detail his state after his father's death, particularly that he held the conviction—common among children who lose a member of their immediate family—that he was to blame for his parent's passing. In his case, however, this belief assumed pathological proportions. He became certain that one can cause the death of a person merely by thought or in a momentary fit of rage. He was convinced of this while the suicides were occurring and believed he could not control his thoughts about some of the victims.

> *I was comforted by the thought that we all have wished death on someone. . . . This is the stuff we're made of, our blood. It happens to everyone that somebody threatens, dominates, humiliates, or takes advantage with no remorse or concern. For an instant, we wish they'd simply be gone. We feel the world would be better without them. When I was a child, I believed I truly could kill a person at whom I was very angry. I tried to quell these thoughts but wasn't always able to.*

He says that after his family moved to Zagreb, he was able to forget everything that happened, or rather he "masked" his real memories with fabricated ones, and only recently, as an adult, had he been able to retrieve the real ones.

People are capable of going to great lengths to survive. Eat shit, steal, beg, lie, kill, betray a friend. When we moved away from the village, the terrifying images began to fade from my memory day by day. At first I felt threatened by this and thought I'd lose myself, and I clung childishly to things and people, everything that was slipping away from me. When I saw I was missing a piece, I'd take from what was there, what still hadn't vanished, from the stories of others. I lied more and more about who I was and gradually began believing my own lies.

The trigger that made him start remembering was, as he wrote, a random insight into the actual cause of the serious Međimurje cases of depression and suicide. He offers a new explanation, one that was not raised by any of the study subjects, releasing himself from all guilt, though no one attributed real culpability to the child, nor could any responsibility be legally proven. M. D. did, however, take full responsibility, explicitly, for the death of the last victim, the boy, Franjo Klanz.

COLLECTORS OF
SECONDARY WASTE

1.

"Come on, cut the crap. You're so full of shit lately. Why would the mall drive you crazy all of a sudden?"

Matija Dolenčec looked away and rolled his eyes.

"A year ago you were ranting about how social media distances people from each other. And anyway, dressed up like that, you look just like an eager consumer."

Gita knew she was being harsh, so after a pause she reminded him how great the book he'd already written was. As far as he was concerned, she may as well have unscrewed his head and spat down his gullet. He didn't listen, pretending to study each window display they passed. Arrogantly, as if he could afford everything. The mall didn't put him off as much as he liked to pretend, as it ought to do to someone who was almost thirty and a writer. The big-city malls looked as if someone had designed them to be exactly like a major European airport, like Frankfurt or Charles de Gaulle. They were a cocktail of perfume, disinfectant, feces, sweat-soaked fabric, fresh newspapers, fast food, uncomfortable chairs that made spending money more appealing, identical spaces with tropical ferns and glass surfaces, corporate art, designer ideals of happiness, and a foreign life. Matija liked malls more than airports because there was no removing of shoes, no patting of his jacket pocket to make sure his passport and boarding pass were still there, and no flight waiting for him, while he pretended the whole time he wasn't scared of turbulence. On the other hand, only important-looking people walked around airports. Running into someone at a major European airport, sharing a latte macchiato, and chatting about the project he was working on supercharged Matija Dolenčec's ego, while meeting someone at the new mall in Savica was merely awkward.

It was late afternoon on one of the first days of January 2011. The media was reporting on what people were eating and the slippers worn by the former prime minister while he was in an Austrian jail, and there were frantic attempts to persuade the nation that a skiing competition in the Zagreb hills was a fabulous notion, not an overblown project to bring a flood of tourists to the metropolis, capitalizing on the idea that Croats are admired everywhere for their famously superior sports gene. There were eight girls pregnant at the Bjelovar commerce high school, and a grandmother in Gorski Kotar had been reimbursed by a bankrupt funeral parlor after they'd forced her to take possession of her prepurchased coffin, which she put in the only place she had room: the middle of her bedroom. She covered it with a tablecloth, a vase with flowers, and a plate of cookies, hoping she'd stop thinking of how she'd have to lie in it someday.

Matija Dolenčec could barely mask his alarm and the dread of losing himself in life's bottomless pits. He'd agreed to take Gita shopping as a gesture of gratitude for her willingness to read something he was hoping would become his third book.

She was the last of three readers of his newest work before he decided whether to send it to an editor. His first two books—a collection of short stories, *The Discovery of Remarkable Organisms*, in 2006, and a novel, *Good Morning, Phantom*, in 2008—were fairly well received by critics and the reading public (meaning that the number of copies sold was just south of four digits). With this third book, things had gone differently. He'd worked on it for over a year, and throughout the process he was dogged by the smell of trash and rot. He knew the story wasn't working. At times he was seized by paranoia that he, too, smelled bad: out of the corner of his eye, he'd see colleagues and total strangers in line at the grocery store whispering awkwardly. That whole year the story never once pulled him in; he massaged the plot in hopes that he might build a more or less coherent collage of banter and feigned pent-up emotional turmoil. The scent of garbage emanated straight from the icon for "novel_2011.doc" on his desktop. The story was about the tragic love between a young Roma man and a Croatian woman, and about a young policeman of mixed Serbian and Croatian parentage who was investigating the man's brutal murder. Matija imagined it to be the kind of book to inspire comments like:

"Holy shit, this is the hottest stuff I've read in years. I wept and roared with laughter. What a scintillating imagination! I can't believe someone I know writes like this."

"Pardon me, you wouldn't be Matija Dolenčec, would you? Did you write that book about the Roma man? Apologies for the intrusion, but it's brilliant. Exactly what our country needs, give it to her straight, spit in the eye of Croatia. Would you be a guest on my Sunday afternoon talk show?"

"In his latest book, Dolenčec gives us the tragic potential of a character from the gallery of the Croatian public's commedia dell'arte."

"The first printing of Dolenčec's novel sold out in a few breathless weeks. This is a moving story exploring hatred toward the Other in all its manifestations in transitional Croatia."

"Having portrayed the impotence of the ordinary man who can be a stakeholder in, but not the instigator of, historical processes, young Matija Dolenčec is a shoo-in for an award from the European Association of Romas."

"David Fincher has begun filming a new movie based on Matija Dolenčec's latest award-winning novel. The plot has been adapted to pre-war Berlin, the protagonists a Jewish artist and a young German woman. Dolenčec, who was recognized last week as Croatia's best-dressed man, will serve as consultant on the film. In the photograph, from the left: Colin Farrell, David Fincher, Scarlett Johansson, and Matija Dolenčec in conversation."

These were the thoughts that helped Dolenčec get to sleep each night after shutting down his laptop. Instead of expressing their admiration and barely repressed envy, however, his three readers advised him to set the draft aside for a spell: there was no vibrancy or sharpness, and, ultimately, no sense of purpose. These were people who cared for him and were sincere; they considered his success their own and couldn't be bribed.

Korina was a friend from his high school days, and for a brief time she'd worked at the same state agency as Matija and shared his convivial scorn for the job. He, however, couldn't leave, while she could and did. She was a particular kind of millennial: no one knew exactly what they did for a living, but they always managed to look chic, socialize with up-and-comers, ski at middling winter resorts while sporting fancy brand-name apparel, drive a tiny designer car that matched their wardrobe, and dine in overrated Zagreb restaurants where the waiters were plagued by chronic bitchiness. By the time she was in her late twenties, she'd already had five jobs, most of them in PR, guerilla marketing, and event planning. She was good at planning events. The only problem was that she'd been hired as an accountant. She ended up working for her dad, who was in real estate on the Adriatic islands, where he sold property to Russians. He created a job that was a perfect fit for her but of no value to the company. There she was finally asked to plan an event and told she would be paid for it, but given a budget of 250,000 kuna, she spent a little over half a million.

She went through periods when she was ready to, as she said, "take on a new challenge." She was carried along by a twisted optimism that each employer would ultimately realize how much good she'd done. No doors were ever fully shut behind her.

She was the first person to receive a hard copy of the double-spaced 350-page manuscript. Matija wanted her opinion as a representative of those picky readers who, if they read at all, read hagiographies of celebrities and success stories recommended by Oprah's Book Club and available at better gas stations everywhere. It would be great for Matija if people like that had his book in mind, in case someone asked them what they'd been reading lately. For instance, a person who made a living commenting on other people's shoes could let it slip that, well, literature wasn't really her thing these days, but she did read Coelho and a few Croatian writers like Dolenčec. Korina had done something similar with Matija's second book. Three years earlier, a weekly paper with a strong yellow bent had run a photograph of a scantily clad forty-three-year-old anchor from one of the local TV stations. She was lounging on a deserted beach sans bikini top, with Matija Dolenčec's book *Good Morning, Phantom* in her hand. The photo revealed a slender wrist, the book a little thicker, and even more generous breasts—in that order. The blurred picture looked as if it had been taken quickly, secretively, from a distance. This was not the case, of course, nor was it accidental that Matija's book was featured.

"Look, this new thing you've written, why don't you let it sit for a while, let it settle. Do something else. Then reread it and start over."

Korina thought editing a bad text might make it good, but Matija knew better. *You can't take a piece of shit and turn it into something delicious, Korina darling. I suppose there's always the shit sandwich,* thought Matija. He didn't ask her what, specifically, she'd disliked. She hadn't liked any of it, he could tell. She probably hadn't even finished reading it. Maybe, thought Matija, the book called for a little more intellectual effort than she was willing to give. He wasn't happy about that, but he was proud of writing a complex narrative, showing he knew how to load his text with a battery of nuanced observations on the current state of affairs in Croatia, genital-fecal events, and the characters' emotional landscapes. He immediately decided his next reader would be Miljac, the smartest person he knew.

Matija had sat next to Miljac in high school. Miljac could easily have been the class bully—in ninth grade, he was already six feet tall and 180 pounds, and he had this big head and low brow. But there was no trace of malice in Miljac. He was an obedient kid and a good student. Two or three times a week, he'd get groceries for his elderly neighbor with dementia who called him Denis and gave him only seven or eight kunas for bread, milk, and the newspaper. Miljac would make up the difference with his own pocket money. Miljac had a threatening air about him, so sometimes he couldn't avoid fights in which he and Matija were regularly trounced. Matija suspected that people were annoyed not only by Miljac's intimidating size but by the fact that he never shut up. In high school, he'd dreamed about graduating and working in his father's computer repair shop installing antivirus software. Two years after graduating he had his own company in which he employed, in addition to his father, four other programmers. He had his own offices, one large car and one small one, an apartment in the Sljeme foothills, and 3.5 million kunas in the bank.

He made his money by creating, just for the hell of it, an online game in which Croats battled Serbs in a medieval setting. Within a year, some thirty thousand gamers were playing it. He advertised on social media and on websites for Croatian and Serbian émigrés. At Matija's suggestion, the game included diplomacy, the option of enemy takeover of resources via the stock market, espionage, the ability to develop weapons, and powerful unnamed allies, so the game took off and people were hooked. Although they had very different jobs, Miljac and Matija always enjoyed each other's company. They gave each other perspective.

"If it hadn't been yours, I'd have stopped reading after twenty pages. It didn't move me," Miljac told him, shutting the fridge with his foot, carrying a bottle of beer in each hand. "Your first two books were . . . wild. I still remember whole passages. But this, I couldn't tell where you were going with the story. But hey, I don't know, maybe I just don't get that kind of thing."

No, Miljac, I think you get it all too well, thought Matija.

There was a slim chance they were all wrong. Neither Matija, who'd written the 350 torturous pages in agony, nor Korina and Miljac—who tried to spot some aspect of themselves they'd never seen articulated before in his story—had been able to make sense of this new novel. Surely Gita would know how to appreciate it, he thought.

She was no literary critic, but for twenty years she'd worked as a journalist on a cultural program that aired on Croatian national TV. He knew she wouldn't beat around the bush, and she had an unerring instinct for how the most relevant critics would read a text. They'd met through his sister, a doctor, five years earlier, right after Matija published his first book. She'd diagnosed Gita with gout (yes, Matija constantly felt the need to show everyone just how funny he was, so he called her Gouta a few times as a joke, but Gita wasn't thrilled about it).

Gita was wearing a pair of platform sneakers that cutting-edge independent research had shown could burn body fat and help people with back problems who wanted, like Jesus, to walk on water. Clearly, she wasn't satisfied to let the sneakers be the only statement of her celibacy, so she'd put on a velour sweatshirt with a tacky pattern of pink, brown, and dark green. It made Matija uncomfortable. Being seen with someone who dressed so badly would make it difficult to be perceived as cool by Croatian literati. In a perfect world, in which contemporary literature had a vital role to play in Croatian society, in which there was the literary version of showbiz that Matija could summon with pagan invocations, they'd be photographed by paparazzi, and what would people see? A literary gigolo, and on his arm a garment worker from the Kamensko ready-to-wear factory, sporting their god-awful tracksuit fashions.

"This thing you've written . . . it isn't much, really. Too many clichés, man. It's not that the plot is predictable, but there's no way to tell where you're going with it. You depict the Romas as if they're unwashed oafs, Neanderthals with this mystical cultural legacy thanks to which they survive, and you give us arrogant roughnecks for Croats . . . And the policeman, he's got his head up his ass . . . Besides, instead of telling a story, you're preaching. It sounds like you started by coming up with a handful of cute sentences and then built the story around them."

Matija agreed with everything Gita said. He'd introduced a butch policewoman, a cussing spitfire, to the plot only because he couldn't resist having the woman say, on her way to the ladies' room, "Off to squeeze the moss."

"Don't submit this. Maybe they'd publish it, there's potential for scandal, but . . . I can already see them saying no one should buy this book, because they're just as likely to find a copy in the trash on a beach. Look, this isn't the end of the world. After two really good books, you wrote something bad. If you ask me, that's better than not writing anything after . . ."

"After what?"

"After the breakup."

"We didn't break up, she walked out on me."

"But why even say that? So you'll feel better, now that you're all fucked up? To justify yourself? What a character you are. I don't know anyone so cruel to himself yet so fond of self-pity . . ."

" . . . "

"Are you and she talking?"

"No. I ran into her a month ago, before Christmas. She was with this guy who was, like, forty-five. He had a salt-and-pepper beard and piercings. I think he paints people turning into furniture, or something. We had a nice chat. As I recall, we debated the difference between LCD and plasma screens for three minutes."

"You've never told me what happened between the two of you."

"Hell if I know."

They were on their way to the parking garage, and Matija, as he walked, felt like his shadow: short and formless in some places, long and frangible in others, but mainly reticent and ashamed. He was so empty that all those things could come creeping into him, things other people—who had some source of joy to protect them—were able to keep at bay.

Matija despised the world that day, himself included. He'd written well before, he knew he had, while he still loved people and saw in them a nobility that made the world livable. That was a time when he was both in love up to his ears and at odds with everyone around him. Now things were different. He'd had no trouble spending a thousand and a half hours writing and hundreds of hours awake when he should have been sleeping. Ever since Dina Gajski left him two years earlier, his damned writing had been the only thing motivating Matija Dolenčec to be human. After Dina, he moved writing to the very center of his being and then lost touch with it—maybe forever. In his search for a good story, there was almost nothing he hadn't tried. He read and wrote, his gaze fixed on the future; he spent days copying passages from classics just to learn an author's voice; he tirelessly jotted down quotes to avoid writing about what was really happening in his story. He tried working early in the morning, then late at night. He skipped meals, fabricated ingenious reviews of his yet-to-be-written book, sniffed glue, found little comfort in porn and clothes shopping, talked on and on about how one should and shouldn't write, wrote barefoot, and developed a urinary tract infection. In short, he assembled a vast opus of untold stories and a stable of characters with no goals or interests. And all that came of this was the occasional sad, incomplete thought and the reek of trash and rot.

While unloading large shopping bags from his trunk at Gita's apartment, his chest tightened because he knew he'd be going back to his apartment and thought he would never again write anything worthwhile. He felt that dread that had been shivering in his gut since Dina came into his life, the dread that there was something sickening deep inside him that was about to burst into the light of day. He could go home and pull at least something worthwhile from the manuscript—the occasional decent passage, the outline for a story—and then erase the rest, but he knew that every new reading of the text would be a fresh humiliation. He had just spent a year as a person who writes. Now he saw himself in the rearview mirror not as a hero in his own story but as a caricature in someone else's.

If there were just one more good book in me, he thought. *Nothing else would matter. I'd never write a word again. Just one more . . .*

At a time when no one but Matija Dolenčec cared about this, he was prepared to do almost anything to write one more good story.

Almost anything. But not to delve into himself.

2.

Dina was hardly a femme fatale for Matija. If anything might be deemed fatal, it was the way he managed to smash the relationship to pieces. In her he had a lover, a fan, a friend, and his greatest ally, all in one. He didn't cause their downfall of his own free will. Rather, he'd let the mask he'd been wearing for two decades—the one he'd mended and tweaked daily—crack, and the things that belonged to him alone, things he'd managed to repress, slipped through. Matija, perhaps because of the dread that he himself was a fabrication, was compelled to reconstruct the biography of every person he spoke with for more than ten minutes, and was uninterested in finding out whether he was right or not. Dina was the only person whose truth he cared enough about that he didn't dare ask her whether his reconstruction was right.

They met at a gala celebrating a women's disease, organized by an international pharmacy chain; Dina Gajski was second-in-command in their public relations office. It was the spring of 2008, shortly after Matija's second book came out. When someone introduced them, they shook hands and politely said, "Pleased to meet you." An hour later, they bumped into each other again outside the bathrooms. She pointed at him and said, "Matija, right?"

He pointed back and said the wrong name. She said she probably wouldn't have remembered his name, either, except it sounded familiar, and she remembered she'd seen his photograph on the jacket of a book she hadn't bought. Now that she'd met the author, she'd go back and buy it. He feigned embarrassment, told her he'd send her both books with a dedication as a gift. The party was loud, they were close together, and he felt her warm breath on his face. Its scent landed in his perfectly fuckable Venn diagram of chewing gum, warm dinner roll, and booze. She said something about food that he didn't hear because he was searching for something to say, before it was too late, to bridge the gaps in polite conversation that led to forgetting. The best he could come up with was: "Admit it, you were hiding in the bathroom. You have the air of the most popular girl at school, but you're not really comfortable here."

She looked at him, serious but not surprised. He seemed to be saying the same thing as a voice already in her head.

"Yes, you saw right through me. And what's your excuse for venturing from your ivory tower?"

"All the beautiful people here! What else?"

"I find that hard to believe."

"Why? Look at them. I'm conducting a brief survey as I mingle. Did you know that more than half the people here have no idea what this event is for?"

"You're no better. You sound like you came to observe the jet set just to convince yourself you're superior."

"Does it sound better if I say I'm here because I'm contractually obliged to appear at events like this, but they're more bearable when I think I might meet someone like you at one of them?"

"Yes, that is better. But not good enough."

Neither of them spoke to anyone else that evening. Matija nabbed a bottle of Plavac and two glasses from the nearest table, and they left the restaurant and sat on the steps outside. In the shadow of a neighboring corporate tower, Dina could not be seen by her colleagues as they entered and exited the building, so they talked for another two hours.

Totally alien creatures passed by, bipeds sucking the food stuck between their teeth, making little whimpering noises, talking about cholesterol, enemas, Buddhism, then getting into their leased cars enveloped in clouds of stale perfume and garlic from the gnocchi sauce. They'd pause to fart at some point between exiting the restaurant and sliding into the car.

"Well, that's that. We're out of Plavac. And I've got to go home," Dina announced.

"The kids' cartoon shows are over for the night, so time for bed. I should be going myself—I start stuttering when I get fewer than six hours of sleep."

"Yes."

"Yes. So look, hey, why don't we trade phone numbers, and then one of us can call the other if so inspired? We'll have more to say about kids' shows sooner or later. Thoughts?"

"Well, okay. I've got a better idea. Here goes. We bump into each other in town somewhere and go out for ice cream. Or try to find a mutual friend so we have an excuse to run into each other. Look, as far as these little dating games go, I'm not interested. I'm pretty binary with stuff like this. If you're unsure, if you need time to think it over, write me little notes, discuss things over coffee, then sorry. Get my drift?"

"Well, no, I'm—"

"You're what? In my head everything's crystal clear. I'm a big girl— no time for bullshit. Can't can, Superman. Capisce?"

"Oof, I thought that might be lurking inside you somewhere. Suits me. Like when the swan developed a crush on a swan boat."

"Pardon?"

"Nothing. I want that, too, of course, I'm just trying not to be pushy, intrusive, whatever. You're a nice person. Forget it. You know what I'm saying . . . I was prepared to play the game for your sake, not mine."

"If it's for my sake, then don't."

The next day, they exchanged thirty text messages before noon, got together at lunch for an orange fizz, and then met again three hours later for a beer. At ten she went back to her place, and he went to his, just to shower and pick up what he'd need for the next day.

For the next three months, they didn't spend two nights in a row apart. She'd been single for a few months after a two-year long-distance relationship, and he'd just broken off a friends-with-benefits thing with a former colleague from the university. Whatever the random sequence of events by which two people fall hopelessly in love, whatever the strange guideposts human nature follows in this clumsy business . . . one thing is clear: Dina and Matija were partners in crime. They goaded each other and sparred like warriors in training. Neither was brave enough alone, but under the scrutiny of their fellow combatant, they were emboldened for destruction.

Jerk, all day long I think about you. I even smell like you. If this keeps up, I'll lose my job.

So be it. Who gives a fuck? Let's go down to the Adriatic and start a monopoly selling seashells on the street. We have too little time together now. You leave the apartment, I brush my teeth and count the hours till you're done with work. I take a shower and count the days till the weekend. I don't know what this is. Nothing matters anymore.

For me either. Think we'll ever watch a movie to the end?

Sure. Yesterday, on the third try, we made it all the way to where the little curly haired Scot's dad is murdered by the English, and the grimy little girl hands him the flower. Almost to the end!

You're the only one who saw that, I already had my back to the screen. I rubbed my knees raw :-).

*

What's that? A kiss? Or an asshole?

Your call.

Before he denied himself her company, Dina was an endless source of new insights into humankind for Matija. He relished her every contradiction and with each new day threw himself, happily, into a puzzle he knew he'd never solve, as readily as he'd always done with the fictitious or real people whose lives he'd invented.

The first peculiar trait he liked was that she carried some of the difficult things from her childhood completely openly, and held them out for all to see, while she buried others that seemed nowhere near as fucked up in that warm darkness of hers.

"That was the worst moment in your childhood? When you kicked a soccer ball and hit your coach's head and they wouldn't let you play anymore? Well, listen to mine: I was this cute little girl, flower in my hair and a pretty dress, but when I was at school I simply wouldn't wipe my ass. I was disgusted by the idea of being near it with my fingers, so after I pooped I'd just pull up my underwear. My folks went nuts. At home after school I'd put off getting undressed, but after going all day like that there'd be this, y'know, itching and burning in my butt, and everyone knew I hadn't wiped again."

"Wow! So how did you get over it?"

"I still haven't! Ha ha. One day my dad'd had it, and he said he'd rub my shitty pants all over my face if I didn't wipe my ass. 'Nuff said."

She spoke elatedly, choking back laughter. But he was more interested in the other part, the part she was withholding from him.

Sometimes, when they'd walk around Zagreb, she'd stop for no apparent reason and stare straight ahead, and then start walking again. It seemed random, like how the elderly cruise through town like ships, never speeding up or slowing down. But sometimes their bodies creaked, and they'd drop anchor and come to a halt. Matija believed this was left over from when she went for walks with her grandmother. Her grandmother was a Zagreb grand dame, and he knew this though Dina'd never said a word about her. Dina had adored her and imitated her in every way, and—he knew this, too—she'd instructed the other kids at school to sit up straight, keep their elbows off the table, hold their cookies between two fingers, and eat over a plate to keep from dropping crumbs on the floor.

Even in their first days together, Matija saw that Dina rarely clashed with people, but she frequently ran into objects. In the morning, when her movements were still partly in the world of dreams, unadapted to reality, she collided with her surroundings. Matija left for work later than she did, so he'd lie in bed and watch her get ready. She tried to resolve her collisions with the world of things as quietly as possible, but didn't always succeed. One rainy morning she yelled at the door handle after bumping it with her elbow; the next day she argued with her iron, said it was a stupid cow and she hated it. This happened because, when she was running late, she'd dress first and then iron her clothes while she was wearing them. Her iron—it had to happen sooner or later—fell onto her foot and ripped her nylons. Matija could no longer pretend to be sleeping so he laughed out loud, and she cheerfully explained that everyone does their ironing like this, nothing weird about it, and besides it feels nice in the wintertime because, you know, it's so toasty. She limped over to the bed and kissed him, and then he kissed her foot where it hurt, and then slid his finger into the nylon tear and went ahead with what was bound to happen anyway. They were both late for work. And from that day on, they called the iron Stupid Cow. Dina's company car was Stupid Horse. The remote at Matija's apartment was

Asshole; Dina sometimes whacked it against the table when it wasn't working. They renamed half the world, and there was always the danger that one day no one would understand them anymore.

She was a true sucker for marketing ploys (this reminded Matija of Nabokov's Lolita), even though, with the nature of her job, she knew them inside out. She'd fall for a lie if it seemed worthwhile. She bought Q-tips because the package said half a kuna from the purchase price would go toward building a school in the Punjab, where the cotton came from. Sometimes she'd speculate aloud about how construction material in the Punjab cost so much less than it did in Europe, so her half-kuna every three weeks was not a negligible contribution. This led Matija to call her the Savior of Punjab. And he never tired of discovering the snowy peaks and verdant dales, sacred sites and industrial zones of that imaginary country on the irregular surfaces of her skin. Sometimes, while sipping her bottled water as Matija drank a glass of tap water, she'd smack her lips and announce that bottled water was purer and tasted better than tap water. She was capable, as she sipped, of envisioning herself atop the very mountain depicted on the label. She could almost hear the designer spring water burbling over the cold rocks. She truly believed the water came from the heart of a thousand-year-old glacier. In some things she was a true-blue do-gooder. So he called her Bleeding Heart.

These perfect asymmetries of her personality echoed the asymmetry of Dina's breasts, which contradicted each other. One nipple pointed straight ahead, and the other gazed sideways, so they reminded him of a lazy-eyed cow. When they fucked, he'd use a hand to right the wayward breast. He found it especially intriguing that Dina, when she was climaxing, slowed, which was the opposite of what he'd experienced with other women. She'd close her eyes or look to the side, go very still, arch her back, and press her belly up to his. And she'd finish with five or six deep, brusque movements, as if they came straight from her heart. Here, too, climaxed Matija's inability to understand Dina. He asked her once why she never talked during sex (because he sometimes felt like asking why the fuck she wouldn't give him head till he finished when she was such a slut, and other dirty things like that, but he didn't like talking when there was no one to talk to), and she asked him if that would turn him on. Well, he said, once, at work, totally at random, just surfing the net, you know how it goes, he'd watched—so what?—this little movie, in which two young people, how should he put this, in which two young people were—okay, okay, let's say making love. So, whatever, it was like, y'know, so . . . intriguing, he thought, how the woman was talking. First, in this commanding tone, she told her boyfriend (maybe her husband, the father of their two adorable kids—who knows) to fuck her harder. Just like that, she actually shouted it, hotly, loudly, as if daring him. This young wife and mother, while they went from missionary to anal, something Matija found even more interesting, dropped the first-person singular and began referring to herself as if she were someone else (*fuck this bitch, yes*). She mentioned parts of her own body as if they weren't hers and commanded him to fuck those, like, parts (*fuck this pussy, fuck it harder, fuck it, fuck it, harder,* then *fuck this asshole, fuck it, yeah, yeah, yeah,* and finally *smack these tits, smack them*). He wondered whether somehow—not every time, of course— maybe Dina might give it a try, because sometimes she seemed to enjoy a sideways glimpse of herself when she was fucking. He'd catch her eyes reflected in the framed etching hanging in the bedroom.

On one Rumpled Saturday (this, in their intimate vocabulary, was when they'd stay in bed until noon, then go out for coffee without brushing their hair), when he finally came out and said she was free to go ahead and talk while they screwed, Dina burst into peals of laughter, and Matija pronounced her Bleeding Heart and pounced on her. They wrestled on the bed, he between her legs, while she chanted in as monotonous a tone as she could, staring past his head into the air: "Oh, oh, yes, here, yes, bang, straight in, noodles, ho, bang, into me, like an animal. Your glans is in my vulva. This is so thrilling. Oh. Oh. I wish you'd do that quicker."

He tickled her, she wriggled free, and without meaning to she kneed him in the balls. He whimpered like a puppy and dropped to his side, turning his back to her. She thought she'd really hurt him and tried to apologize with a kiss. He didn't react to the first or second attempt, so her voice went serious, and she said, "Are you okay? I'm sorry. What should I say now?"

He flipped over, climbed onto her, and grabbed her by the wrists, and then she began chanting again in a monotone: "That, that, ah, ah, there you go, stallion, oh yeah, oh yeah, you're a king, a legend, bang, harder, yeah, punish me, punish, I deserve it, thank you, thank you, for fucking me, thank you, I don't deserve you."

He couldn't stop laughing, and when she flashed him the grimace and mimicked the deep moan he made when climaxing, he nearly doubled over. She'd repeated the grimace and moan ever since, each time he tried to explain something serious to her and she refused to take him seriously.

Rumpled Sunday, Bleeding Heart, o-face, salty anchovy, peopleships, the lazy-eyed cow, the remote known as Asshole . . . this was their mythology, their connective tissue. The pathways they'd laid in case one of them lost their way and needed to find the route back.

Things he'd long forgotten began to surface, one by one, in presentiments and dreams. At first he thought they came from the present, not the past, and that they belonged to someone else. It began with nightmares. He clung to the idea that the amounts of happiness and unhappiness in his life ought to be in balance; this was a precondition, he felt, for each new day with Dina. He'd wake in the middle of the night, groggy, and sit in bed and stare into the darkness. He'd grope frantically for the light, try to focus on some real object, and convince himself there was no ghost. He couldn't make sense of his dreams, though he felt there was something to them: a twisted logic, a truth hidden from the world. Dina would wake, too, because she wanted to be a part of whatever it was he couldn't articulate. She'd press up against him in the dark like a small wild animal, not to flee danger together but to be together no matter what, until Matija was no longer scared to go back to sleep. At times, he dreamed he was standing by a river and watching a boy he didn't recognize with a large head of tousled hair who stood waist-deep in the water. The boy would stare at him for a while. Then he'd open his mouth like a person screaming. No sound came from him, only dark, velvety blood coursing down his chin, over his chest and belly, into the murky river. Sometimes, still delirious, Matija would mumble, "There, they're here, they've found me." Dina felt there must be another side to this man who seemed endlessly lighthearted. A dark side, something he kept hidden. She thought this because of his unexpected reactions, the occasional blast of rage he'd later try to walk back, and other moments when he seemed to withdraw into himself, staring, entranced, into his darkness.

"I like when you do that."

"Am I tickling you? I can't cover it all with spit."

". . ."

"It's hard. By the time I reach the tip, the part below it is dry."

"Doesn't matter. Really. I like that you aren't doing it just so I'll feel good. You have a plan: cover it all with spit. I'm witnessing the work of a master."

"I'm an apprentice before this masterpiece. The first part always dries."

"Like memories."

"Like what?"

"Memories. That's how they fade, too, like brushstrokes . . . Such a loony. Loony Gajski. It's all loony tunes inside you. But I'll cover them, too, with spit."

3.

"What?"

"Nothing. I'm watching you."

"What, you're watching me do the dishes?"

"No, I'm watching your ass wiggle back and forth while you scrub the frying pan. It's sexy."

"This is sexy? Sexy like a T. rex-y?"

"Sexy like those panties you're wearing today. They're so . . . retro. Are those heritage panties from the Gajski clan women? Passed down from one generation to the next by the mature members of the dynasty, since the conquest of the Avars? I find things from the past sexy in general. Not just the undies, but the T. rex thing. Since when have you been into rhyming jokes?"

Dina often came up with rhymes in idle chatter, when she had nothing in particular to say. She'd repeat the last word said and add a rhyme to it with no concern for logic. Matija thought of this as her grandmother's influence.

"Rhyming jokes? Up in smoke?"

"Since you got saddled with this pig in a poke?"

"Do they annoy you? Bug you? Are you about to dump me? For another woman? Go ahead, be my guest, you philanderer. Get lost, piglet. Who gives a fuck anyway? Nonsense. Garbage. Just wait, you'll see. What's that thing they say in Međimurje? Every butt knows the way to the toilet?"

"Every ass ends up on the crapper. That's what they say in Međimurje. And don't you forget it if you want to be a Međimurje daughter-in-law."

"What kind of a Međimurje man are you? You only say you're from there as an excuse for your bad spelling. Or when the people of Zagreb begin sounding like conceited smart-asses. And when were you last there anyway?"

". . ."

"What's this now? Nothing to say? Am I getting to you?"

"No. Every day you amaze me. In the morning, you bump into things and iron the clothes you're already wearing, you toss out this lucid gibberish, your Dina-isms, and I spend the whole day wondering where they come from and what's going on in your head. It's as if something a really long time ago got turned inside out, and now nothing works exactly how it's supposed to, but everything still functions at some deep-down level. No way do you annoy me."

"You know, sooner or later we'll get on each other's nerves for this or that stupid thing—you know that, don't you?"

Now Dina, still washing the dishes, was almost totally serious as she spoke. As he listened, Matija could imagine, the day before, Dina's colleague, a maybe slightly older blonde from a small town, talking about her sad marriage of many years. Things just weren't the same anymore, she said. He walks right into the bathroom in the morning when she's brushing her teeth, sits down and starts taking a shit, and asks her what she's planning to cook on Saturday, green beans or kale? And he sees nothing wrong with this. And it's so wrong for her that she doesn't even know how to say it. After that, how could she possibly find him attractive? So they haven't had sex for months, Dina's make-believe colleague and the colleague's probably very real husband.

"Look, you're already messing with me. I mean, who goes around in granny panties like that?"

"These are my dish-washing panties. I wash the car in my thong. No, seriously. I seldom wax pathetic, but what we have is really good, and that's making me a little crazy. I want to know you won't pack up and leave. I know I won't."

"You know I care, don't you? I mean, I can't hide it. No matter what . . . This really matters to me. I wouldn't just walk out. Okay?"

"I guess."

"Y'know what? Let's make a list right now—instructions in case of emergency, or whatever. The three or four things we have to do if one of us loses interest, snaps, or something. I think people break up because they forget what it was that brought them together. And remembering is so . . . easy. Okay? A plan."

"An emergency plan."

"Right, in case of emergency. We'll do everything on the to-do list, and then ta-da—we'll be back where we began!"

"To-do, ta-da. Yeah. Okay, but you do the writing, I have a few more plates. 'In the eventuality of a breakup . . .'"

"Wait. Right. 'In the eventuality of a breakup, the undersigned, Matija Dolenčec and Dina Gajski, agree to have sex.'"

"Come on, I was serious."

"Hey, I'm serious, too. It's one of the three things that binds me most to you. You know how before . . . I dunno . . . You know how people always put on an act. Like in everyday life. I was anxious, I realize now, that during sex someone would look into my eyes and see who I really am. With you, I'm not afraid of that."

"Really?"

"Really. And not just because you mock my o-face."

"Okay, you wriggled out of that one. But I will absolutely not have sex with you if the reason for the breakup is cheating! I'll drink your blood, damn it. Two. 'In the eventuality of a breakup, each party has the right to ask three questions, and the other party has to answer honestly.'"

"Fine, but you already have that."

"Well, I guess. Sometimes you can get a little secretive and dark when your moods get the upper hand. And who knows what might happen down the road. We go on living our lives in this relationship . . . People change. But they stay together with the illusion that the other person is the constant."

"Three. 'In the event of a breakup, they must go to the following places together: where they first met, where they first kissed.'"

"Where they first held hands, where they first knew the other person wasn't some ethereal being whose sweat smelled only of flowers."

"What? When did that happen?"

"That time we were waiting for the tram, after the reception at the museum."

"Seriously?" He wanted to know.

"Yessss. You reeked. Sour. A man's man."

"Wow, awkward!" he shot back. "You've never smelled even a little sour to me. Wash less. And, finally, 'the place where one of them realized that nothing would ever be the same as it was before.'"

"The place where the world turned upside down for one of them." She smiled.

"On the steps."

"On the steps."

"We'll go back there and say everything we said that night. We'll wear what we wore to the gala. After that, if we need to, we'll repeat the rest of it. The text messages the next day, the orange fizz at lunch, and everything in the same order right up to the day when the problems began," he said.

"We'll keep repeating the same story, if we have to, all our lives."

"A hundred thousand times."

"Hey, let's make a list of things we have to do to stay together." She grabbed a pen.

"Sure. Go ahead, write."

4.

"First: every day we have to think of a good thing. Before we go to sleep each night, we'll remember something nice and invite it to lie down in bed, snuggle under the covers, and sleep with us. We'll remember a story we made our own."

"Okay. And we should never go to bed angry. Ever."

"What's wrong?"

"Nothing."

"Nothing? Then why haven't you looked at me in the last two hours?"

"Because I can't stand the sight of you right now. I'm tired. I want to go to sleep. I have to get up at seven tomorrow, and your friend Miljac is really a pain when he drinks. I like him fine, but fuck his stupid YouTube videos of jackass clowns at one thirty in the morning. Leave me alone and take us home."

"Why are you so pissed at me? You were all sweetness and light with everyone else."

"Look, I've had it. No more talking, just drive."

"Young lady, we're not going to talk like this."

"No? Then how should we talk? You'll just say I'm being dramatic."

"What the fuck's wrong?"

"Fine, I'll tell you what's wrong. The crazy story you've told me at least ten times about when you and your friends were sailing and a storm swept you off to some island where you ate fish and drank tons of wine at this old guy's place and passed out in the kitchen in his shanty. You made that up, didn't you?"

". . ."

"I asked the guys when you went to the bathroom—we didn't have much else to talk about—and they just looked at me sideways."

"Oh, c'mon, Miljac was so drunk he wouldn't remember his own grandmother."

"No? I looked like an idiot. But what I can't figure out is why you made it up. Or why you sold it to me like it was true. Write a short story, man. Don't lie to me to make yourself sound cooler."

"I'm not going to talk about this. You need sleep. We'll pick it up tomorrow. You're a little drunk."

"Don't talk to me like I'm an idiot. I wouldn't say anything if this'd been the first time. But when we were out bowling, I asked Prle about when you and Miljac beat up those punks who grabbed your beers in the park. He stared at me, then at you, then at me. And then he just muttered something, and you changed the subject. I guess the punks, unlike the old man on the island, at least were real, but they beat you up, not the other way around."

"Look, he wasn't even there. How would he know? Maybe you should be a little less creative in interpreting people's glances, the tone of their voice, and shit like that. Any more brilliant questions? Miljac and I have given as good as we got—"

"I couldn't care less! I wouldn't give a fuck even if you'd been pounded to a pulp, or if you'd never done a single exciting thing in your whole life. It doesn't matter at all to me! What I care about is why you have this need to, like, make things up. We're not in high school. I've heard of guys who lie to their girlfriends that they're going on a business trip, and instead they're banging an ex at some hotel. That kind of lie I could understand. But these . . ."

"Screw that. I don't lie, and I'm not talking to you when you're like this. I'm driving you home, and then I'm going to my place. I'm out of underwear anyway."

"We won't start sentences with you never and you always. I read that couples who do that in serious conversation often split up in the end."

"You always have the best ideas, sugar."

"You want to?"

"What?"

"You know, *do it.*"

"No!"

"Come on, there's no one on the beach."

"No way! You're crazy."

"Oh, c'mon. Let's get a little wild? Shake it up? It won't hurt anyone."

"You'll get some at home. And anyway, your cock's all salty from the water."

"So what's wrong with that? A salty anchovy. There's only so many salted nuts a person can nibble. C'mon, give it up, I know you want to."

"You're terrible at this, cowboy—you should write a book about how not to hit on a girl. Today you're coming up dry. Y'know what I've always wondered?"

"What?"

"What the story is with your missing toes."

"I told you."

"You told me you were in the woods at night when you were little, with friends, and you stepped in a puddle and froze, and they had to chop your toes off."

"Well, there you have it."

"But the day before yesterday, your mom said that you sleepwalked when you were little, and that one night they found you out in the yard and took you to the hospital, where they had to amputate your toes. She tells it . . . you know . . . with a bit of humor. You could've frozen."

"Oh please, Mom doesn't know. I wasn't sleepwalking; I had a secret club with my friends, and we met at night to swap Animal Kingdom cards, and I locked myself out."

"So they amputated your toes?"

"No, that wasn't when they cut off my toes. I mean, I should know. We were in the woods."

"I guess she mixed it up. You told me about your secret club, but you said you were, like, on the lookout for treasure or something."

"We did all kinds of shit. I can't remember half the stuff we did."

"Well, I bet you had a great time. What were your friends' names?"

" . . . "

"So why don't you ever go back to Međimurje?"

"Um . . . we sold the house and . . ."

"But you still have family there."

"We do . . . but we're not in touch anymore, since we came to Zagreb."

"Why?"

"You're really pushing it today. I don't know, we haven't seen them in, like, a hundred years. No one's been pushing for us to get together."

"I'm not pushing it—I just want to know. And what about your friends from the secret club? Are you still in touch with them?"

"Why do you care? No, I'm not in touch with anyone from Međimurje. What more do you want from me? I haven't been there in twenty years. It's crawling with rednecks and hicks. I don't know what I'd do there or who I'd talk to."

"What does that mean?"

"It means you're giving me the third degree, the sun's burning my skin, and yesterday we overdid it with cocktails so my head's pounding. I've had enough of the beach. Can we go?"

"We just got here an hour ago. What's wrong with you?"

"Oh, for fuck's sake. You always stay on the beach until you're, like, cooked. I can't just sit in one place for a couple of hours, I go bananas. I get nauseated."

"What's going on with you?"

"I'm going home. Call when you want me to come get you. Bye."

"Fine, go—you're acting weird anyway. There's always something going on with you. What a crank."

"We have to be honest. Lay out the brutal truth, come what may. Likewise, we have to be good at separating the big things from the minor shit. No sweating the small stuff."

"It was hilarious, you should've seen it. Book events are high-society shindigs in these backwaters. The middle-aged ladies—teachers, the doctor, the registrar—go to the hairdresser's to have their hair done and then dress up for the evening . . .

". . . and they make their mediocre absent husbands put on suits they can't zip up anymore. They hover by the tables with the hors d'oeuvres and drinks . . ."

"They're all stiff and have sticks up their asses, like they're at the theater and not at some talk about a book. You should see it. They're all poised, like, what's going to happen next? And you were totally cool, so sweet."

"Oh, I know, I can't help myself. Yes, like Dina said, they don't laugh so they won't spoil the performance, the scene—who knows how they see it?—and only applaud after the reading, and when it's over and they go eat."

"And talk about how literature was at its best in Balzac's day, and how now everyone uses crude terms, they curse, they write about sex for no reason, they use all these English words—no respect for the Croatian language. Hey, tell them about the guy who began reciting."

"Oh, right, the local sheriff, old as the grave, came to a reading at Matica hrvatska, got a little tipsy and started reciting Tadijanović, but got it all wrong. He was rocking back and forth on his feet, holding a glass of Sauvignon—a real catch for the over-sixty-five set."

"And one of them says, 'You can see he's a real gentleman. His pants are perfectly tailored.' I'd bet you money the old geezer got lucky that night."

"And you should've seen Dina, she was doing the supportive girl-friend thing. She grabbed my book, cozied up to ladies by the hors d'oeuvres, and then she's like, 'Honey, remind me what you were think-ing about when you wrote . . .'"

"When was that, exactly?"

"What do you mean, when? Last week, at the book event. C'mon, you were in fine form . . ."

"Right, I remember the event, but I don't remember saying that to you. Don't overdo it."

"C'mon, Dina, there's no harm in strutting our stuff . . ."

"Right. Of course. With your 150 copies, you're the bestselling author on Šišićeva Street, and I'm your groupie."

"What do you mean? C'mon, we're just messing around. Your friends want to hear what your life is like in the Croatian literary fast lane. People, this is, like, totally high society, you have no idea. Chivas Regal, Dom Pérignon, snorting that white stuff."

"Don't lay it on too thick, love."

"You should've seen Dina the rock star. She talked to the ladies about how tough it is living with a writer, how restless I get, how I work all night, and the next day I'm so—"

"Okay, hon, take it down a notch. When did I say that?"

"Well . . . when you were standing with the ladies by the hors d'oeuvres. You don't remember . . ."

"What kind of jerk are you? Holy shit, do you even know how much you lie? Tell me, do you even know you're lying?! Or do you believe it yourself?"

"Hey, what's wrong? I'm just teasing. Try to remember, the three ladies—"

"Seriously? Now you're making up my memories, too?! Are you out of your mind?! You can't tell me what I remember! I know who I am and what I did and where I was. Unlike you!"

"Every day we have to tell each other one thing that upset us and one thing that pleased us."

"I'll listen to all your stories."

"I hope you're patient. I can talk a lot. And when I run out of new things to say? What then?"

"Then start again at the beginning. For the hundred thousandth time."

5.

After she let him have it, they all stopped talking for a moment. Not knowing what to say, they each sipped their drink and looked around the bar, and eventually someone changed the subject. Dina and Matija stayed another fifteen minutes or so, finished their beers, pretended they always bickered like fashionable lovers, briefly feigned a quarrel about whose turn it was to pay, and then, smiling, left. In the car, suddenly somber, they said nothing. Something had finally snapped. They say lies are what keeps a couple together. For Matija and Dina, it was lies that were driving them apart.

He was precious to her because, thanks to him, she was part of things she otherwise never would have understood. He was her link to a world she'd watched from the sidelines since she became an adult, trying to make sense of it like a kid watching from a balcony to see who was playing below in the street. The enticing world of culture and art was, strange as it might seem, tied in her mind to humanitarian work and the environment. All that was foreign to her, and that's why it could all fit in the drawer where she shoved everything new, along with a few poems she'd read in her literature classes (over the years she'd forgotten both the poet's name and the poems' titles; all that remained were orphaned lines of verse, probably misremembered), broadcasts of the Viennese Philharmonic's New Year's performances, and a poster of a Klimt reproduction. Before Matija, she'd never known anyone connected even remotely to that world, aside from the so-called celebrities who systematically appeared on posters for animal welfare organizations, flaunting their humanitarian sentiments to promote themselves. The only solid link she had was her bank account, from which she paid fifty kunas a month to UNICEF, and her copy of Janson's *History of Art*, and Bulgakov's novel *The Master and Margarita*, which she reread at least once a year. Needless to say, Matija went wild when she confessed this to him. Dina had an image in mind of the colorful "alternative crowd": women in scarves and men with beards and linen trousers who worked for nonprofit organizations, watched slow-paced, opaque European and Iranian movies, bought books, climbed mountains, and persuaded one another that unknown bands with weird musical stylings were the world's finest. Matija was her link to that world. As if lacking inspiration herself, she outsourced to Matija the job of compensating for her totally irrational feeling of intellectual inferiority.

She'd anticipated Matija's unpredictability and even expected his creative attitude about the truth. At first she romanticized it. She never asked him about the story he'd mentioned when they first met, the one about the swan and the swan boat. She filled the gaps in her understanding with assumptions about herself and her lack of familiarity with the world. At first. But by now her colorful imagining of Matija's creative world had grown dark and cold. She'd catch an odd gesture at the end of a grueling day, a whisper to someone invisible, when he'd come to the end of his rope, when something raw peered out from beneath his playful exterior. He'd be suddenly skittish, shifty, edgy, and silently pained. She knew he was hiding something from her when she came home one evening and saw him kneeling on the floor, one hand punching a pillow, the other over his mouth and nose as if holding back something that was burning in his throat. He made a sound, a howling from deep down inside him. They weren't words she'd ever heard; later she remembered *hhhhsuh*, *dellllik*, and *znalllk* or *znarrrrk*. Terrified, she tiptoed out of the apartment and called him from the street a half hour later. She didn't have the courage to face what was happening, but the outcome was inevitable. Matija was becoming more a part of the material world, the world of things she so often collided with. She became aware of the possibility that even Matija might seriously harm another person without meaning to, simply by living as he always had.

He called her at work first thing the morning after they argued in front of her friends.

"Hey."

"Hi," then silence. After a moment, Dina said coldly, "So, what's up?"

"Not much. I just wanted to check and see if we're good."

"Can't talk now, I have a meeting in five. I don't know if we're good."

"I'd like us to be. I reached for you last night."

"I don't know what to say. Since you never call me at work, I assume you know where I am?"

"Sort of, yes. I know something's been bothering you, but I don't get why. People always embellish a little now and then, spice things up. I don't know why you went crazy over it."

"First of all, don't talk to me about crazy. You lose it, like, every few days. Last week, when you screamed at those kids playing around in front of the building? So who the fuck are you to talk about crazy?"

"Whoa, don't go—"

"And second: It's one thing to spice up a story a little. But you tell a story one day, and the next it's totally different. And then you try to convince me you didn't say what you said, and . . . I don't know . . . And all the damned off-limits subjects. Fuck, it's like you don't remember anything before high school. What's that about? If I hadn't already caught you making up stuff about your childhood, it wouldn't matter, I'd believe your memories started when we met. See? I wouldn't care. But now, damn it, now I have to know, because . . . I need to understand."

"I don't know what to say. I know who I am, but every day it strikes me a little differently, and I, like, come to it a different way each time. And that thing yesterday—so what? People exaggerate, y'know, everyone does that. Tell me your dad doesn't embellish his war stories a little. As if they actually hung grenades instead of ornaments on the Christmas tree—please. But the story's good, so we laugh and nod and don't give it another thought . . . I'm no different."

"Seems to me you are. Or maybe I care more. You're making it sound like I'm this Gestapo bitch overanalyzing what you said and how you said it, like I'm nitpicking, but no way. Fuck, got to go."

"Wait, are we seeing each other today?"

"Don't know. Not exactly in the mood."

"No need to be in the mood—I'll perk you up. I have a bottle of rosé with your name on it. And some good jazz. What do you say?"

After a pause, Dina spoke clearly and firmly. "Okay. I'll come to your place. But without the rosé or the jazz. I'll come around eight, and then please, tell me about yourself. Seriously. As if you're talking about someone you don't like. Cut the bullshit. Whatever happened, happened. You're not an addict, you're not in debt to loan sharks, you don't beat women, so far as I know you were never in jail, and you probably don't have the plague. Everything else I can handle, I know I can. But I have to know. See? From now on . . . You tell me everything, the way it happened. If you're up for that, we're good."

If Matija had said, "I am," he knew it would have sounded fake.

"See you tonight," he said and felt his balls swell.

Matija did what he had to at work, he was unusually cheery and flippant, and on the way home he bought the rosé. He spent no time at all thinking about his lies and how he sometimes overreacted. Most of the time he believed he was no different from anyone else. Sometimes he'd say something happened that didn't, sometimes he'd say something happened to him when it happened to someone else, sometimes he'd do a little of both. But tweaking his history was like covering a song, he thought, and everyone did that. He knew Dina was sick of it, though, and that he'd better stick to one story. *Piece of cake,* he thought. Most of all, he thought about how he'd fuck her.

She arrived around eight thirty in a hurry, no time for a kiss hello. They sat at the kitchen table without even taking off their shoes. *Who cares? I'll fuck you in your heels on the table,* he thought. He went first.

"Okay, here goes. I can't tell you my whole life story, that'd be impossible. Most of it's forgotten, but that's true for other people, too. So ask me whatever. I think you're taking this a little too seriously, but so be it."

"Okay. Tell me your life backward, starting from today and going back to the first memories you know are really yours."

"What? You mean day by day, hour by hour?"

"Whatever works."

"Wait, what do you actually want to hear?"

"All of it."

"All of what? You want to know when I came home, what I was wearing, how I crossed the street, what the cars looked like?"

"All of it."

"Fuck off. Why not just say you came to fight and dump me?"

"I didn't. I came because I'd like—"

"Oh, I get it. You want me to list all the women I've slept with. You want to hear whether I'm in touch with my exes and if I meet them every now and then for coffee. Look, I don't go around asking you who you've fucked."

"No, that's not it, because those aren't things you'd lie about," said Dina, and added, as if speaking to an invisible third person, "I can't believe what a weirdo I've fallen for." Addressing Matija again, she said, "You know, you have three different stories for everything that ever happened to you."

Maybe because she'd said she'd fallen for him, or because there was so much tenderness leaking through her vehemence, he began to yearn for an end to the torture. Matija planted both hands on the table, leaned forward, and began to talk, looking her straight in the eye. He talked for what felt like an eternity. He confessed a series of unpleasant things: the way he and Miljac used to be beaten up when they were in high school, that his family was impoverished after his father died, and how he'd started pretending to have a better life by, among other things, saying he'd had such a fabulous time sailing his family's yacht. He said he had no friends until his family moved to Zagreb, and that's why he made up the secret club. He told his new friends these stories so they wouldn't think he was a weird loner. After the move, a good lie was a lifesaver. He talked about his father's death. He said he found it easier to see how pain impacted his mother and sister than face his own fears. In high school he said that his father had probably been killed in Germany by Serbian secret agents because he'd helped to prepare Croatia for the war, so not much was known about his death. His father, in fact, had died of leukemia. Matija's voice spontaneously quavered in a few places, he was so moved by his own story. Even Dina, he thought, teared up a time or two. At university he'd lied and said that his book was coming out for a year before he even submitted the manuscript. He was relieved when it was accepted for publication, because he'd used it to seduce a woman who was, like, way out of his league. He admitted trying to come off as more clever and more important than he really was at work. His title had enough cachet to flatter his intellectual snobbery, but it was boring enough that people didn't ask him much about it. An ideal position for training and promoting frauds, imposters, and fakes. There you have it.

"There you have it," said Matija. He'd mortified himself so completely that he was almost certain they'd open the rosé any minute now, and then in no time he'd be removing her panties. He'd paid his dues.

"So many personalities in one person, right?" said Dina, visibly softened.

"But aren't we all? Maybe you just never noticed, but—"

"I have more. Don't get upset. I asked your mom to send me pictures from when you were small. Just a few random snapshots, whatever caught her eye. I printed them out. I'd like to know what you remember about the pictures. That's all I have left to ask."

"Go for it, get the pictures, and I'll pour us a glass."

Dina pulled out a manila envelope, and Matija poured two glasses of wine. She placed several photos on the table. Matija glanced briefly at the first and told her all about how it was taken, if he remembered correctly, while his dad was still alive. They'd gone to the coast at Orebić, but it had rained almost every day, hence the overcast sky and the fact that they were all in T-shirts. The other people were Slovenes his folks had gone sailing with a few times. They'd gone together to hear music on the hotel terrace, and there, out of pure guest-worker mischief, they'd stolen the wineglasses. He laughed aloud at the next photo because, he told her, it was taken when he was helping his uncle with the grape harvest, and Matija and his friends had gotten so drunk that some women from the nearby vineyards had had to herd them home like livestock. He didn't recognize the third photo right off the bat, but then he realized it was of his mother.

"Oh ho ho, now will you look at this? I'd forgotten. Look at her, wearing socks with sandals. Motherrrr." Matija laughed and said it was taken in Germany when his parents had gone to an amusement park with colleagues from work; he and his sister must have stayed home with their grandmother. Dina took out the next one.

"Look at that hair. They let me grow it so long when I was a kid, I don't know why. It probably amused the guests. That was in front of our neighbor's house in Međimurje. They had two horses—see, behind here—and I sometimes helped feed them. Then they'd make me grated apples with sugar and cinnamon."

He was so caught up with his stories that he didn't even see her tears. He didn't know it, but not one of the photographs was genuine. After her meeting, Dina had googled, despondent, *honesty*, *memory*, *remembering, childhood trauma.* Matija rarely spoke about his childhood, and when he did his voice changed completely, as if he were flattening all nuance. He'd stare at the ceiling, as if searching for a clear image there. His mother and sister were also quiet on the topic. They deftly changed the subject whenever it approached the events of their lives before Zagreb, and Dina had been too polite to press. For this very reason, she knew she should start with them.

She called Matija's mother and told her she was putting together a scrapbook and needed some of Matija's childhood photographs. They had coffee and cookies, and then she went home, where she scanned the pictures she'd chosen and digitally cut out the figures of Matija, his mother, his father, and his sister.

In various combinations she inserted these figures into backgrounds she found online. A stretch of open ocean seen from a road in Manila, a house and yard in a town in southern Sweden, a road alongside railroad tracks somewhere in rural Sandžak. Places where she knew the Dolenčec family had never been. After that, she added some random adults and kids in stovepipe jeans and shirts with floppy collars, which she'd dug up when she googled "family photos from the late seventies." It took her several hours to tweak the collages she'd assembled and print them out. She knew it would be hard to explain why she was so determined to do this. No one would understand that perfect happiness in love is, in fact, beyond reach. As far as Dina could tell, the prognosis was bad no matter how you looked at it. Great love either faded or became extremely painful. This first outcome she'd recognized while observing a couple in a café staring silently into space; doing so was less painful than saying something and getting nothing back. Only their elbows, their spines, and the people around them propped up their listless bodies. As far as the second outcome, it happened when people cycled between hurting each other and having makeup sex. This first scenario was acceptable to Dina—she considered it an asceticism of sorts. The second—absolutely not. That's why she wanted things to be clear, even if this meant resorting to duplicity.

She'd show Matija the collages. If he said he didn't remember where and when the pictures had been taken and didn't know the other people, he'd be telling the truth. If he launched into stories about the pictures and the people in them, she'd leave him that night. And he did make a story up for every single photograph. How thorough he was! He even added the odd detail for authenticity. She hated him for the bit about the grated apple.

While talking about the sixth photo, as he described how his sister and cousin were sledding and Matija was trying to pelt them with snowballs, he finally looked up at her face.

"Jesus, what's wrong? Hey!"

Dina didn't answer. If she'd spoken, her voice would have quavered, and the situation no longer allowed for that.

"Whoa, what's wrong?"

Matija offered her a napkin. After a time, she began speaking softly. "These aren't real photographs. I photoshopped them myself. The people here . . . you've never met them. You've never been to any of these places. You never threw a snowball there, you never fed any horses. I wanted to see if you'd lie no matter what, or if you'd admit you didn't recognize these pictures."

Matija felt his whole body go numb. The space around his chest folded over for a moment and formed a shape physicists call a wormhole. The wormhole vanished immediately, but the space around him stayed forever crumpled, like a handkerchief. Matija's life began to ooze out through the microscopic opening, and it might be said (though science has yet to prove it) that his biological demise began at that moment.

"A test? I suppose I deserve it. But I told you how things come to me. When I see a picture, for the first three seconds I don't remember anything, then I see my face and a familiar detail, and then things start occurring to me . . . and I just start talking."

"What's wrong with you?"

"The things I told you earlier, they are 100 percent true . . . But from when I was little . . . I can hardly remember any of that stuff."

"But then why did you say anything?! Why not just say you didn't recognize them?!"

"Because you wouldn't have accepted that. What do you want from me? Look, that's me. I can't explain it, not to you, not to myself. I see dirt on my sneakers, like when we went for that walk along the riverbank, and I know it has something to do with the eyes of a horsefly, but I have no idea what that means now. Then the next day I see an old wooden toy, and I feel a surge of rage, but I don't know why. All my memories are like that. Broken. Shit, that's why I make up stories."

"I see, you've got amnesia. I've read about that. Serial killers and politicians pull that out as their excuse all the time. What've I gotten myself into . . . Who are you, damn it? A man with no past?"

"That would make you a woman with no present—damn you and your police investigation."

"Did something happen when you were little?"

"Sure, aliens abducted me and experimented on me. Does that line up with what you read in *My Secret*, or whatever? Why the fuck're you doing this?"

Dina went to the bathroom and retrieved her toothbrush, deodorant, perfume, and the emergency tampons she'd stored there. Then she went into the bedroom. Matija was still staring at the fake photographs, hoping he'd find a detail that would by some miracle prove he hadn't lied after all, but he could hear her opening the drawers with rough, brusque movements—heartfelt movements—and packing her belongings into a cloth bag.

She came back into the kitchen, steadied herself for a few minutes, and, without a trace of a quaver, said, "Why did you lie to me? Why is it so damned difficult for you to tell the truth, even though you see how much I love you?! You idiot, whatever you'd said, if you'd told me you'd stolen, begged, been abused—if it had been the truth—I'd have loved you even more. Why can't you understand this? What could that six-year-old child have gone through that was so terrible you can't tell me about it, even when you see me leaving?!" She waited another ten seconds, saw that Matija wasn't going to say anything, then took her bags and opened the door.

"You're leaving," said Matija, plainly, with the hollow realization of finality.

"I'm leaving you. You can put it that way. But you were only halfway here."

6.

That autumn marked the beginning of his slow decline into everything painful, dirty, and shameful. From the outside, he appeared to be holding up well. He explained the breakup to Miljac as a result of incompatibility. "She was from the corporate world, you know." Matija's voice cracked, and he stared at the ceiling.

Deeper down, things looked different. His heart skipped a beat when he found a forgotten can of anchovies, he became a bumbling mess when he ran into someone from her circle, and sometimes he drove himself mad with thoughts of someone else fucking her. A better man than him, with a hairy chest, who knew his way around cars and wines, who remembered absolutely everything. He thought of her often. He jerked off with his left hand while imagining that in his right he was cupping one of her big lazy-eyed tits. Sometimes he loved her with true desperation. He tried to convince himself that he merely loved the memory of her and wouldn't desire her so intensely if she'd stayed.

At first everything seemed under control because he had the perfect chic dodge. That summer, he could finally give himself over to writing. He couldn't have anticipated the hell that awaited him. Summer stretched into fall, and he spent the next year looking for a story worth writing, then the year after that telling himself he'd found it.

Although he'd initially decided to write a moving story about a soccer player who realized he was gay, by Christmas he had only a half a page of notes.

THE GAY SOCCER PLAYER—POSSIBLE TITLES:

Bend It, Bench, Score: "Bend it" suggesting a soccer pass, possibly the protagonist's nickname; bench for the second-string players—also a metaphor for social outsiders. The bench will be where his first caress is exchanged with a fan. Show how tough Bender is getting some—no one will expect that.

Dropping Out of the League: When a soccer club ends the season at the bottom of the league; also suggests when the penis slips out during anal sex—that keeps happening to the protagonist because of his lack of experience.

Fistful of Balls: The courage needed in a repressive society to come out of the closet; also when, during missionary sex, the one on his back (Bender) has to lift his balls so his partner can penetrate him.

Epilogue title: Referee Overtime. This, like . . . are we as readers capable of judging his decisions and shit like that?

He didn't get much further because of numerous and welcome distractions. On his way home from a late beer, he'd rail at himself and go to sleep promising that the next day he'd definitely write a full page. One Sunday morning he downed a bottle of wine before noon and started writing, though he knew he couldn't handle more than three glasses. He got going. He stopped returning to the beginning of each paragraph and erasing all the stupid sentences; he stopped wandering off into endless tedious digressions. The next morning before work, he read what he'd written, his stomach clenched, still tipsy from the night before, and it wasn't half bad. It was something people who wore hipster glasses and bragged about how well-read they were might actually read. This was the voice of someone angry. It was like he was watching someone else's dream. And since it was morning, he felt he might slip back into his reverie, so he sat at the computer and tried to continue. If it began to really take off, he thought, he'd call in sick and write all day. *A dream should be so powerful that it sucks you in.* But it didn't.

In early 2009, his old friend Korina persuaded him to have a professional photographer take headshots and make an album for him like the ones actors and models had. He agreed, hoping this would get his creative juices flowing, and spent 4,500 kunas on clothes and tattoos before the session. He didn't really understand what was so cool about being the millionth person in the world to wear an olive-drab T-shirt with a red five-pointed star and Che Guevara's profile, or get your name tattooed on your arm in Chinese.

His regular physical masturbation was soon joined by the mental equivalent. He held imaginary interviews with himself and came up with all sorts of incisive repartees to questions about life, the world, politics, and art; he had fantasies about how, when his magnificent book came out, buxom journalists would ask him for his opinion on some inanity. He wrote out quotes from his not-yet-existent book and imagined how one day they would appear on news websites, alongside other quotes from famous people. He imagined Dolenčec in alphabetical order among other famous names (Dickinson, Doderer, Dolenčec, Donizetti, Dostoevsky, Dumas). He pored over biographies of famous and successful writers, especially the parts where they were miserable. Supposedly Balzac drank forty cups of coffee a day and could work for fifteen hours straight on the vast *Human Comedy*. He'd eat something around five or six, sleep until midnight, then get up and write for hours. Sometimes he wrote naked. Schiller pulled the curtains, soaked his feet in cold water, and stored rotten apples in his desk drawer.

Matija was certain an idiosyncratic detail would tilt the scales, a particular way of writing that his future biographer would offer as a curiosity from the life of the magnificent Dolenčec. He began writing barefoot, as if to keep himself awake and focused. For two days, he wrote a moving story, barefoot, about a porn star from Vratišinec. Actually, he spent two days in front of the computer going from one porn site to another, all the way down to the darkest parts of the information superhighway. On the fifth day writing barefoot, just when he'd finished revising the first paragraph, he noticed it stung when he peed. He'd gotten a urinary tract infection. Several nights in a row, he woke thinking he'd heard someone call his name from the street. Half asleep, he was afraid to see if there was anyone actually out there at that hour.

In the spring they tore down two buildings across from his. They dumped all the debris in a heap, and that same day two twenty-year-old vans full of dark-skinned people began circling. These collectors of secondary waste made daily rounds through his neighborhood with the nonchalance of vultures. Matija had the impression that every retiree within a six-block radius had befriended them as if by collective agreement. They found one, whose name was Pajdo, to be particularly appealing. He'd gesture to every passerby with a thumbs-up and shout, "Giff me fife." One day he shouted this to Matija, and Matija had no idea what to answer, so he said, "Good morning." They repeated this exchange every time they met. Giff me fife. Good morning. Matija found Pajdo disgusting. He didn't want to be infected by the man's aura of failure.

With the construction project, the dust in his apartment became increasingly onerous. He often felt the need to blow his nose really hard, so with his left hand (because his right was on the keyboard, poised to write down the next ingenious thought to come to him, any minute now) he'd pull a T-shirt or sweatshirt from his laundry basket and blow his nose into it. He was sure the snot would vanish in the washing machine, until one day in the middle of a meeting—around the table were seated Coffee, Monday, Toothpaste Smell, and Suppressed Morning Erection—he noticed a glob on the sleeve of a shirt that had been washed and ironed, living proof that his nasal buddies were resistant to laundry detergent and wouldn't be so easily forgotten.

Most of the time he was furious, and he soothed himself by walking. He spent several nights wandering through the city instead of sleeping. He peered through the windows of a house in Cvjetno naselje because he thought he'd lived in a home a little like it when he was small, in Međimurje. It had dark-red roof tiles and a gray-yellow facade; he could tell, though only a streetlamp kept the form of the house on this side of wakefulness. He stood for a while because he seemed to recall a game with a string and a ball, but suddenly a white hand appeared from the gloom behind a window and, fingers splayed, rested on the pane. There was no way to see who it belonged to, but behind the phantom hand flitted a throng of white shadows. Matija stood transfixed for a few more seconds before he ran back to the well-lit street. He saw the hand again with perfect clarity when he shut his eyes in bed. It was milky-white and blue, cold, like the hand of a dead child.

Summer neared. He read and fitfully copied passages out of Houellebecq, Walter Benjamin, Franzen, Updike, Frisch, Murakami, and Pamuk. He wasn't particularly interested in how they wrote, but he read them because he could no longer bear being unable to drop their names at fancy-schmancy receptions.

He despised every cunning plot twist, every perfectly original observation. When he read the passage from Murakami's *Sputnik Sweetheart* about a girl who loses her tram tickets, he thought he might be able to tweak it a little and use it himself, and then later swear he hadn't plagiarized it if anyone asked. He persuaded himself that no one would ask anyway, and it could be presented as the sort of cunning inter-textual game that might entrance a beautiful student of anthropology and Czech and motivate her to talk about it with her well-endowed girlfriends.

He gave that up quickly. He observed himself becoming a scaven-ger, a collector of secondary waste. He was even prepared to steal if it would get him writing. He thought this was similar to what Pajdo and his crew had been doing over the last months around the neighborhood. Like them, he didn't care about the people from whom he was taking everything. Damn the collectors of secondary waste. Their passive dis-regard, their carefree brashness.

One morning he kept tightening his tie until he could no lon-ger breathe. He watched his face change without blinking. The veins popped out on his forehead, and his mouth sagged open because he couldn't swallow the saliva pooling around his tongue. He began black-ing out and loosened his grip, but the tie didn't loosen. He fell to his knees, coughing hard, and had to yank with both hands to pull apart the knot. All the next week, he was reminded of this incident by heart palpitations, pain when he swallowed, and red scratch marks on his neck from the scrape of the collar. He had a terrible feeling that this hadn't happened of his own free will, that something was driving him from a hidden place.

For several days when he left work, he ran into a faceless man, always dressed the same way, who said Matija's name while walking by him. The man was fat and short, shaped like three large cube-like lumps that had been tossed together by an unskillful hand. The first few times, Matija turned, but the man just kept walking. On the fifth day, in the same spot, Matija asked where he was from. The man stopped, shoved his dull gaze into Matija's face, and in an odd dialect full of open, lazy vowels, he calmly answered he was from a place where you could see lights in the forest at night. Matija never saw him again.

At some point in August of 2009, he finally gave up. After months of insomnia, he was totally disoriented. He'd walk into a room and forget why he'd come. Although he couldn't prove it, he was certain he had not sent the relatively young, feminine department head an email with his notes for the novel about the gay soccer player. How could he have? Matija stored his notes in a separate account linked to his private email. But there it was, from his work address, and on the document, under *Properties*, Matija was listed as the file's author and owner. The whole thing became more dramatic because the department head saw this as an insult and reacted accordingly. After Matija carefully explained (never mentioning the words *gay*, *provocative*, or *sensitive*) that he was a published author who, in his spare time, was always looking for a good story, the department head chose to reduce his salary by 10 percent for a year and placed him on a two-year probation for bullying.

As he slipped off his shoes at home that day, he admitted his life had long since fallen hopelessly to pieces and that he had to snap out of it, no matter what. His conclusion was reasonable enough, but he'd misunderstood the cause. He gave himself an ultimatum: if he didn't get himself together within a month, he'd seek professional help, and, if need be, stop writing. He thought up the story about the Roma man and the Croatian woman. Only a small part of him believed he'd succeed.

For the next year, until Gita's conclusive assertion that the novel was a bust, Matija's fears were contained in the realm of reason. The unusual encounters and bad dreams were less frequent, but he carefully concealed how he was slowly being devoured by what he saw when he was alone.

It would be wrong to say he'd had a change of spirit. He'd changed shape. For a time, he joked about his every fart to his colleagues, certain he was so beloved that they'd only love him all the more for it. He came up with cruel nicknames for people, and lied about how much he was cooking for himself at home. When he was with friends, he pretended to be someone who was forever commenting on world events, an over-bearing know-it-all. His companions simpered politely.

And, finally, sometimes, only sometimes, just before he shut his laptop, feeling pleased he'd done something useful that day, he'd read the last words he'd written backward. He didn't mean to do any of those things, and this last one he did as if being compelled by a fierce invisible force. *Ecreif. Elbisivni. Ecrof.*

7.

Once he'd unloaded Gita and her groceries, he felt as lost as he had the last two years but now had nothing to hide behind. He stopped at a neighborhood dive, a bar where there weren't any chairs, so when the drunks could no longer stay upright by leaning on the counters, they threw themselves out. At least in theory. The dive was called Lord, probably because it had been imagined as a place where a man could feel like a gentleman, smoke cigars, sip cognac, and discuss world markets and foreign affairs. But the actual customers had lost every chance they'd had in life, yet they still seemed to feel that life owed them something. The fiftysomething waitress—wearing Borosana shoes that looked like open-toed high-tops on heels—still hadn't taken down the Christmas and New Year's decorations. This suited the people who drank there perfectly. They were celebrating something that was long over, and more than alcoholism, they shared a constant surprise at what had happened to them. They were living only part-time. The rest of the time, they imagined the lives they thought they deserved. And that was better than remembering when they still had hope.

Matija might have walked right by the bar without even looking in, but that evening he needed to see people who were more miserable than he was. That's why he went in when Pajdo waved him over.

"Lookee, lookee, it's Mr. Goodmorning. Come in for a beer, neighbor."

Pajdo was clearly worse off than he was, if by no other measure than the duration and quality of his loserdom.

Walking in, Matija said, "What are you drinking, gents?" to Pajdo and his friend, a bearded older man dressed in dark-red socks and a floor-length black coat that showed the stains from several meals. There was something hoglike about the old man's face, and apparently he hadn't been able to speak for some time. Matija didn't fit in, but he didn't care. This place was no different from any other place on earth.

"I'll take a spritzer, Janja."

"And I'll take whatever you have on tap . . . Janja. So how've you been, Pajdo? I haven't seen you . . . must be a year," said Matija.

"They sent us packing. While we were collecting debris, someone stole the iron manhole covers, the ones on the street, and then one of your neighbors had an accident when he drove over the uncovered manhole. But it wasn't us."

"I'm sure."

"Now we just scavenge for copper, tin, that sort of thing. Maybe old paper, too. If you have any . . ."

"Not me, but at my work. We have tons of old paper. Usually we put it out for the recycling truck, but I could arrange for you to pick up a load. Come on Monday, noon, Maksimirska Road across from the outdoor market. I'll tell the porter."

"Boss, you're good to me. Now it's my turn. Janja!"

"No, no, I still have some."

"All right, later then. What do you do?"

"I work for a government agency. Boring, really. But I used to have a nice hobby, I wrote. Novels and short stories."

"Not anymore?"

"No, today I'm quitting. I worked on a book for two years, and no one can stand it. So that's it, I capitulate. A year too late. I should've been doing something else," Matija said, then took a big gulp.

"No, boss, that's not capitulation," said Pajdo, shaking his head. "To give up on your dreams, that's not for just anyone." Matija looked him in the eyes for the first time. "For that, you need gumption." Pajdo assumed the voice of a well-meaning auntie reading fairy tales to children. "I'll tell you how it goes. I am an expert in this. First you only think about things you don't like, about what you want and can't have. Just the bad side. You seal yourself off in your cave, stop talking to people. That takes time—six months, maybe years, depending on the person. You see, when you're a kid, you divide everything into good and bad. Good things seem beautiful and strong, they smell nice, and you want them. You feel like you already have them. Then you're older, and you see you've somehow become all the things you thought of as bad, weak. They're there, and you can't get rid of them."

"Mrs. Janja, pour us another. Whatever's on tap."

Pajdo kept talking in this hypnotic tone, and Matija drank his beer. One by one, everything around him slipped away. The bar, the older drunks, then the younger ones, the ashtrays, and the bad attempts at portraits of generic English lords on the walls. After a while, Matija could no longer feel his face, and he began thinking that he, too, was slowly vanishing. Only Pajdo and his voice, and the silent old man in the socks, were left. Objectively, maybe his companions weren't real. Was he actually talking to Pajdo? Who cared, this wouldn't be the first time he'd invented someone to talk to.

8.

While part of his brain was trying to place the face in front of him, another was reconstructing the dream the face had plucked him from. It was about a town of strange people on a hill covered with dark-green conifers. The hill was actually an island, because when night fell the water rose and turned into this immense lake, and no one could get on or off. First the dogs started dying, then the chickens and cows, and then, in terrible agony, the people. By dawn only Matija was left, waiting for the water to ebb.

When he woke, he was on a sofa in his sister's place, and it was late afternoon. His sister's husband was facing the stove, putting water on to boil as quietly as possible.

"Well, where have you been, Mr. Life-of-the-Party? Why drink when it causes you pain?"

Matija couldn't force cheeriness. He was wearing a T-shirt bearing the logo of the bank where his sister's husband worked, and pajama bottoms.

"What time is it?"

"Late for some of us. We called in sick for you. Don't forget to mention your one-day flu and very high temperature. Drinking on a school night, eh?"

"Wait till you hear where I got plastered. Lord. You know, that dive by the post office?"

"Geez, hear that?" his sister's husband chuckled, leaning on the stove.

His sister laughed. "I've never thought of you as a Lord type. What, you got drunk with the desperadoes? I'm not going to hook you up with the doctors at Vinogradska, the hospital for alkies!"

Matija grinned weakly.

"Listen, please don't tell Mom. You know what she's like."

"Okay, sure."

"Don't give me that 'Okay, sure' stuff. You know she's afraid I'll crack up . . ."

"Well, okay . . . But look, was there a particular reason?"

"As if I need a reason. But if you want, I'll dig one up . . ."

His sister gave her husband a few instructions about shopping and the importance of timing for getting the food in the oven, and he headed out. She poured two cups of coffee.

"So, now, what happened? For real this time."

"Gita read the manuscript. She says it's crap."

"Oh, come on . . . You didn't get drunk with her, did you? I've told her to stop that shit, but you can't teach an old goat new tricks . . ."

"Don't worry, she wasn't there. Gita has things under control. I was with her yesterday when she went to pick up her sleeping pills."

"Oh, okay. Well, so she didn't like the story about the Roma guy and the ugly girl? Well, I guess that's a good reason to get plastered. I haven't had time to read it yet, but I have it on the computer . . ."

"Forget it, delete it. It's not worth the time."

"Hey, don't start with the pity party now . . . Relax a little, hang out with friends, watch a couple of mindless movies in that new 3-D theater, take a trip somewhere. Forget yourself for a while."

"That's been the problem."

"What?"

"Nothing."

"Listen. You have two books behind you, and now you're reassessing things. I mean, I don't know much about writing, but I know you'll snap out of this. Best to let sleeping dogs lie, like Granny would have said."

"But I can't remember."

"There are first-rate writers who hadn't even started at your age. And ones who only wrote crap for years. Fuck. It's a waiting game."

"I'm not one for patience. I'm just a smidge overbearing."

"Then, brother dear, it's time for you to focus on other things. I understand you like it, but you can't live off writing, so it's a hobby, right?"

"Yeah, just like collecting baseball cards or sticking pins in a world map."

"Oh, come on, don't start with some story about writers as precious jewels or whatever. I'll lose it. Have you ever wondered why you need this anyway? Are you happy? I don't think so."

"No, but I can tolerate myself when I write. It's only then I can see things clearly."

"How sad." His sister barked a laugh, clearly angry. "You're just a pathetic version of yourself. Now, I'll tell you something. I got test results for a kid who's twenty-seven, younger than you. A brilliant chemist, came out of nowhere, central Bosnia, he doesn't even know where his parents were killed in the war, works at the Ruđer Bošković Institute and volunteers, in his spare time, to tutor kids from poor families. And he came in this morning with a headache, turns out it's a brain tumor, inoperable, and he's got three months to live. Over the coming weeks, he'll lose function after function as he slowly fades. On Monday he's coming back, and I'll have to break the news. And now I'm listening to you whining about your lost-cause writing. Who cares?"

"Hey, why ask if you don't want to hear about it?"

" . . . "

"Look, I feel sorry for the guy. What's his name?"

"Stjepan Hećimović. Fuck. The first time you see something like this, you think things just have to be that way, you'll get used to it eventually. But that's not how it works. You get to the point where you control your voice and the expression on your face. But the knot in your gut is still there."

"So what will you tell him?"

"What else? Tell him there may be a new experimental treatment and trick him into taking aspirin. Send him home, lock myself in the bathroom, curse."

"If he's a chemist, he might see through the fake treatment."

"Maybe not. People believe all kinds of shit when they're scared." She was angry and sad. Over time, she'd learned that only the first emotion was okay to show others. People stopped listening to the sad ones after a while. "But you should pull yourself together and be grateful for the gorgeous life you have."

They both stopped and smiled weakly.

"Okay, so, what else is new? Other than getting drunk at dive bars? You seem as if you're in a weird place."

"'Weird' is putting it mildly."

"So tell me. I won't yell at you, I promise."

"I don't know. It's just that there are these . . . things that weren't there before. Maybe they don't have anything to do with each other, but . . . I don't know. It started while I was with Dina. It was as if I couldn't tell her about anything that really happened in my past. And the further I think back, the worse it gets. I don't know how to say this: I tell stories about things, they seem to be right there, but I don't actually remember anything at all. Dina was furious about it. It turns out that . . . I'm lying all the time . . . I don't know."

His sister stared at him and said nothing, she didn't even nod. Matija—busy trying to come up with some insight into his twisted life—didn't notice she was having trouble breathing.

"I started feeling afraid and reacting strangely. Like, I'm walking, and a car passes behind me, and it sounds familiar somehow, and then I'm suddenly in a bad mood, and feel cold inside . . . I can't sleep. My dreams are fucked up. And I feel like someone's following me. Maybe I'm . . . seeing people others can't see. You know, like in a B horror movie. Man, I'm saying all this out loud for the first time, and I sound crazy. I know it's stupid . . ."

His sister said nothing, she just downed her last swig of coffee and sipped some water. After a time, Matija said, "And I don't understand my own behavior. It's as if I'm imitating something I can't see. I don't know. Well, it's not all bad. Maybe I'm depressed, so this all comes up on its own. I'm not as bad around other people—at work and stuff, I do okay. I think it's because I can't write. When I started writing, in high school—"

His sister interrupted him. She spoke quietly, steadily, and deadly serious.

"Not high school. You started writing when you learned the alphabet. Why are you looking at me like that? Jesus, you really did totally lock away everything before we moved to Zagreb. That was probably good, you switched channels and survived, but now it's time to find your way back. I've got something for you."

She stood up, slipped on her clogs, and left the apartment. She came back a few minutes later carrying a cardboard box. There was a smudge on her sleeve from a brush with dust, so Matija figured she'd been down in the storage locker. She took out a pile of children's drawings on yellowed paper and several sheets covered in an awkward scrawl and tossed them down in front of him without a word.

"Are these yours? Mine? What?"

Matija glanced over at the drawings, and after an initial numbness, he felt a growing chill. They were a child's sketches of brutal scenes of mutilation, abuse, maybe even death, but definitely agony and pain. In one, a child knelt in the middle, with big black eyes, one hand covering his mouth, from which red blood was dripping, and the other holding a red lump. Matija thought it was a heart. Around the child stood five or six figures, their heads turned away. Either that or they had no eyes. The drawings were done with crayon, mainly in black and red. The strokes were quick, and the surface of the paper was almost scored, the crayons had been pressed so hard. The circles weren't closed. The skies were, as a rule, filled with black-and-red streaks; there was no sun in any of the drawings.

In the second pile were sheets of paper, and on them were messages, half of which were in the local Međimurje dialect, and most of which he couldn't read due to the illegible handwriting or perhaps a sudden spell of dizziness. One sheet read:

> *Too many strange things are happening around me, and I'm scared I'll be lost in our house or garden because the things and furniture and trees and animals aren't acting like they used to. Each thing is fixing to tell me something. They're always talking, all at once. I can't stand listening anymore, I'll go crazy.*

In a flash Matija was at the toilet, where he vomited until all that was left to expel was yellow-brown liquid. When he came back, he was at a loss. The drawings didn't look familiar, but they resonated totally with his terror.

"You left those on Dad's grave," whispered his sister while he stared at the table. "I took them because I was afraid of what people would think. I didn't want them to be afraid of you, though you were strange with me and Mom after Dad died. A weird little kid, no two ways about it. I was scared of you, and I was scared *for* you. You were how old? Six? And you'd ask us out of the blue if we'd still love you if you'd done something really bad. Or you'd ask me softly, so Mom couldn't hear, whether I'd go with you to dig up graves. A boy of six. You talked to yourself. Once I found you standing in the middle of your room, staring into the corner of the ceiling and talking, half in some strange language I couldn't understand. I remember you said some words . . . *undal, brokesto, safuntteo* . . . and then you nodded and smiled. When you realized I was watching, you said to the ceiling that I was your sister and they should 'leave me alone.' And then things started getting even harder. You stopped eating, everything disgusted you, you were afraid to stay home alone, you were afraid to go out in the yard, you wouldn't tell us what was scaring you so bad. You wet your bed at home, and you wet your pants at school. Once I woke up in the middle of the night because I sensed someone in my room, and it was you. You were in your PJs, shivering, crying, and whispering, 'They're here, they've found me.' You'd get better for a few days, and then Mom would find bruises and scratches on your ribs and back, as if someone had beaten you, but you wouldn't say who. You threw stones at the neighbor, spat at people, set fire to things, hid stuff. You'd always swear that it hadn't been you. That you didn't know who it was, but it wasn't you. Once I saw you throwing rocks at the cherry tree in our yard and punching it until your hands bled. I asked you what the fuck you were doing, and you finally said you were mad because Mom had thrown this wooden box away, and it was better to hit the tree because you were afraid you'd do something bad to Mom. You ran away from home, don't you remember? In the middle of winter, someone found you on the banks of the Mura, nearly frozen. You were in your pajamas and a jacket. And then later you ran off into the forest. That was when they had to amputate your toes. You must remember that. When you were in the hospital for two weeks and got pneumonia?"

Matija stared at her without blinking.

"You erased it all, and that's that. Well, we were scared shitless for you. We thought social services was going to take you; the people in the village had started talking. Then you calmed down for a few years. But then . . . when the suicides began, one after the other, remember that? Jesus . . . you kept showing up near someone, and then they'd kill themselves. Mom and I were . . . skeptical. Fuck it, I guess you can't understand what's happening until you get distance from it. Perspective. We moved away because of you, not because Mom found a job in Zagreb. Everyone was scared of you."

Matija was barely breathing. His sister went on, still whispering.

"You didn't start writing in high school. The only authentic stuff you ever wrote was earlier, when you were a child. Later you were good at it because you'd learned how to lie about what you didn't want to remember. Mom and I are partly to blame. Whenever you'd make something up and switch it with something that actually happened, we just nodded and smiled. Everything you've written—the short stories and the novel—all that is good, but it's a by-product of the fact that you had to invent a childhood. But understand: Your obsession with writing won't end, even if you write a hundred stories you think are good. It's not the writing you're aching for."

"This is all totally . . . incredible."

"Know what? Take a sedative to calm down, then have a shower because you reek. Sleep here. Tomorrow you'll go to work, pretend you're fine, and after you'll go see a friend of mine whose job it is . . . to help deal with the serious stuff in life."

"Please don't send me to a shrink, I beg you," said Matija, though there was no fight left in him at all.

"He earned a degree in psychology, but he hasn't practiced in years. Okay? You'll go out for a drink, take a walk, whatever. C'mon, do it for me. And don't forget Stjepan Hećimović, the guy with the worst luck of the decade."

9.

"My sister informs me you're no longer working as a psychiatrist. You're on the young side for retirement."

"Let's drop the formalities, all right? Yeah, it didn't work out, me being a shrink. I had a practice in the Upper Town for a while, but I started losing patients. My fault, I'm sure. I told them they were crazy. Since then, I've pretended to sell art, but my wife supports me. I told her, too, that she's insane herself, putting up with me the way she does."

"So were they crazy? Your patients, I mean?"

"Who isn't crazy in their own way? I'm just sorry I didn't get more money out of those pompous assholes. I should have told them what they wanted to hear: That their parents were to blame, that everything will be fine if they spend fifteen minutes a day repeating they're worthy, beautiful, and good, and reality is whatever they make of it. The new-age bullshit some young psychologists are selling these days. I'm an old fart."

"So who's right?"

"Neither. But when faced with a complicated problem, people shouldn't lurch off into esoterics. I hate the idea of promising people they'll be successful, healthy—fuck it, forever young—if they buy into something . . . You can't just manifest a change in something rooted so deeply in a person that they can't reach it. I have a friend who spent the last five years of his life in front of a TV because he was certain everything would turn out fine seeing as he was visualizing success and love."

"I thought . . . I assume you're doing this as a favor to my sister, so I'd be interested to know what she told you."

"I may not be a shrink anymore, but that doesn't mean I'm not interested in human nature. Your sister only said that weird things were happening to you, and you haven't been yourself lately—nothing more."

"I came because my sister asked me to, and because I can't figure out how to move forward. I wasn't sure I'd be able to be honest with someone I don't know about such personal stuff. But now that I'm here, I'm . . ."

"You have no idea what weirdos I've listened to: lawyers, politicians, business leaders . . . and their kids! I promise I won't tell you you're crazy."

"Well, okay . . . I feel like I've been receiving signals from the past . . . This has been happening a few times a week for the last two years . . . I see people, and I'm not sure whether they're actually there."

"Are they always the same?"

"The same one appears a few times, then stops. I saw an old woman standing in front of my building, always wearing the same apron. A fat man says my name as he walks by. And sometimes I feel like I'm supposed to be someone else. I don't know how else to describe it. And then sometimes I see something real, like a car or something, and for no reason I'm suddenly really angry."

"Okay, you really are crazy. Kidding, kidding. Well, you're probably not delusional—you're way too lucid for that."

"I'm almost sure these are things I repressed years ago. I remember very little of my childhood, before we moved to Zagreb. Yesterday my sister told me about some weird things I went through, and I thought I might be able to remember them now. I'm pretty sure I'm not scared of what I would remember. I just want to know what really happened."

"I don't know whether it's possible to access the original experience—perhaps by hypnosis, though even that isn't a sure thing. But how do you know this is about the past and not a distorted perspective on what's happening now? Maybe you'd find it easier to project your feelings back into a mysterious past."

"I know this isn't proof, but all of it . . . feels like something terrifying, something only I know. And it doesn't seem random. Sometimes I can link two of the elements. For instance, never a face and a name, but a yellow short-sleeved T-shirt and the fact that it rained that day, stuff like that."

"I see. Well, why not try to accept these random isolated signals for what they are: fragments of a whole you can't access? Why try to understand? It's highly unlikely things would change significantly for you if someone were to show you a film of your childhood."

"These episodes, these visions are . . . getting more intense. At first I ignored them. I thought, I don't know, maybe they'll just go away. It's like I'm living in a house where there are some doors I can't open because I don't have the keys, and I don't know what's behind them. I thought maybe these things would show themselves in time. But nothing's happened, except I can see that I've started avoiding certain places, while obsessively visiting others. I know what my sister told me, but even still . . . I've made up all sorts of stories about my childhood . . . and I lost a person who was important to me. Because of the lies. That's why I need to understand. And besides . . . I don't know how to explain this . . . They have power. They're frightening. They're catching up with me, and they don't mean well. They're controlling my behavior, impeding me. There's this primal malice."

"Good old Sigmund would have loved your story. He'd have sniffed a little of the white stuff and said, '*Ja, ja, sehr gut,* Matija.' Look, what you've told me is troubling. I am 100 percent certain there's a mechanism by which what is left behind goes right on affecting us, controlling us. But how, and how much power it has . . . no one knows. Going back to an original experience, the 'real' memories . . . It's not possible. People think that when you experience something, you form a memory that's like a photograph of what happened, and then, when you recall it, you distort it a little, fail to mention some things, add a few others, and that's that. But we know that memories aren't really distorted as much as they're always re-forming. Each time you retell something, you're erasing the old memory and rerecording it, and the next time, you start from your most recent version and modify that, and so on. Describe the plot of the last book you read, and then read it again. You'll see you've changed things, yet you're certain that is what you read. When that American space shuttle—*Discovery*, *Challenger*, whatever—exploded . . . a group of elementary school children were assigned to write essays about where they were, what they were doing, what they were thinking, what they were feeling, and what they said when they first heard about the tragedy. Twenty years later, they brought the same group together and asked them to rewrite that essay. None of what they wrote was consistent. Every person wrote an entirely different story about what he or she was doing, thinking, and saying that day. When they gave them back the essays they'd written twenty years earlier, the reaction was mainly 'Yeah, sure, that's my handwriting, but I didn't write that.' Human memory can rarely serve as evidence. I clearly remember paying some jerk €270,000 for an apartment that wasn't worth half that. But I also remember the asshole snickering as he got into his car. What I'm getting at is that I may have added that part myself. I can't be sure. As soon as there are feelings in play, particularly negative ones, a person tends, I think, to tell a slightly changed story. Disgrace, fear, guilt . . . These are the most fickle of narrators."

"My sister told me I was a weird kid and she was frightened of me, both right after Dad died and later."

"So there, maybe that's it."

"I'd like to know what happened. You mentioned hypnosis."

"There are all kinds of things—hypnosis, regression, there are even meds for this—but I think they can only lead to a brief moment in the construction of the self. What you're dealing with isn't amnesia, it's repressed-memory syndrome, and it hasn't been well researched. The people who work on this think you can only really reach a memory when you have a trigger: a smell, or taste, or something else that ties you to it. But it's controversial. In your case, I think you should focus on the negative feeling that's associated with the memory. Maybe something will open up for you. Be brave, give in to it, see what happens. I don't envy you. The key, I think, is when a person realizes he can't escape himself and the things he's hidden. The trick is to embrace them. If a person learns to live with his full self, carries around his suitcase packed with repressed, shameful, bad things, opens it once in a while and has a look, and then takes a long moment to process all the debris . . . he'll understand himself better, if nothing else. And be happier for it. And, probably, more fair to himself. Whatever you've been through, now you're here, you've survived, you're standing on your own two feet, with all your baggage and your demons. You need to take the first step, that's all."

"All that's swell. But . . . I don't know where I'm supposed to be going."

"That's not a problem. You said they control you."

"Yes."

"So let them. Let them take you there."

10.

When he came home, even before taking off his shoes, he poured himself a generous glass of whiskey, downed it, then filled the glass again. He sat at the table and leafed through the drawings and messages. He tried to arrange them in some kind of chronological order guided by elementary logic: first were the drawings on their own, then drawings with names over the figures, then drawings with sentences, and finally sentences without drawings. Nothing proved to him he'd really written and drawn them. He tried to imagine the kid and the world that made that kid the way he was. It was a terrifying world full of clocks and bitten-back words, full of shame and defeat. He could clearly imagine the boy watching him from a snowy field in early morning, whispering, "Have you come for me?"

His hell might have gone on forever. He'd tried letting his demons take the lead, but this hadn't gotten him anywhere. He could ask his sister for the details; she would tell him, unlike their mother, who would've twisted the whole thing beyond recognition to avoid the hardest parts. He could get into his car, right now, half-drunk, drive to Međimurje, and cruise around the village. Maybe something he found there would jump-start his memory. One of his cousins still lived there. He knew this because a few years ago, out of the blue, he'd received an invitation to a wedding, and he hadn't even had the decency to RSVP.

He'd imagined himself in a house full of people with whom he shared genetics and nothing else, drinking when the obligatory toasts were made, pretending that the city was inferior to village life, playing down his accomplishments so as not to cause envy, and to keep from coming across as pompous, he'd praise the decor and go on about how he didn't have a family of his own yet. Maybe now he could tolerate wearisome conversation with people he had nothing in common with so he could find a little space to ask, after a time, perhaps even laughing a little, what he was like as a child and why everyone was so frightened of him.

No way.

In their reconstruction, there'd be a moment when he'd glimpse a face clearly, hear a few words echo, but it would all be strange to him. These were not the things calling out for help in his dreams.

False memories ruled the whole nasty evening until, while poking around in his box of photographs, third glass of whiskey in hand, he stumbled on a high school class picture. Seeing it sent a hot flush rushing to his cheeks, like the painful sting of an insect, and he shut his eyes. When he opened them again, the blaze on his cheeks lingered; what he'd glimpsed swirling behind his eyelids was cold and shameful, and totally his.

A kid named Franković's father had been killed in a car accident, and the whole school was on their way to the funeral. They all stood there, solemn and hushed in little groups in the hallway, waiting to leave for the Miroševac cemetery. The boys were talking quietly about sneakers, the girls musing about how painful this must be for Franković. Korina said her old man was a creep, but she'd die if something happened to him. Everything was fine until Matija blurted out that he didn't give a shit about Franković's old man, who'd been a terrible driver anyway. The chatter stopped, and Matija suggested they all go for a drink instead of to the cemetery. He snickered sourly, and the others eyed him, startled and disturbed. Someone said, "Hey, what the fuck," then another said, "You moron," and "Dolenčec, shut the fuck up." He sneered. He pretended to be enjoying himself: "Hey, for God's sake, lighten up, we get to trade the chemistry and math classes for fun things like Formula One or Stanley Kubrick or, if you prefer, Franković's old man." No one laughed; Matija rolled his eyes and acted like he was the only one with the balls to speak his mind.

It was shameful and sad, and it had taken until this sorry moment for him to admit to himself why he'd done that. They were all feeling sorry for Franković, but when Matija's dad died, no one felt sorry for him. *It's way tougher to lose your dad when you're small than when you're almost grown,* thought Matija then, *and we were left on the verge of poverty. Who cared how things were for me then?*

This must be the key Mr. Shrink was talking about, thought Matija.

That evening more tangles unraveled, and he crept closer to his misery. The alcohol had begun heating him up, and he was starting to probe the warm, silty river bottom. He let himself sink. This was the only way to delve into it without caring. Instead of seeking a victim in the mirror, he felt himself craving someone else's pain. He fell asleep, eager for morning, wanting to catch a glimpse of the golden boy who was condemned to die. *Don't forget Stjepan Hećimović. Please, how could I possibly forget him?*

He was burning to see this man before Hećimović learned he was doomed, to soak up his every gesture, to see how carefree he acted, thinking he'd have another forty years. They might even meet, and Matija could ask him, innocence incarnate, how he was feeling. If the chance came up, he might just give the man the worst news he'd ever hear. Matija could watch him as his face changed when he learned he had only three months to live. The thought that he might witness another person's downfall made Matija grin. He stopped waiting, passive and frightened, for the forgotten stuff in his head to spread across his sky. Once he'd broken the news to Hećimović, he'd be prepared to look at the disturbing drawings of that kid he'd buried in his memory so long ago.

He googled Stjepan Hećimović and found him listed on the website of the Faculty of Science at the University of Zagreb. Hećimović's field was inorganic chemistry, and he'd be teaching the next day at nine thirty in the morning. This suited Matija because the next day was Friday, and Fridays at his state agency were the days when the staff ran errands, met with people at government ministries, and drank countless macchiatos, chatting sourly about their likelihood of landing another job.

Stjepan Hećimović was an unusually tall, gaunt young man with a boyish air. His stubble, the shaggy hair that hung over his ears, a few zits, and his well-worn jeans made him look even younger. There was hardly anything to suggest this was a person who was deathly ill—only the dark circles under his eyes, which reminded Matija of slices of bologna kept too long in the fridge. But it was there in the way he moved. First Hećimović couldn't decide whether to place his materials on the desk or the lectern, so he put some on the desk and the rest on the lectern. Then he realized he'd rather stand and switched the piles. He started, "Today we'll . . ." and then realized the room was a little too dark, so he went back to the door to turn on the lights. He spoke quickly, but would often stop midsentence to take a labored breath, and then enunciate the rest of the sentence slowly, speaking clearly. He started listing chemical compounds, with six in mind. When he'd twice listed only five, he stopped, turned to the board, and counted, whispering, on his fingers. After a long moment, he turned back to his class with a triumphant grin and gave them the sixth. The students' anxiety could be cut with a knife. They didn't laugh, Matija noticed. He was really looking at a person struggling with disease, his complexion sallow, his ears red. He'd try to draw a straight line, and against his will his hand would trace a curve, but this was not, for Matija, enough proof of the tumor. It would have been much more gratifying if Hećimović had, for instance, clutched his head and moaned in pain, if he'd vomited, if white foam had bubbled from his mouth, if he'd lost his balance, or, say, gone suddenly blind. Nothing like that happened, and Matija began feeling impatient. He sat in the last row and doodled in a notebook he'd bought at the bookstore. He thought about how Hećimović would spend his last three months. Matija should go up to him today, while the man didn't know how sick he was, while he was still unaware. *Štef, can I call you Štef? You may be wondering what that odd feeling is, that tension in your temples? Well, my friend, you've got this lump in your head, and it's inoperable!* It might be time to set up one of those Facebook support groups, reach out, raise money . . . and maybe . . . maybe he'd offer to write a book about Hećimović's farewell to this beautiful world! Matija would follow Hećimović to the bitter end as his ghostwriter, registering every deep thought he had about death and life and all that shit. He'd follow him while the young scientist slowly faded. It would be the most intense near the end. His sister said Hećimović would lose cognitive functions. He'd start saying things, babble nonsense, lose his memories, not recognize members of his family. *Hey, now that would be bringing harsh reality to writing, something no one has ever done before! I can already see myself shedding a tear on Oprah.*

He was woken from his mental masturbation by a sentence that seemed totally random.

Hećimović was trying to speak from memory and read at the same time, so he interspersed definitions among his stutters:

". . . and other compounds, such as . . . um . . . butanediol . . . and . . . well . . . um, well . . . ahem . . . are used industrially for manufacturing certain kinds of plastics, elastic fibers, and . . . um . . . plastic fibers and so on . . . not um . . . and polyurethane! And besides . . . heh heh . . . for kids like you . . . um . . . well . . . I'm not so old myself . . . heh heh . . . may result in disorders in the neurotransmitters, changes in mood like depression and anxiety . . . so people who work with chemicals like butanediol have to take precautions . . . the problem is probably because the compound is . . . um . . . soluble in water, so it can easily permeate groundwater in greater quantities, but usually factories have built containment systems . . . and so on. So, as I said 1,4-butanediol, also referred to as BD, um . . ."

Butanediol rang in Matija's head a few more times. *Loidenatub.*

He started so intensely he lifted the desk in front of him with his knees. He was on the verge of blacking out, he could see little more than the outlines of the world around him, so out of the lecture hall he staggered.

11.

He crouched over the first bench he saw and began scribbling in the notebook, then went sprinting toward home. Whenever he ran out of breath, he'd lean for a moment against a wall. It was freezing cold, the sky went dark, and rain began to fall. It would have been reasonable to expect everyone to lean forward and hurry along. But they all seemed hopelessly slow to Matija.

In the center of town, he jumped into a cab and alternated between urging the driver to go faster and scribbling like mad. Sobbing and laughing, hunched over behind the passenger seat. The tidal wave of information surging from this one word he hadn't heard in over twenty years was unbearable. He wiped his sweaty forehead with his sleeve.

A little under an hour later, back in his apartment, he finally sat down, shut the notebook, and switched on his computer.

It was easy to find two or three reliable sources to confirm that butanediol had indeed been and still was being produced in Lendava, not far from the northern Croatia-Slovenia border, at an artificial fertilizer plant. This substance—this very 1,4-butanediol—had psychotropic properties; it could exacerbate depression and hallucinations and contaminate the groundwater. He quickly changed into dry clothes and then drove—forcing himself to focus on the traffic—to the state agency where he worked. He said hello to the doorman and headed to his office. He reached into a drawer and, after fumbling around, pulled out a sealed document, which he ripped open.

Two weeks earlier, he'd been leafing absently through a report about a research project studying an unusual series of suicides in the early nineties. The report had lingered at the margins of his consciousness, nothing more than a curious footnote. Which was strange because the study was conducted in the very village where he'd grown up, in northern Međimurje, and the conclusion specifically mentioned local people linking the deaths to a boy, a seven-year-old, whose initials were M. D. But Matija had been obsessing over what Gita would say about the novel, so none of this had raised a red flag. He'd skimmed through the report, taking breaks to surf the internet. He jotted down that the project had had an equal number of male and female subjects (within a 12 percent deviation, as required by EU regulations) and stuffed the report in a drawer he cleared out every three months. For the rest of the day, he'd felt dismal, loathing everything around him, but that was nothing unusual.

Now he devoured sentence after sentence and began cursing under his breath while scribbling, already on the seventh page of the notebook.

When he left the office, it was evening. The street was quiet. Nothing particularly remarkable had happened that day in Croatia, bad news had been taking a long weekend. The only item of interest was of an unusual blue-and-red flash of light that appeared in the sky between 7:30 and 8:15 p.m., which could be seen from almost all of northwestern Croatian and a part of Slovenia. Several photographs of it circulated across social media that evening, and several people who'd seen it described it for the late news. One of them said it was incredible that the aurora borealis could be seen this far south, others wondered what the hell it was. The next day the papers ran a few of the pictures and a brief commentary.

The scientific fact of the butanediol freed him of the blame he'd been carrying.

85

He walked calmly, as if actually seeing the city around him for the first time. He was all tied in knots. It's not that he felt relief—that would have been too strong a word. He felt clear. What he'd written and what he'd write over the next three days, only stopping to sleep when he had to, when he nodded off inadvertently, was all addressed to Dina Gajski.

He walked into the apartment, locked the door, and took out his cell phone with his left hand because he was clutching the pad he'd been writing on in his right. He called his sister's friend, said, "It's Matija," and, without waiting for a response, went on:

"I thought I'd killed them. That's why I forgot. Things you've forgotten bide their time. They keep an eye on you, poke each other in the ribs, and snicker softly so as not to disturb the sanctity of the delusion. They only start getting louder when you begin to stagnate, when there's no forward movement, and that's when they go after you, seething because you've forbidden them from coexisting with all the new things you neatly pack into the storage unit known as your life. I can finally see them clearly, and I'm walking toward them. Still . . . I can't help but wonder . . . what if this is just another lie? Well, even if it is, what recourse do we have? We only settle for a lie that's good enough."

The voice on the other end of the line tried several times to interrupt the groggy, insular flow of Matija's words. What made sense to Matija was just a garbled string of syllables to the person on the other end of the line. But that he was speaking backward didn't matter. Because he was writing forward.

I turn and see a gallery of familiar faces, like portraits I painted fast, with no skill, in the heat of the moment when I thought I'd have them with me forever. When the models were right there in front of me, I slopped on the paint, thinking I'd refine the faces at some point, so none of them would ever get away, but every single one of them is lost. Now I suddenly wish I could rework them all, if only I could have one of my canvases back so I could finish it properly. I'm sure I'd make my one and only masterpiece, if only I could have the sketch back.

And no, that's not why I'm writing, I'm not that rude. I'm writing because now I think I can tell you the one story about myself you wanted to hear. You've earned it. I'm writing to you, to myself, to the stranger I've been carrying around inside me all these years, to everyone who has been touched by this, whether living or dead or somewhere between . . . And I'm burning to tell all of us—whether or not I'm to blame—that I'm sorry, so goddamn sorry. This is my excuse for confessing. If this story is about anything, it is about a time when I knew courage, seeking, fear, and ultimately—always—love. Now I feel as if I have been loving only in fits and starts with an imagined, alien self, hoping to gloss over the dark, accursed part of me that no one (except you, a few times) has ever seen. And that's the only part of me that's able to love fully. Only that part can.

HOW TO DRAW YLENOL

1.

It would be impossible to describe the strange occurrences of my child-hood, some of them truly bizarre, without first recounting a legend told by the people living in the region of Croatia known as Upper Međimurje. There in the North, the older folks often told a story about how, in the beginning—when the world was still light and young and made so much more sense—God gave each of his children one part of Earth. He divvied it all up, save one little chunk that he kept for himself. The loveliest and greenest place: a highland with rolling forested hills, redolent with the fragrance of resin and green grapes, and a lowland with meadows, hayfields, and rich tillage. These lands were divided from the rest of the world by two tame, clear-running rivers: the Drava to the south and the Mura to the north. Satisfied, when God saw he'd finished his work, he breathed a sigh of relief and sat down on Mohokos, the highest peak in the beautiful terrain. He soon felt something wriggling between his toes. These were the smallest but also the hardest-working and friendliest people who, not wishing to disturb their good Father, had begun to till the fields of God's land. The only one who spoke was a child, who whispered: "Dear Father, dear God, how will you reward us for our loyal service?" God was sorry he'd forgotten the dearest and humblest of all of his children, so he gave them the piece of Earth he'd set aside for himself. And so it was from that day forth that this gentle place was known as Međimurje, meaning "land lying between waters." It was home to a peaceful people who never left their little piece of earth except when forced to by hunger and privation.

However, peace and prosperity don't last forever. From the north came big, wild men, ogres, with no home of their own (for they'd never been God's children). Mercy was foreign to them; they had long stringy hair that had been tangled and matted by sweat and dust, their eyes were bloodshot, their bodies were caked in mud, and their arms were crusted to the elbow with the gore of people they'd slaughtered in their aimless wanderings. They rode giant horses and astride them forded the Mura. Ever since that day, the river had become murky and was rife with dangerous eddies. This was because they'd rinsed the blood of the innocents from their arms and their swords and their axes, and turbid and rusty the water remained; the ruts gouged out by their immense horses in the riverbed had made the currents unpredictable and treacherous. The Mura often shifted course, as if impelled by the uneasy eternal sleep of the innocents. In its whirlpools and sudden drops in depth, many had disappeared, and many a parent mourned a child who'd been swept away by the river.

The ogres traversed the plain of fields and orchards where the humble people lived, and settled in the forested hills near the village. For they shied from the sun and the light of day, while the local folks loved it and lived near the river. At first the folks were afraid of the newcomers, whose language they didn't understand, but they welcomed their guests because their good Father had taught them to be generous with every living creature. They gathered what they had and greeted the newcomers at the forest's edge with wine and honey. The newcomers took what was offered, but gave nothing back.

The ogres didn't wait for the villagers to come again, but came out of the forest and took whatever they desired. Every household offered up something, they shared freely what God and the fertile fields had given them. An old woman even gave them candles she'd made herself.

The people of Međimurje had learned how to make candles from the first Christians, who used them to bring light to the underworld so souls wouldn't be cast adrift in the dark. One of the ogres grabbed a candle and bit down on it, and saw this was not something to be eaten, so the grandmother showed him how to use it. The ogres were pleased—now they could come down at night from the hills and easily take from the orchards and farmyards. After that, lights could be seen flickering in the darkness among the distant trees in the place where the ogres camped, and the local people watched the forests with growing apprehension.

The village's oldest grandfather showed the ogres how to bake bricks and build walls of mud. Soon their wild forest encampment grew into a fortress, a grim fortress, and at night the screams of the ogres reached the village as they worshipped their cruel gods.

One day the most beautiful girl from the village, seeking respite from her work in the field, went into the forest to find a cool, shady spot. The older villagers had warned her not to go near the trees, but she believed no living creature would harm another without a reason. Seven ogres found her and ran her through with spears. They juggled her head all the way from the forest to the village and dropped it at her mother's feet. For three days and three nights, her mother wept bitter tears. The third night she died of grief, and they buried her by the river, just downstream from where the women scrubbed their laundry. The old people say that even her dead eyes wept, and when the next morning dawned, a new branch of the river had sprung from her tears, which has been known ever since as Grieving Mother Mura.

The sorrow and fury of the peaceful folks mounted, and they gathered their kin from the neighboring villages and set out after the ogres. As they had no weapons, the men took with them hoes, pitchforks, and picks—anything they could lay their hands on. The women and children listened to the screams, tramping, and blows echoing all night from the forest, and many good men lost their lives.

At dawn the ogres slew young Janko, a decent, God-fearing boy, a lad beloved far and wide. He was the son of the old woman who'd fetched the ogres the candle, and the very child who, many years before, had said, "Dear Father, dear God, how will you reward us for our loyal service?"

This sparked the wrath of God the Father, and he sent three angels, who cut the ogres down to their very toes. The angels towered over the ogres and lopped off their heads. Their headless bodies were buried there in a vast pit in the forest, where the feet of three hills meet, and this place is still called Angels' Slaughter. A few of the ogres escaped to the river, but they drowned in the depths they themselves had dredged with the hooves of their giant horses.

Some say the forest was cursed that night. The people, especially older folks, say that even today when the fog rises from the Mura riverbanks on autumn evenings, one can see lights flickering at the edges of the forest. They say these flickering lights are the will-o'-the-wisps, lit by headless bodies rising from their unmarked grave. The ghouls silently pace the forest, candles in hand, waiting for their day of revenge. Perhaps they're waiting to pounce on stray villagers. Each Međimurje village claims that the great battle took place right where it now stands.

In one village, the one closest to Grieving Mother Mura and Angels' Slaughter, they say the courageous lad Janko was buried beneath old linden trees at the place where two paths converged at an angle, one leading up from the riverbank into the hills and the other leading to the other Mura villages. The lindens are long gone, but this is the place where all villagers are buried when they die.

2.

Many years later, at that same burial ground, I swear there must have been eight hundred people gathered to pay their respects to a man everybody thought of as a fine fellow, and whom they remembered as always flashing his warm smile. He was scarcely forty when he succumbed to his illness and left behind his wife, his fourteen-year-old daughter, and me, his five-year-old son.

Looking at the crowd, I felt there was something frozen about the scene, something eternal that justified the disquiet that, though I didn't know it then, would haunt me to this day. It was this feeling that everything I was seeing was staged. The whole thing made me queasy. A sour taste kept rising to my mouth from the bologna in the sandwich I'd wolfed down that morning as people gathered in our yard with black umbrellas and white handkerchiefs. I felt all collywobbles and remembered Dad saying on the way to the coast one time to think about something else, at least until the next rest stop where we could pull over. I didn't know what else there was for me to fix my mind on, so I threw up all over the car window, my sister, and the rest of the back seat in an effort to spare my mother—sitting in front of me—the contents of my stomach. I didn't want to puke all over the grave, so I watched people and tried to remember their names to fix my mind on them. I was surprised to learn one of the mourners was named Vajnč, even though everybody called him Poison because he'd had to go to the emergency room one Easter after drinking rat poison by mistake. There were also men who, if you asked me, looked as if their name ought to be Miška (they had these bushy whiskers, drove lawn mowers, and in the summer came to the front gate in just an undershirt), and others I imagined just had to be named Joža (they had big earlobes, didn't shave often, and sometimes even dared to say "honest t' God"), but their names, of course, were totally different.

I was still small and didn't know much about how things appear and disappear in this world, but I did understand how you could get stuck with a nickname if you showed off, or kept saying the same thing over and over, or were different. Somebody comes up with it, says it, and everybody laughs. The nickname sticks like tar to the person who's marked by it, and to those who use it. And it wasn't just anybody who came up with nicknames. Some of the nastiest ones (Serf, Stinker, Corpse and his entire family—the big and little Corpses) were cooked up by Imbra Perčić, who probably enjoyed the privilege because he was our only electrician and so we had to put up with his ornery ways. Because they feared acquiring a nickname, people seemed to watch what they did, what they bought, how they dressed, and what they said. If they'd seen me picking my nose, they might've dubbed my whole family the Boogies. Somebody might crow, "Lookee, lookee, here come the Boogies." Everybody would laugh, and the name would stick forever. Then again, they might name me after a soccer player from Germany or Italy if I scored a goal for the Miners, the local soccer team.

Julika, known as Stockings, breathed through tightly clenched teeth at the funeral. Her late brother had worked as a mason somewhere near Klagenfurt and died there when he fell, drunk, off the scaffolding. He'd always worn his pants tucked into his socks because he said he didn't want to catch his toe in the cuff, stumble, and, God forbid, fall and smash himself to pieces. A little farther from the grave, by the cypresses near the mortuary, a man we called Samanta—because he was always talking about the singer Samantha Fox at the bar—wiped away his tears. He was good at painting, and he painted portraits of Samantha Fox from pictures he'd cut out of magazines. He did a fine job painting her face and torso, but not her arms, so Samantha always had them behind her back, as if she were being arrested. Next to Samanta stood a widow who was known as John Deere because she drove a little tractor.

Next to her stood Đura, head of the village. He had clasped his hands in front of him, but his face was so twisted from holding back his sobs that his chin and nose nearly met. His wife, Mirica, pressed her purse to her chest and bowed her head so nobody could see her face. They were communists, and they didn't cross themselves or say prayers. My granny told me the commies didn't believe in God and didn't think good people went to heaven, and she said all the baddies (including, according to her, the commies, anyone who stole, and those who worked on Sundays) went to hell. Đura and Mirica were the only ones who played their part well, I thought. If the believers actually believed my dad had been a good man, they should be happy now that he was better off than us in heaven. Granny told me you don't have to do anything in heaven, nobody makes you eat or go to bed, and you get whatever you want.

Next to Đura and Mirica, who, as village heads and commies, probably didn't need nicknames, stood the Ciphers. We called them that because a long time ago they'd had this cow everybody adored named Cipher. According to Granny, the cow was almost noble, with her stately gait and her hide, which was covered with beautiful brown spots, but she was most remarkable for her humanlike gaze. She'd look you straight in the eye and snort as if saying howdy. When Cipher died, Granny said, sadness settled over the village. The teachers at school assigned the children to draw a "cow or another domestic animal during the National Liberation Movement," and several people wanted to hold a requiem Mass for her, but the parish priest wouldn't have it. He explained that an animal couldn't have a soul. "We don't have to call it a requiem Mass, let the Father call it what he wants!" said somebody, but the priest did not oblige. Still, in his heart of hearts, he knew what sort of animal she'd been. At Mass the next Sunday, he spoke so movingly about the animals that kept baby Jesus warm that people were dabbing their eyes during Communion. The cow's owner had been called Cipher long before the cow died, but he didn't mind the nickname. They called his wife and kids the Ciphers, and later they even bestowed this nickname on his son-in-law, who'd come from Slovenia, just over the river from Prekmurje, and who'd had nothing whatsoever to do with that particular cow.

No one standing there on other people's graves, right on top of the genuinely dead and buried, crying as they leaned on the marble headstones, had any idea that I knew the score, that I could tell the whole thing was a farce. I was onto them. To be clear, I was no child genius. Everything I knew about the past was just lumped together in my mind. For all I knew, Emperor Augustus commuted to work in a car. Jesus and Josipa Lisac, the pop singer, watched cartoons together as kids. The will-o'-the-wisp folk Granny had told me about had their own soccer club but didn't make it into the big leagues, so the owner and the coach had a fight. I thought earthworms turned into snakes when they grew up. In Afghanistan, which we kept hearing about on TV, people went to midnight Mass through deep snow and to Hungary to buy their groceries. I frequently wondered what the pope watched on TV, whether ants could see microbes, and if they could see them, did they torture them the way I did ants? And when I was missing the words for something, I'd just point. I knew other people didn't understand me most of the time. It's strange, the number of things in the world I'm missing words for has changed. It's so much bigger.

I wasn't particularly sharp, but I was no fool. I knew what funerals were supposed to look like. They looked a lot like this—a pile of flowers and wreaths, a big hole in the ground . . . but as far as I was concerned, the coffin was just a big wooden box that could have been a decent wardrobe, and everybody was pretending, for my sake, to be burying my dad.

It was all a show put on just for me, an audience of one. The sobs got louder when our neighbors—Pišta, Vest, Rumenige, and Mario Brezovec—began lowering the light-brown coffin into the ground. They sweated and groaned as though with real effort. Pišta slipped and almost fell with the coffin into the open grave. Vest (who didn't play soccer, but drank a lot and picked fights) was panting, "Fuck, fuck, hey wait, slow down, Pišta," because the rope was slipping through his hands. The priest coughed delicately to cover up their voices, and just at the right moment because I could have sworn that Mario Brezovec farted from the strain. Things like that don't happen at real funerals, I reckoned. Angels lend a hand at those.

And, I should say clearly, I had seen my dad's body. When the big black car with German plates pulled up, and they set the coffin down in our living room by the TV on a makeshift bier, everybody fell quiet. Mom was flustered, she looked out the window and said something to herself. Everybody but me cried, even my big uncle. I wasn't sad, I was happy because I knew this heap of pale flesh, this dead doll with a bluish double chin and hands crossed over his belly, could not possibly be my dad. Everybody should have been able to see this, even Granny, who bumped into furniture all the time, groping her way through life instead of seeing it. Maybe death was with us, but not on that bier by the TV. Death was smoking cigarettes, sipping coffee, listening to the conversation about how *the spuds ain't doing so hot this summer* and *it's high time we started digging the ditches so's we can pipe in running water.*

One by one, mourners picked up a clod of dark earth, gave it a kiss, and dropped it into the grave, where it landed with a thud. The power of their performance stirred in me, if nothing else, a sense of awe.

I had a few ideas for how to explain everything. Maybe he'd left us for another family in Germany, and now everybody was pretending he'd died. I'd seen them do the pretending thing before when I'd wanted a red-and-white lollipop and they told me the factory had closed. Then again, maybe he didn't have another family. He loved Mom so much he was always kissing her, to my horror, on the mouth. More likely, he was angry at me because last spring, when he was working in his workshop, I told him he smelled bad, and now he was punishing me. If I apologized, he'd come back for sure. The whole village would come over when I hollered, "I knew you were pretending!" and I'd figure out where to punch my uncle so it would hurt the most. Then there'd be a barbecue, and the grown-ups would smoke cigarettes and drink wine spritzers. We'd open presents: my uncle would get a new set of monkey wrenches, my sister would get something for school, and I'd get a toy I couldn't care less about. The next day, Mom, Dad, my sister, and I would eat at the fish restaurant in Čakovec where I'd be allowed to have a second Coke if I cleaned my plate.

I could only apologize to him, though, if I knew where he was. I asked my sister about it the day before the funeral when she was washing coffee cups and shot glasses—never enough of them in those days. She wouldn't look me in the eye, said something about angels and how the dead are always by our side. But then a coffee cup fell from her hands into the sink. She rested her elbows on the counter, dropped her head so she could be inside herself for a moment, and then said, angrily, "Dad's dead, he's gone, you can only talk to him if you pray or visit his grave." Maybe she meant I could leave a message for him on his grave and he'd get it. That's why I bugged her to teach me how to write: *I'M SORRY.*

Maybe he just wanted to see what I'd do if I thought he was dead. He'd snuck in among the black cornfield of people standing at the cemetery and was watching. If I looked sad, he'd know I cared.

The priest talked for ages. I searched for Dad among all the people there but couldn't spot him. Maybe he was hiding behind the cypresses, or maybe he'd disguised himself to look like somebody else, like in that

TV show, *The Saint*, about that Simon Templar guy. But if I could see his eyes, I knew I'd recognize him.

That was autumn 1988. After that, I learned how to write and read, I learned it's impossible for a person to write, draw, or say everything inside their head, I learned what friendship is, how thoughts can be dangerous, and, finally, about death.

3.

After the priest was done blessing everything in the world, Feri, the gravedigger, and his son shoveled dirt onto the coffin, and people began drifting away. My aunt and grandmother had made cakes, coffee, and stiff drinks at home. I played with my cousins in my room. I was quiet, but impatient. Once in a while, someone would come in with a coffee cup or a shot glass and say something like "Don't you be sad now" or "Your daddy'll always be with you, even if you can't see him." I'd bite my tongue and drive my toy car behind the bed.

They were all quiet, but nobody cried until Godmother went to the car to get lollipops and Milka chocolate for the kids. She worked in Germany like my dad, and I was the only one who called her Godmother—everybody else called her Ljubica. Through the window I thought her sweater was the same one my dad had always worn, and when the door opened, I said, "You're back!" Everybody stopped talking for a moment, and then Godmother came in, closed the door, took out her already wet handkerchief, and buried her face in it. She knelt and hugged me, and the chocolate and round plastic box of lollipops slipped to the floor. Without a word, she went into the bathroom and didn't come out until it was only my mother, my sister, me, and the smell of the funeral wreaths left in the house.

The dark came, and it felt like it went deeper into the house that night. I lay in bed, thumbing through a picture book about Iva and Ana taking a plane. My sister said I had to brush my teeth, so I followed her to the bathroom. She opened the door, then quickly closed it and said, "No brushing teeth or washing feet tonight. Put on your PJs, and I'll tuck you in." When my sister had opened the bathroom door, I'd seen Mom sitting on the toilet lid and Godmother in front of her holding her head. Mom's face was red and puffy, and she was crying in a whole different way than people had been crying at the graveyard. No restraint. Her hair was stuck to her forehead, her eyelashes were matted, her mouth was raw and red, and her arms shook even though they were resting on her knees. I heard her whisper, "How'll I do this all alone?" and then they looked at the door, which my sister quickly shut.

My sister helped me pull on my PJs, tucked me in, and left. I watched the shapes of shadows cast on the uneven ceiling by the weak light from the hall. I prayed to the guardian angel my mother told me was always looking over me and tried to fall asleep. After a while, I got up and opened the kitchen door a crack. My sister was at the table, her back to me, taking photographs out of a shoebox. One by one, she held them gingerly, brought each photo to her lips, kissed it, and set it down to her left on the table. I went back to bed and stared at the ceiling.

4.

For the next four days, I didn't have to go to kindergarten. Everything was almost like normal when Dad was away in Germany, except Mom was wearing black and she'd had her hair cut short, and my sister's eyes were glassy and she said very little, and only in a hushed voice. In the evening the TV would be turned on as if to justify the hush that filled the house, which I was finding more and more difficult to bear.

Wisps of fog floated all day long between the houses around ours, dispersing when the rain came down. Mom told me I couldn't go out. I mostly looked at picture books and the ceiling, and through the window where the world was shifting from downpour to shower and back.

I perked up when Mom said she'd be going to the graveyard. I asked if I could leave a message for Dad on the grave, and she said I could. Since I still didn't know how to write all the letters, I drew myself, then the house and the workshop, and Dad, with his hands and face dirty. Finally I drew water flowing out of a spigot, and a bar of soap. I knew he'd understand.

I'd only started kindergarten that fall, but during the hours I was there, the world outside my classroom became, in my mind, an endless series of miracles and delights. The same thing happened when Mom and Granny decided I was old enough to start going to Sunday Mass. All the best shows were on at the same time as Mass. On the Slovenian channel, there was the cartoon *Živ-Žav*, and I watched a Serbian kids' show, *Musical Toboggan*, which I liked because they used Serbian words I hadn't heard before. For example, they called children *deca* instead of *djeca*, and called rice *pirinač* instead of *riža*—the way we said it at home—and for paper they said *hartija* while we called it *papir*. I stayed home once thanks to diarrhea, and another time I faked whooping cough and got away with it. One Saturday after my bath I told Mom I'd rather go to Mass on Sunday evening instead of Sunday morning. She asked why, and I told her about *Živ-Žav* and *Musical Toboggan*. She said Jesus hadn't chosen watching cartoons over dying on the cross to save us all. This was no consolation as far as I was concerned. I told her Granny said Jesus was already old when he died on the cross, older than thirty, so maybe he'd watched cartoons as a kid, too, and then still had time to die for us all later. In the mirror I saw a look that meant she was mad, and I knew that in a few minutes I'd be sent to bed even though it was only seven thirty.

Everything outside the church became enticingly delightful as soon as Mom or Granny sat me down on the pew and crossed me with the holy water. It stopped seeming so tempting as soon as I heard "Go in peace." After Mass there'd be Sunday dinner—yuck—so no way could I go in peace. In those first weeks of kindergarten, the way I imagined everything outside of school also changed. As soon as I stepped through the front door, before I even sat at my desk, a giant seesaw, huge swings, and a trampoline would rise up from the ground, and on it the fat postman, Joža Popić, and Milica, the saleslady with a mustache, would be jumping, eating chocolate and ice cream. Buses would be waiting to take everybody swimming and out for hot dogs in Petišovci. There'd never be news, weather, or cooking shows, but always *Tom and Jerry*, *ALF*, or *Knight Rider*, with KITT, and movies with Terence Hill and Bud Spencer. Farmland would transform into soccer fields, and farmers would play one-goal hockey using hoes as sticks and potatoes as pucks. We would all drink our cocoa cold so there would be no creepy skin from the cooked milk. As soon as I left the classroom, however, my fantasy world evaporated, and everybody pretended to go back to living their boring lives.

In the days after the funeral, I saw how wrong I'd been.

By the third day, I was getting angry that Dad hadn't shown up so we could go to pick up some milk at the store, fiddle with the car, go to a soccer game and later down to the Mura ferry, where he'd have beer with the grown-ups and I'd slosh Cockta or an Ora soda around in my mouth. I was so angry at him that I probably wouldn't have run to him if he finally showed up at our door.

Still, I wanted to bring him home faster. In secret I did the things that usually summoned grown-ups (sometimes I thought I had an invisible brother telling on me). I wiped my nose on my sleeve, but the only person who saw it was my sister, who rolled her eyes and walked away. With the door to my room open, I'd put one of my Legos in my mouth, which always infuriated my parents, who'd remind me, yelling, of a nameless boy from a nameless village who choked to death doing that. This time—nothing. Both Mom and my sister walked by a few times, and I eyed them, legs crossed and the blue number eight right there between my teeth for all to see.

Then I thought of something that would be sure to work. Dad seldom got mad, but he'd gotten furious once when I made a mess of things in the workshop next to the garage. He told me I was bad, gave me a time-out, and sent me back to the house. That was the only occasion he ever used all three punishments at once.

So after dinner one night, not long after the funeral, I snuck out. I left the door to the workshop open. Everything was organized the way Dad left it: the nails with the nails, the nuts with the nuts, the screws with the screws. I dumped out the boxes and grouped the rusty nuts, nails, and screws in one box, the dark-gray ones in another, and the almost-white ones in a third. Out of the corner of my eye, I watched for his shadow to cross the window. My heart pounded when I thought about how furious he'd be. But the only thing breaking the silence was a tractor on the road. I dumped the three perfectly rearranged boxes onto the floor, then added a big box of monkey wrenches. Again I looked at the door. Nothing. I took the biggest screwdriver, the drill with a cord, and a set of paint scrapers, added them to the unusual pile, and, finally, sprayed it all over with WD-40. I was more and more impatient. I must have said something out loud, because a shadow fell across the doorway.

"What? Have you lost your mind? Into the house, on the double!" The days had been so hushed I'd forgotten what it sounded like when Mom raised her voice. As I raced past her, she reached out and grabbed my shoulder. I ran straight into my room and threw myself onto the bed.

I ached, suffered the way kids do. I was overcome by a sullen, sad mood and would burrow deep down into myself. Away from the world and into me. Granny sometimes said I was pensive like my grandpa Matjaž, whom I was named after. He was a bit odd, stared at his feet, talked to himself, and paced around the village. I'd go into myself so deeply that I no longer experienced what other people did, and I saw and heard things others didn't.

The disturbing and tedious performance of the days after the funeral hurt me because once, when we were playing, Dad had spoken of treasure buried deep in one of the dark forests above the village. He stopped short of telling me where it was, so I threw a tantrum and said I hated him. He told me that if that was the case, the two of us wouldn't go searching together for the treasure. I was sad and angry and, maybe, hard to say (because I didn't articulate it or draw a picture of it), maybe just for a second I wished him gone. And maybe, somebody somewhere heard my wish and granted it. The thought that I'd killed him had been hiccupping in my mind for days, and I bounced between that and the conviction that he hadn't actually died at all.

Dad often sang a song about people who lived in a valley of dreams, where this boy and girl first kissed. He whistled the parts where he didn't know the words, and sang the loudest when he came to the part about the valley. Until then, I'd taken this to mean that the two of us would leave the valley of dreams to find the secret treasure in the hills. Now I wasn't so sure.

Mom came into my room, but I turned to face the wall so she couldn't see my eyes. She said now it was just the three of us, and I had to do what she said and be good. I mustered all my strength and said: "Would you still love me if you knew I'd done something bad? Not like messing up the screws—something way, way worse?"

"What? I'll always love you, come hell or high water. Spit it out, what's this bad thing you've done?"

"I can't say it, I'll never tell."

She let me go visit Granny, a few houses away, closer to the Mura. I was relieved, I could no longer bear the hush of absence in the house. There was always a subtle feel of absence at Granny's (probably since Grandpa Matjaž died), but I was used to it there.

I helped Granny get the chickens settled in for the night, and then I played in her room while she knitted and watched TV. Her house was smaller, but more fun than ours. On the wall by the bed hung a rug that showed two deer drinking from a stream and a needlepoint tapestry of big rabbits, and in the kitchen there was a sizable picture of Jesus, a long-haired fellow with a beard and mustache in a red-and-blue robe. Through the red you could sort of see his heart, and he was pointing to it. I thought maybe he had a T-shirt on under the robe with a picture of a heart on it.

I loved my granny so much that I'd even watch the quiz show *Numbers and Letters* with her and pretend it was interesting. I wondered if maybe she was only pretending to like it for my sake. That didn't bother me, maybe we both watched it because we loved each other. Mostly we didn't say much except when I convinced her to tell me stories. I had to promise I wouldn't have nightmares (as if that were something I could promise) and that I'd pray a decade on her rosary beads with her. As she put the rosary down beside the red-and-white polka-dotted enamel cup, her dry lips brought to life stories about the ghoulish will-o'-the-wisp folk, about the Mura maidens who drew young men to the river's silty bottom, about the knight of Malekoci, who hurled his mace all the way to the next village, about the little girl from a song whose father drowned in the Mura though she escaped death, about the ancient church that sank long ago but poked up at times through the river's surface, and about miners who were still buried deep down in a shaft up there in the hills.

These stories didn't scare me when I was with Granny, because she seemed essentially fearless. She'd survived hunger and disease and the war with the Germans and the Russians and the Cossacks of Cherkasy, and she wasn't afraid of bad weather or the future. Still, there was one thing that gave her nightmares: pop singer Josipa Lisac. Lisac wore weird clothes and stared intensely at the camera. Granny wasn't really scared of her, she was really scared of hell, because she thought that if Saint Peter balanced Granny's scales wrong, Josipa Lisac would send her to the fiery depths wearing spikes on her head and a metal corset.

That evening she told me about the invisible children. Adam and Eve had many children, and when they heard God was going to visit, they started washing their grimy offspring. They didn't have enough time to wash the whole kit and caboodle, so they only showed God the clean ones. God knew they were hiding some so he decided that everything they hid from him, he'd hide from them. Ever since then, those children have been invisible.

It still wasn't totally dark out, so I urged her to tell me the blood-chilling story about the Mura maidens again. How odd that all her scariest stories somehow ended up in the Mura. I personally didn't think of the river as threatening. I loved tossing pebbles and leaves into it, and running along the shore following my little boats. But none of the grown-ups liked the river. It flooded often, and chilly fogs rose off it in the fall and made the frail older folks sick so sometimes they died before Christmas. In summer, clouds of mosquitoes rose up from the bogs and gave off the peculiar, fusty stench of stagnant water, so choking that people couldn't even talk on the street those evenings and had to retreat to their homes. And every so often, word got around that somebody had drowned in the river. The most recent was Milan, a Roma man out for a good time on a humid August afternoon. Before him, a fisherman had drowned. The only things that were found were the fisherman's bicycle, earthworms, and a three-legged stool that looked as if it were peering into the water waiting for him to reemerge. People joked that maybe he'd gone swimming with the Mura maidens, as he was quite an old coot.

Granny and I talked till dark that night. Before Mom came to get me, I asked what happened to the young men who were dragged down by the Mura maidens to the river's bottom. She said they were still waiting there, beneath the riverbed in total darkness, for someone living to be traded for them. Perhaps she shouldn't have told me that.

5.

I didn't really like kindergarten. I had only a few friends among my classmates. The rest, I could tell, didn't bathe every Saturday, and some had grime under their fingernails, which I thought was disgusting because my mom and sister said it was. Some were boring, and some were rough and loud and laughed for no reason. And somebody who laughs for no reason is a dimwit. There weren't enough toys. When our teacher opened the toy cupboard, we understood, briefly, what life would be like for a very poor child. The toys looked as if our teacher herself had played with them when she was little. The teacher had a big bosom, which I liked looking at, and crooked brown teeth. When she walked, she left a lingering scent of cigarettes, coffee, and vegetable stew, beans, green bean casserole, or goulash, depending on the day of the week. The tables and floors in the classroom were old and crumbling, and sometimes I'd inadvertently bring home a fragment of the classroom furniture or flooring in my hair, socks, or sweater, or under my fingernails. If I'd gone to school enough, I'd have ended up taking the whole place home with me. The teacher and her friends always wore the same clothes and stood in the room they called the teachers' lounge and smoked cigarettes as if they had no idea what was fun. Or maybe they knew exactly what was fun, and had chosen to do everything else. Out of nowhere, these harlequins and clowns would show up, and they'd dance and sing about how the greatest riches lay in friendship and how our Yugoslav seacoast connected all the peoples and lands the world over. In my opinion, they were total nobodies. The teachers read us a story about a girl who was persnickety and headstrong. The teacher said she was flighty and capricious; the girl had red hair in braids that stuck out on either side, and she did weird things just because she felt like it. This made no sense to me. Why tell us a story about a girl like that? If she'd been in our class, nobody would've wanted to be friends with her, and the teacher would've punished her. If I'd been in charge, we'd have been singing songs about ninjas and their throwing stars and reading picture books with KITT and Simon Templar in them.

We learned we were supposed to say that nowhere is life better than in Yugoslavia, because everybody here is happy and free and equal. Still, none of us knew what our country had done that was so important after—all by ourselves—we sent the Krauts and that Napoleon guy packing (which was enough for me to be ashamed of my German pencil case and felt-tip markers). We learned two big words: *socialism* and *camaraderie*. Camaraderie was the most precious treasure, and socialism was when everybody helped everybody else and there was no one in charge to tell you to do anything. We learned to sing a song about camaraderie, and the teacher asked what we thought about it. I didn't know what I thought, so I said that what mattered most was when everybody was friends, and it was best when we all played together and helped each other and had camaraderie. She praised me, so I relied on that principle to answer every question I was asked all the way—now that I think about it—through my university studies. I didn't think any of my classmates actually thought camaraderie was such a big deal. Maybe only Silvija Jambrožić and Suzana Perčić, who always played at pretending they were teachers. Nobody wanted to be their students, so they took turns being teacher and student, and were very strict with each other. Camaraderie, the most precious treasure. I wanted to tell everybody that my dad was getting me remote-controlled cars from the

Quelle catalog so they would fight over who could be my friend and have that dumb camaraderie thing with me.

I also didn't like kindergarten because some kids were bullies. The worst was Goran Brezovec, who, on our first day at school, made up a ditty about Damir Noklec, who was fat. It didn't even rhyme, but everybody repeated it and laughed, and it stuck. The main point was that Damir split his pants when he bent over, though as far as I knew, that had never happened. Goran Brezovec was the biggest kid in the class, his dad was village head, his mom worked at the post office, and everybody wanted to be in good with him. I, too, sang the ditty a few times. I was afraid if I didn't he'd make up one about how a bird pooped in my mouth and that's why I didn't know how to sing.

There was a mean song about a girl when the teacher found lice in her hair. A quiet boy who wore glasses was nicknamed Kiss-Ass. I didn't know what Kiss-Ass meant, but I imagined it might be a person who kissed his own, or maybe someone else's, ass. Of course, I had no idea that when I grew up I'd kiss someone else's ass, and it would be very, very nice.

Somebody made up a cruel song about Dejan Kunčec, who sat next to me in class and was my best friend. He pooped in his pants. We had just started drawing a forest and a river, when beneath the odor of the markers there was the smell of poop. The teacher was the last to notice, and she quickly sent Dejan home. He flushed red as a beet and lowered his head, and his tears fell directly in front of the light-brown stain that had dribbled down his pant leg and onto the floor. Goran Brezovec and a few others hooted with laughter, and the teacher opened the window, and then she asked us to raise our hand if we'd never peed or pooped in our pants. Nobody said a word except Goran Brezovec, who mumbled something about how he knew where the toilet was. That's when I loved the teacher, because she stood up for my friend. She was fair-minded, and that was enough for me to believe that Yugoslavia, too, was fair-minded. At the end of the day, she told me to take Dejan his things. This was a few days before the long black car pulled into our yard, before the weird funeral performance happened. He told me he'd only barely felt something bad in his belly, and he'd had no idea this would happen. I knew just what he meant. To be at kindergarten meant constantly feeling bad things in your belly and having to go to the bathroom all the time.

"I felt this fart coming, and then everything was warm between my legs. And it was sliding down."

"So why not say, 'May I please be excused' and run to the bathroom?"

Dejan gave a heavy child's sigh.

"Once I pooped just a little at home, and nobody even noticed for two hours. I thought it wouldn't be that long till the teacher let us out."

"Goran Brezovec made up a song, and he'll tease you." He parked his toy truck between the armchair and the cupboard, without saying anything. "But I won't," I said, and really believed I wouldn't.

Dejan shot me a grateful glance.

The next day we were playing Chicken Laid an Egg on the playground, where everybody crouches in a circle, and one child runs around and puts a handkerchief or a rock under somebody. When they ran past Dejan, a few held their noses and the others laughed. I'd never really understood the game, so, to hide my ignorance, I laughed, too. Dejan glared at me. The next day he didn't want to walk with me to school. I went to bed a few nights really sad because he was mad at me, and I didn't know how to explain to him why I'd laughed.

After Dad's funeral, something changed at kindergarten. Everybody was kind to me, and, most important, Dejan wanted to be my friend again. With the naivete of a child, I saw the finger of fate in this. Maybe Dad had left so the other children would be my friends and so Dejan would forgive me for laughing at him, and then Dad would return after a while. He knew nobody made fun of a child whose dad died. So my first day back at school after the funeral was one of my very best days at kindergarten.

That day I was in a good mood, and I couldn't keep quiet any longer, so at recess, in confidence, I told Dejan what was happening and that my dad wasn't actually dead. I trusted him because maybe he wasn't complicit in the circus everybody else seemed to be part of. Sure, Dejan's parents were commies and they didn't go to church, but he'd told me he believed in God and ghosts. He said he hadn't been baptized, but he'd been vaccinated when he was little, and for commies that was like being baptized. I tried to explain to him that they weren't the same thing, but he yelled that they'd had a tree, too, just not for Christmas but for New Year's.

He didn't understand what I told him, so he told me a story about a man everybody loved who had died. Everybody was sad except his wife, who tried to convince people he had just fallen into a deep sleep and that it had happened before—he'd fall asleep for a day or two, hardly breathing, and then wake up as if nothing was wrong. They had to tie the woman to a chair so she wouldn't throw herself on the coffin, but everybody who went to the funeral heard her cries for help. The next day, at the crack of dawn, a gravedigger happened to be walking by the new grave and heard pounding from deep under the ground. He knew that the man's wife had begged them not to bury the man because she thought he was alive, so the gravedigger called out to people who were heading off to work in the fields to come dig up the grave as fast as they could. It was too late. The man's suit was torn to shreds, and his fingernails were bloody, broken, and twisted across the tips of his fingers. His legs were doubled up under his chin, as if he had been trying to push up the coffin lid. One of his arms was unnaturally bent behind his head. On his face was the grimace of a man who ached to breathe one last time. That was ages ago, said Dejan, before the two of us were born. Only after that did the village begin holding vigils over the dead for at least one night, and sometimes—and I knew this, too—they'd put this little tin bell in the coffin. I let him tell the story all the way, though I knew he hadn't understood me.

"I ain't saying my dad was buried alive."

"No?"

"He wasn't buried at all, dummy. I saw what they buried, and that was no person, and no way was it my dad."

"But they all saw—"

"Oof, what they saw. Did you? Me, I sure didn't. The whole village pretended like he was dead, just for my sake, though I don't know why. Maybe they think he abandoned us so they refuse to go looking for him."

He saw I was serious.

"You gotta help me find him."

"But where will you look?"

Good question. I didn't know.

Later that day, I thought I saw my dad from behind as he was going into a neighbor's house, and then later I saw a man with hair and a mustache like his leave a store. I knew he was close, but I couldn't figure out where he might be.

I told Dejan I thought maybe the government had kidnapped him. Granny was always warning Mom that the government would take our house if we built a weekend cottage because that would mean we had too much money. And every time Dad came home from Germany, men in suits would come to ask him about what he'd been up to and who he'd been with there, where he'd gone to church and how long the Mass had lasted. I knew Mom and Dad went to German Mass in Germany, because there was somebody at the Croatian-language Mass who handed out pamphlets (I pictured these as being little videocassettes) against Yugoslavia. If the government had taken him, I reckoned, it must have been because they thought he'd built a cottage or gone to Croatian Mass in Germany. I knew I had to tell somebody from the government that it wasn't true.

I knew that the people working for the government were police, customs officers, and aunties at the bank and post office. The aunties at the stores in Čakovec seemed suspicious to me, too. They were equal parts brusque and rude. They addressed everybody as *honey* and touched the slices of bologna with their bare hands. There was something comforting about the single-party system and the thought that there were no alternatives . . . that's roughly how I remember that government. On the other hand, we also had God, and the parish priest, the chaplain, and the sacristan all worked for God. The ministrants were working for Him, and with them was a pile of invisible players—the angels, archangels, saints, and the like. Although they told us at catechism that God was the most powerful, stronger even than Yugoslavia, there was no talk of God at school except when the teacher asked who was going to church and made a list of us (until she realized it was easier to list the two kids who weren't). The socialist system and God had some things in common—the Young Pioneer Club for the little kids was like first communion, and the youth brigades for teenagers were like confirmation, but as far as I could see, God and the government weren't the best of friends.

Dejan said we could ask his dad. His dad was a car mechanic and a member of the party, so he'd probably know somebody.

But what if the government hadn't kidnapped my dad? What if he was hiding in one of the other villages along the Mura? What then?

At the time, I thought the Mura flowed in one direction, and the Drava flowed the other way, with Međimurje between them, a little like an island, and I was seriously worried that Međimurje—for I wasn't entirely certain how heavy it was or how deep it went—might come loose and spin around like a boat with no anchor. And then Železna Gora would end up where Črna Mlaka used to be, and Črna Mlaka would be where Žalosni Klanjec had been. The only thing that made this fear bearable was that I might be able to sit in a boat without oars or a rudder in the marshy backwaters of the Mura and watch as my world spun around. Then I'd switch all the names, and I'd help everybody move to where they'd been before, and everything would be fine. After the funeral I was worried that all of Međimurje really was turning and that Dad, when he came back from Germany, might've gone to the wrong village, where maybe they'd taken him prisoner. At a soccer game once, I'd heard shouts that people from the neighboring village were "rotten" and "thieves," so that seemed a genuine possibility. I asked the grown-ups when they came to Granny's, pulled the doily off the TV screen, and watched the evening news. If they'd said, "Listen, we pretended to bury him because we have no clue ourselves of his whereabouts," I would've been the happiest boy alive. I asked them whether all of Međimurje could turn around. From the semidarkness, five pairs of eyes lit by the glow of the TV turned to look at me.

"It can't turn inside out," someone said.

"Not inside out, I mean around itself, because of the Mura and the Drava." None of the adults understood what I meant, but my sister did and explained that it wasn't possible. First of all, she said, both rivers actually flowed in the same direction, and, she added, Međimurje was not an island. Everybody turned back to the evening news, and for the next few years I thought islands in the Adriatic Sea might float away and spin around, and then woe to the tourists and the street vendors who sold water pistols and swimming goggles.

There were times when I didn't understand what the grown-ups were saying at all, the sentences seemed to roll out one after the other without anything linking them together. *Everybody ought to talk in a straight line,* I thought, *like when Granny tells stories.* I could hardly wait to be older, when one morning I'd get up and the whole world would finally make sense.

6.

I grew up and forgot everything, so I often thought that children had no patience and couldn't focus on anything that wasn't entertaining, and that's why we perceived them as self-centered. Now I remember everything. I know things aren't like that at all. Their patience is hidden. Their devotion is boundless. In those days I thought almost exclusively about how I'd find my dad.

One Sunday I woke up early and spent the morning in a state of anxiety. When no one was watching, I snuck spoonfuls of vitamin C powder and Kraš Ekspres cocoa. At Mass, I counted everybody wearing coats, and everybody who had mustaches, to pass the time. At Sunday lunch, I could only eat a little soup, and that was enough to send me to the bathroom in a sweat. It was so painful that I promised God, there on the toilet seat, that I would never eat powdered beverages with a spoon again.

Later, at Dejan's house, we had a contest to prove who could stare at the sun longer, and who could spin with our arms out without falling down. Then both of us felt sick so we plunked down on the steps and watched Dejan's father disappear farther and farther under the hood of the neighbor's Opel Kadett. He was burly and tall, with black hair and thick, fleshy fingers that looked like armrests. He spoke in such a deep voice that every other word was lost in an animal-like rumble.

"MNHMMNJcarburetorMMHNAOMNdamnitalltoMNOA. Come on, Stanko, crank up the motor."

I was already feeling anxious, but Dejan was in no rush to talk with his dad. Jabbing around in his nose with his finger, he told me a story about how a man ("near Čakovec") lost his son in a car crash, but then when the man got home, he saw his son sitting in the kitchen, smoking a cigarette. First he thought it was a ghost, but the body was real, just a little grimy from motor oil.

"So, what happened then?" I asked.

"His dad poured gas all over him and set him on fire."

"Because he was scared?"

"Nope, because his son was smoking in the kitchen. And he was right. I'd have poured gas all over him myself and lit him on fire," declared Dejan. Ever since being teased at school, he'd had this thing about over-the-top violence.

Dejan's dad wiped his hands on a rag and came over. He pulled out a cigarette from the bottom of the pack, instead of the side with the filters, and lit it with dirty fingers.

"Hello, son, you come over to play a spell?"

I didn't know what to say when grown-ups asked obvious questions. When a neighbor was starting their lawn mower, someone inevitably passed by with a friendly "My, my, mowing, are you?" The answer was always yes, with the obligatory addition of "a bit," probably so the other fellow wouldn't feel guilty about the amount of work to be done. The answer of the person passing by then had to include words of praise like "nice going" or "keep up the good work."

"My, my, mowing, are you?"

"A bit, the grass is getting mighty tall."

"Nice."

Within fifteen minutes, the man who'd passed by would be revving up his mower, too. What would people say if he didn't mow his own lawn? In the next quarter hour, three more mowers would start up around the neighborhood.

"Hello, son, you come over to play a spell?"

"I just stopped by."

"Glad you're here. Stay as long as you've a mind to, visit every day if you like."

He was about to pass between us into the house, having nothing more to say, when Dejan finally piped up: "Dad, about criminals, if a person is a thief or steals a tractor, then the police come for 'em, right?"

"Yep, if they figure out somebody really stole something," he said calmly, and I could tell he'd answered this question many times before.

"And then they lock him up?"

"Yep, in jail, till he gets better. But there's no reason for you to be worried. You're a couple of troublemakers, but I won't be reporting you." And the three of us laughed, one with the voice of an 18-wheeler, and two with sparrows caught in their throats.

"But what about if somebody, like, hasn't stolen anything, but, say, wants to build himself a cottage because he's got so much money, or he goes to Croatian Mass in Germany, or says something bad about Yugoslavia?"

Dejan's father got all serious and crouched down.

"Why ask me that, boys?"

"Just because," said Dejan, and his eyes slid inadvertently over to me, then quickly back to his dad.

Dejan's dad looked up into the air as if considering what else he might put on the grill, then started to say something, then stopped.

"If the man's got a good soul"—he looked at me, then paused, then spoke again—"well, he's got nothing to be 'fraid of with the police. If he has money and wants to build himself a cottage, well, he ain't stolen it from nobody . . . Somebody who goes to Mass, he ain't stolen from nobody . . . But against your country, you ain't supposed to say bad things, you know? Never ever. Your daddy . . ." He sighed and then went on more slowly and gently. "He was a good man, and the police've got no call to arrest him. We people here in Međimurje, we work hard, nose to the grindstone; we ain't troublemakers, and we're happy with our lot, see?" He looked toward the road, and I thought he wouldn't be saying that if other grown-ups had been around. Men didn't talk like that. They cussed the unions and the local government and talked about how the ref was a jerk and should go to hell.

He stroked me on the back of my head and, louder and sounding relieved, said: "Now, why're you asking me silly stuff like that?"

Dejan had his answer at the ready. "Oh, no reason in particular, we just wanted to know what happens to people who say things against Yugoslavia. Not Međimurje people, but, y'know, the Slovenes from across the Mura, or folks from over in Zagorje. Or Hungarians and Italians."

Dejan's dad stood up and turned to go back to the red crocodile of a car and muttered: "First they're taken to the police station in Čakovec, then maybe to jail in Lepoglava, or maybe to Goli Island. That's where they send the ones who are enemies of the working people."

As Dejan made his toy car pounce on the Parcheesi-piece enemies of the working people (and Goran Brezovec), I sat at his desk and pretended to inspect the countries on the globe. I didn't have a tissue, and sniffling would have exposed the fact that I was crying, so I cried into my sleeve. Dejan, without looking away from the Parcheesi men he'd carefully lined up, declared: "Tomorrow we skip school. I'll take the money out of Gramps's wallet, and we'll take the bus to Čakovec and go to the police station. By next Sunday, you and your dad and me and mine'll be at the soccer game, drinking sodas and talking about how the ref is a jerk."

The next morning at seven thirty, Dejan and I were standing at the bus stop with our backpacks. Other kids walked by and looked at us, and some waved, surprised, but nobody asked anything. Somebody would tell the teacher they'd seen us there, I was sure. The only other person waiting was a high school student who was late getting to Čakovec and was looking tensely through her notebooks. Dejan said the driver would probably ask us where our parents were.

"Right. So what do we say?"

"Dunno."

"Well . . . maybe we go to Čakovec tomorrow, maybe my uncle can drive us," I said, scared and overwhelmed, just as the bus came around the corner, brakes screeching. The high school student got on and flashed her monthly pass. I froze, but Dejan, as if this were nothing unusual, looked toward a store and spotted Katica Fiškališ coming out the door with her basket. He waved to her and called: "Bye, bye, Granny! See ya!"

Katica stood on the threshold and waved uncertainly back at us. Dejan stepped onto the bus and showed the driver a purple five-thousand-dinar bill with Tito's face on one side and the city of Jajce on the other.

"Čakovec?"

The driver pulled a small handle twice, and out popped two tickets from the machine. I passed the driver, eyes fixed on the floor.

"Boys, will somebody be there to meet you in Čakovec?"

"Yep," I answered, "my daddy." The bus pulled out. I sat in the third row of seats on the right side, happy we were on our way. Dejan reached into his bag and took out a bologna sandwich. Dropping crumbs all over the seat, he explained he always had to eat when he went on a trip. The two of us talked and giggled with nervous energy all the way to Čakovec, and people turned to see who was gasping so loudly with laughter.

At the imposing state building, we walked past the guard at the front door, the two of us little boys with our checkered schoolbags, and stood there for a spell, watching the police. I suggested that we stand in line at one of the windows. Dejan didn't know how to read yet, but I already knew most of the letters, so I managed to make out most of the sign for the line for "__EHICLE REGISTRATION."

"What are you doing here?" asked an irritable woman's voice from somewhere above us.

"Hello," I said, turning toward the source of the unpleasant sound. "We's here for ehicle registration." Above us, leaning over the counter, loomed a large policewoman. She was almost as big as Dejan's dad. When she leaned over, I saw she had a pistol on her belt. Her thick black hair was in a ponytail, with one lock hanging down on either side of her face, not quite touching her chin. She glared at us sternly and asked question after question, paying no attention to the other people waiting.

"Who's with you? Where are your parents? Why aren't you in school?"

We couldn't speak, we were so scared, so she came out from behind the counter, grabbed us by the arms, and steered us into the hallway, then took us into a room with a few desks covered in files and a big old-fashioned filing cabinet. She set us down like pups, each on a chair. There were two young policemen waiting there; one was skinny and pale, the other was chubbier. Unlike the behemoth who'd dragged us in, they talked normal, like us. Later I heard someone call the first guy Dragec, and the other Stankec. Their funny nicknames made them sound familiar and friendly, like neighbors. Stankec had tousled hair with a cowlick, as if it were running away from his red-flushed face. He seemed nice enough, though; I decided as much as soon as I heard him talking like us.

"What's up, Milena, rustle up a coupla suspects? Enemies of the state?" We sat, perched halfway on the chairs because she hadn't let us take our bags off. "Whose are these little skeezickses?"

"How would I know? What are your names? Where are you from? Can you talk?"

"My name's Dejan Kunčec."

"And I'm Matija." I had to swallow hard before I could finish. "Matija Dolenčec."

"What are you doing here?" she yelled louder.

I started to explain, but she interrupted again.

"Where are you from? Boys, explain to me this minute what you're doing, coming to a police station! Or do you not understand what I'm saying to you?"

"Let 'em be, Milena. They're scared to death. Slow down. Dejan, right? Dejan, tell us where're you from and what you call your mom and dad. Where are they?"

Milena sat across from me. She huffed impatiently, making her chest swell and her nostrils flare. I thought she was going to punch me. I looked her straight in the eyes because I was suddenly beyond caring. All the rooms I'd ever been in merged into that one space, all the lumpy wallpaper, all the creaking parquet floors and the shabby furniture. This was just how I'd pictured the room where the government would be holding my dad.

Dejan gave his father's name and said where we were from, and Dragec suggested that Milena find the phone number and dispatch a patrol car to fetch our folks.

"So tell me, boys, what could have possibly brought you here by yourselves, all the way from home?" Stankec asked, offering us wafer cookies from a box.

"The bus," I said.

Dragec guffawed and thumped his fist on the desk.

"And? What for?"

Dejan glanced at me, and at first I didn't know how I could explain it, so I muttered: "I don't care, go ahead and lock me up, too."

"Now why would we do a thing like that? Did you filch something? Break a window somewheres? Run a person over?"

"Naw. I came here to tell you my dad ain't never said anything against the government, and he only went to German Mass at church, and he never built a cottage. Never did none of that!"

While I was speaking, Dragec and Stankec glanced at each other, and their faces darkened.

"Wait a minute, hold your horses now. What's your daddy's name?" Stankec asked me solemnly.

"Gusti."

"Dragec, look for an August or Augustin Dolenčec." Dragec stepped out, and we were left alone with Stankec. He offered us pretzel sticks, and we nibbled them in silence for a bit. "Matija, where'd you come up with this? Anybody say stuff like this to you?"

"You locked up my daddy 'cause you reckoned he was saying bad things against the government and going to Croatian Mass . . ."

". . . and building a cottage, right. But why? Did somebody come and take him somewheres?"

"Nope, in the village they said he's dead just so I'd think he was, but I'm sure he's alive. I came here to get him, and my granny says the government takes you away if you've got too much or you say bad things against the government or . . ."

". . . or you build a cottage. I know, so you said. Matija, I'm pretty sure we ain't locked up your daddy."

At that point, Dragec and Milena came in and called Stankec over. Milena no longer looked as if she'd eat us alive. She even winked. They spoke in hushed tones, but since I was nibbling pretzel sticks and wafer cookies, I didn't hear most of what they were saying.

". . . if that's the guy, he's died . . ."

". . . don't say nothing to the kid . . ."

". . . right, let his mother do the talking . . ."

". . . no need for social services . . ."

I didn't care what they were saying. I was happy I'd had the gumption to go as far as I had, and the room was even beginning to look a little less awful.

Stankec finally came over, and this time he was even kinder.

"Boys, nice of you to come by, but your parents are waiting for you outside."

Dejan trembled a little, but he stood up and went to the door. Milena extended her hand, so we could part as friends. Stankec took me by the shoulder, leaned over, and said: "Friend, hey, boss, hold on a minute. Listen. Believe you me when I tell you your daddy ain't in jail. The government wasn't after him, not a bit. You oughta be looking for him somewhere else. Talk with your mom, and . . . do you go to school?"

"Kindergarten."

"So talk to your teacher, too. Okay?"

"Okay."

"Ask them whatever you've got to ask. Off you go."

In the lobby, Mom was disheveled and tearstained, and she held me by the shoulder and said I must never-never-never do that again and that nobody knew where we were. She'd had something to drink, I smelled it on her breath. In the corner, I saw Dejan's dad slap him. In an inhumanly deep voice, he explained that there are bad people who steal kids, take them to Italy, and make them into soap and sausages. Dejan said I made him do it, and I didn't hold this against him. His legs were shaking so bad he could barely stand. I guess that was when I understood what they meant when they sang that camaraderie was the most precious treasure, but I doubted anybody had a friend anywhere near as good as Dejan.

When we were on our way back home in the patrol car, each of us stared out the window. I wished Dejan would burp so we could giggle. Mom told Dejan's dad she'd reimburse Dejan's granddad for the bus fare by the end of the week, and he told her not to worry about it, he'd see to it. Through tears she said, "Thank you." When she and I got home, she knelt down and asked me why I'd gone to Čakovec, and I was so scared I almost told her the truth. She was breathing hard and shaking her head. Although it wasn't Saturday, she said I could take a bath, and she made sandwiches with cheese and mayonnaise, and we ate them in silence. I lay down on the floor of my room and drew a picture of the prison, the police with pistols, my dad sitting in a cell, myself, Dejan, and his dad slapping him with his big hand. Mom was ironing and putting things away in drawers. I paid no attention till I noticed she'd stopped and wasn't moving around. I peeked through the door. She was sitting on the bed, holding black socks in her hand; she must have missed them when she put Dad's things in the attic after the funeral.

7.

"So if the government ain't locked him up, I guess he won't be coming back home and he's down there under the ground," said Dejan, trying to stick a piece of paper to his pencil with snot. It was recess, everybody had eaten their sandwiches, and they were chasing each other around the classroom, spreading the smell of bologna.

It's difficult for me to explain today, but I simply could not believe he'd gone when we buried that wooden box. Maybe I'd have understood it if somebody had really explained it to me. *Your father stopped living after his organs failed. His heart stopped pumping blood, so the cells in his brain began to die. After a few hours, his body became stiff, and the microorganisms in his digestive tract began producing gasses. His body temperature dropped, and a process of rot and decomposition began that would end only when all that was left were bones, nails, and hair. These last two go on growing after death, so the corpse looks like a starving drunkard.* There, if they'd told me all that, that this is what happens, some people die sooner, some later . . . I wouldn't have gone on looking for him. They might also have said that death is not the end and there's something after it that's beyond our grasp and continues a person's existence beyond their body, in another place, in cracks and fissures we cannot even grasp most of the time. If they'd talked to me that way, maybe I'd have believed them. But what the grown-ups told me was confusing and unclear. Mostly they'd say he'd left, that he was with other members of our family who'd died, that he was waiting for us, that he could see us.

"He's underground," I said, finally. "So that's where I've gotta go looking for him."

"C'mon, what'll you do? Dig up his grave?"

"Not his grave. He ain't in his grave. We'll go to the Mura after midnight and tell the Mura maidens to give him back."

Dejan snickered, closed his eyes, shrugged, and turned his head away, like grown-ups did.

"Hold on. He was never one for night fishing. How could the Mura maidens pull him under the water? And I don't even believe they're actually real."

"Really? So why doesn't anybody in the village go night fishing?"

"They got better things to do. At night, they're either asleep or going at it with their wives."

"My granny says the Mura maidens are too real. They guard the entrance to where the dead folks are, the ones who still haven't made it to paradise. My dad's there, I know it. At night, they lure boys into the water with their breasts and then pull 'em down to the bottom to drown them."

Both of us were disgusted by the thought. We were certain we'd never do those things ourselves, whatever that meant, though Dejan once told me his plan was to live with a woman who had soft breasts and long red fingernails. He'd touch her breasts, knead them, maybe they would sleep in the same bed and watch TV together in the evening, but that was it. They wouldn't make babies or anything like that.

"Breasts. Yuck. We definitely won't be jumping in—we don't care about that stuff, do we? We're only going to ask them what they want with my daddy."

"Okay. But I still don't think they're real."

"Then you won't be scared to go there at night. Or are you?"

"Scared? Take that back, or I'll sock you. See you there, at midnight."

I didn't know what the maidens looked like. I imagined they wore long white gowns that drifted across the water and had black hair plastered to their pale faces. Their eyes were completely black, and they could see into a man's soul, to steal what was warm in his heart. I didn't know how I'd stop myself from running away when they appeared, nor how I'd ask them what I had to ask, but I knew the answer they might give me. My granny told me: a person can return from the land of the dead only if somebody alive is traded for them.

We agreed to meet by the old mill, where we'd heard the fisherman had disappeared a few years back. The mill was spooky by day, nobody had used it for a long time because the marshy backwaters of the river were dead, the water stagnant, the riverbanks boggy with water lilies and water striders. If phantoms were going to appear, this was the place. Dejan already knew how he'd sneak out of the house because he did it whenever his parents were grilling something and sent him to bed early. He'd stolen the extra key and hidden it, and after a while his parents stopped looking for it. I couldn't go out the front door, but I was sure I could climb out the window. I was calm and settled that evening, I did everything I was supposed to without whining—I ate my whole omelet, brushed my teeth, and went to bed on time. I waited a few hours for my mom and sister to fall asleep. I shook when I remembered that outside the night would be dark and silent, and I wasn't sure I wanted to go. If I could've, I would've let Dejan know we shouldn't go just yet. Still, I didn't want to ditch him after he'd been punished because of me. So I snuck to the door of my mom's room and listened for her snoring. Then, over my pajamas, I pulled on tracksuit pants and a knitted sweater. I couldn't get my sneakers so I pulled on two pairs of socks instead, one over the other, and closed the door softly. I moved two flowerpots from the windowsill to the floor and stood on a stool to reach the latch. I clenched my jaw, hoping the sound of my teeth grinding would stifle the creak of the hinges.

I raised the blinds slowly and felt coldness wash over me. There was something hellish in the outside world, as if a great evil were stirring that night, something that had compelled people long ago to build what they later called walls. I dropped down from the window and felt my socks get damp and cold. I glanced back. I probably wouldn't be able to climb back in. Out on the street, I realized I'd have to walk past fifteen houses before I got to the turnoff that would lead me through the brambles to the riverbank.

I remember how each step and thought in the dark of the village was like a soundless creak, the kind you feel head to toe, like the shuddering of the support pillars that quiver and break when we feel terror. I clearly heard the air filling my lungs, held it back, then exhaled slowly. My feet and chest hurt from cold and fear. As I moved farther from the house, I became able to see more clearly. Outlines of homes and wooden fences loomed in the darkness. Each object had a ghostly calm. That night I came to understand the meaning of the word *prickle*. Later I often heard it described as *tingling*, but the two things are not the same. When your skin prickles, it's like being sprayed with boiling and freezing water, a mix that's neither hot nor cold but very uncomfortable. It's when you become aware that you're not all alone, and somebody who's as lonely as you are wants to tell his story.

I figured out why the dirt around the village was always so dark, nearly black. Dark mother earth. When night fell, the thick darkness must have soaked into the ground. But the ground couldn't absorb much more. I thought for a time that the blackness would hover above the ground and dawn would never break again.

The river reflected the brightness of the half-moon, creating more light than there was in the village. Still, this illumination was sinking into the petroleum-hued water more than shining from it. Everything had the smell of damp grass and manure. It was peculiar how such a large body of water could be so cursedly still. The river was to my left, but I was so afraid of ghosts that I chose to look to the right, into the pitch darkness. I walked as fast as I could, ignoring the bumpy ground aggravating my feet, which were beginning to feel as if they'd been sewn onto my legs. I tripped a few times, stumbling over roots or tall grass, but I was far enough from the water that I didn't fall in. The voices I sometimes heard in my head when I was scared—mainly the voice of my uncle, probably the strongest man in the world—these voices had vanished. After a few hundred yards, I saw the dark outline of the old mill in the distance. I froze and fought the urge to run home. Since I wasn't sure how I was going to get back into the house, I squinted and took the next step. Finally, like a child carved of wood, I mounted the concrete foundation on which the mill stood, went around the shabby hut, and sat where the mill wheel used to be. The particular smell of rot, the union of wood and stagnant water, filled my nose and lungs. I sat with my back to the mill and stripped off my wet socks. I waited for a time, shivering, and then I heard a rustling. I whispered, "Dejan?" a few times, each time softer than the last because my voice had frozen deep in my throat. Finally I saw my friend's silhouette, it couldn't be anybody else. I'd never been so glad, but when he came closer, we were both just as scared and alone.

"Waiting long?"

"Dunno."

"Hey, you're shivering. Are you scared?" asked Dejan, with a spark of hope.

"Cold. I couldn't put on my sneakers, or I would've woken up Mom."

Dejan pulled off his brown shoes and socks. He put his shoes back on and gave me his socks. We sat there like that and stared at the water.

"See anything?"

"Nope. But I wasn't looking too close."

"I can't see nothing," said Dejan grumpily, and I had the impression he didn't want to stay long. He was scared, like me, but of other things. If his father found out, he'd take my friend's head off. We sat there in the middle of the night, morose.

"I wanna go home," said Dejan. He'd had the gumption to show up, and now he wanted to leave. Meanwhile, I was staring into the water, and my father's face was looking out at me, clear as a bell. It wasn't the living face I remembered, but the bluish-pale puffy face of the dead doll on the bier in our living room. I thought of the valley of dreams and the treasure in the hills, the fish restaurant, and the monkey wrenches. The voice in my head was whispering that I was scared to go home and ring the doorbell and see Mom crying and shouting that she didn't know what to do with me and why wasn't I like other kids. If I was going back, it had to be with Dad.

"Hold on. They'll come."

"Who'll come? Are you crazy?"

"They're in the water, we'll call them . . . One of us needs to jump in, then they'll come."

He turned to look at me. Now he knew why I'd asked him to come. If I wanted them to give me back my dad, I had to have somebody to trade. And it couldn't be me, because then I'd end up dead, and Dad would be back among the living, so we'd miss each other. I wasn't scared by the idea of going in, but it couldn't be me. Simple. So it had to be Dejan now, I reckoned, and then later I'd return with somebody else and bring him back. I'd bring somebody old, somebody who was fixing to die soon enough anyway, or a bad person nobody liked. I knew this was a big favor to ask, but I'd swear on my life that from that day forth I'd be Dejan's servant once it was all over—I'd do his homework for him and keep his bedroom clean. Of course, I could have traded my granny for Dad. I loved my granny, but I had the feeling she'd be willing. She already had her name engraved on Granddad Matjaž's headstone, with the dates: *1913–19__*. Uncle would tease her that he wouldn't be paying for another headstone if she lived beyond the year 2000, and she'd snap, "I'll be glad to be gone. I'm nothing but a burden anyway." Sometimes she told me she'd be dying soon, and she'd look me straight in the eyes. I thought she wanted to see how I felt about it, so I'd hug her and say she was never going to die. That cheered her up, and she'd pat my head and give me grated apple with sugar and cinnamon. So that's why Dejan was here.

"Listen. Strip down and stand in the water here. Hold on to this stick, and I'll pull you back up when they come. The water ain't that deep here."

He stared at me frozen, then began moving slowly backward. His back was against the wooden wall of the mill. Now, on top of my own breath, I heard his. The socks were snagging on splinters.

"Come on, let's do this. The sooner we do it, the sooner we can head home. See? We'll all have our sodas together at the Sunday soccer game, just like you said."

"Quit it, stop."

The sweeter my voice, the more he inched away. I grabbed his sleeve.

"Come on, we agreed. It ain't deep around here, not, like, over your head."

Dejan tried pulling away, but I managed to grab him by one arm. I just wanted to explain.

"Wait, wait."

Dejan lunged to run, but he tripped and fell onto the wooden board closest to the water's edge. I let go of his arm. I stood over him so he couldn't get up unless I stepped back. A weird feeling, I can only barely remember it. I stood over him and looked at him; he was no longer my equal, but a means to an end. It felt like his existence didn't matter as much as mine.

"I'll come back for you," I said calmly, leaning forward to push him into the river.

At that moment, a force pulled me up into the air and threw me down so I hit the ground flat on my back.

"What? Are you crazy? You goddam sonofabitch!" roared a voice from the darkness above me. Dejan's dad. He lifted his son into his arms, hugged him close, and whispered something I didn't hear. He grabbed me by the scruff of the neck, still holding Dejan, and pulled us back a good ten feet from the riverbank.

"Crazy . . . plumb crazy . . ." He sobbed and panted over and over, and Dejan and I eyed each other in the dark.

He held us tight and set off for his house. He must've heard Dejan sneaking out and followed him. I knew what it must have looked like to him, as if I actually intended to kill his son.

Strangely, I felt warm in his sturdy grip. He carried us through the dark village all the way to their house, stopping only a few times to catch his breath, never letting us out of his arms. When he opened the front door, Dejan's mother was in the hallway, gaping aghast at her husband, then her son, then me. Someone had woken her, and she couldn't tell whether the world she'd woken up to was the same one she'd gone to sleep in hours earlier. Dejan's dad put me down, but he didn't let go of Dejan. He pulled a cigarette from his pocket. We looked at each other in the hush of the hallway, in the middle of the night. Dejan's mom fetched two blankets, one for Dejan, one for me.

"Where were they?" she asked.

"By the Mura, at the old mill," said his dad. His eyes were open very wide; they were red with rage and relief.

"Mother o' God." Dejan's mother covered her mouth with both hands. She said she'd put Dejan right to bed and they'd take me home, but his father said he wasn't leaving Dejan alone and we'd all go together. I stopped shivering. As we left the house, I glanced at the wall clock. It was two o'clock in the morning. I'd never been awake this late, not even when we celebrated New Year's.

Dejan's father had to ring and ring our bell before a light came on. My mother called to my sister, and after a while there was a voice behind the locked door.

"Who is it?"

"Don't worry, it's just Đura Kunčec here. Open up, everything's okay!"

My mother and sister peered out with the same expression of terror on their faces.

"What's going on?! Where were you?!" yelled Mom when she saw me.

I walked past her into the house, and the Kunčeces came in after me, silent. We sat in the kitchen.

"I found them by the Mura, at the old mill."

"The Mura? When?"

"A half hour ago. Your boy and mine."

"He made me do it!" hollered Dejan with a voice that rang through our cold, empty house. He sobbed, and his father hugged him and quieted him.

Mom turned to me.

"Matija, tell me what you were doing there. This minute."

I said nothing and stared at the floor. They wouldn't understand anyway.

"Have you lost your mind? What's wrong with you? What am I supposed to do with this child?" Her voice gave way to sobs.

Dejan's mother said: "But that's not all. There's something else you need to know . . ."

They sent Dejan to the car, though it was freezing cold outside, and I was told to go to my room. Our eyes met as he was leaving, and I could see he was done with me.

I got out of my wet clothes, lay down, and pulled up the covers. I could hear what they were saying in the kitchen. Dejan's dad tried to speak softly, but his voice was so deep that he couldn't keep it in check.

He said that I'd tried to talk Dejan into jumping into the water, and that I was going to push him in when he refused. Dejan's mother interrupted, agitated and loud. She cried wildly that she was afraid for her boy, that he was her only child. Her husband tried to interrupt, but she couldn't stop until she'd said she was sorry, but Dejan and I couldn't spend time together after this.

Mom kept asking them to forgive her, saying how ashamed she was. They left without saying goodbye. I quickly switched off my light and pretended to be asleep. My mother and sister came into the room anyway, turned on the light, and sat me up.

"Don't hate me," I repeated, but Mom didn't reply.

"Tell me what you were doing there. You are not going to sleep till you tell me what you were doing," she said, furious.

I looked her in the eyes and said nothing. The first slap didn't surprise me as much as the second one, from my sister. Then the third, and more, came from my own hand. Mom grabbed my wrist and spat, "You're gonna tell me what was going on out there, or I'll beat you into the dark, dark earth."

"We was out looking for Daddy."

My mother and sister, shocked, stared off in opposite directions. Something might've snapped in them if their gazes had met.

"We went looking for him because I think they're holding him in the land of the dead. So I was going to trade Dejan for him. But I was going to come back for Dejan, and . . ."

"Listen up, now." She held me tighter. "You won't find him. He's dead and he's gone. There's no place on Earth you'll find him, so stop looking. You've got me, and you've got your sister, and he's looking down on you from heaven, and looking after you, but he can't help you if you don't help yourself! Act like a normal boy, otherwise . . . Otherwise they'll take you . . . They'll think I ain't looking after you like I should, and they'll take you away, understand? Stop looking for him!"

For a moment, I wanted to believe her. If I believed, everybody would be nice to me, and they'd forget what I'd done. If only I could believe. The next morning at school, it was clear I was on my own. Dejan walked right by me, saying nothing, and sat on the last bench at the back of the room with the boy we'd called Kiss-Ass. That was when the loneliness started.

8.

Those days I barely spoke to anyone at school. Silvija Jambrožić and Suzana Perčić spoke to me a few times; they thought if they wanted to be teachers, they should practice talking to the kids everybody else hated. The others eyed me strangely, I thought, though I didn't believe Dejan told anyone about that night. Granny, Mom, my sister, my uncle, and his wife treated me like they always had, and I made an effort to be especially good and to do everything they told me without complaint. I made two drawings around then, one of the river showing Dejan and me, and my dad's face watching us from the water, and in the other I'm sitting on a bench while other children are playing. I went with Mom to the cemetery and left my drawings there under the graveside lantern, or in the little trough behind the headstone. The next day the drawings were always gone, and that was enough to convince me he was getting them. Traces of Dad's presence disappeared bit by bit from our house. Reminders of him appeared now and then in unexpected places. Mom put his deodorant by the toilet for us to spray after pooping. My sister found an old note in a drawer saying he'd gone off to our neighbor Tonči's to pick up tires. I was finding it harder and harder to wipe the painful grimace from my face, and several nights I dreamed I was vanishing. In my dream people came to see the vanishing boy. They tried to grab parts of me, but I always slipped through their fingers.

A few days after the night by the river with Dejan, when Mom and I were at the store, I thought I saw the two women at the end of the aisle talking in hushed tones with the saleslady, who was pointing at us. When we got closer all three said hello loudly, oozing friendliness, and talked brightly with Mom about how the harvest wasn't great this year, and how the community ought to get a better fertilizer for the people who were farming. This was the topic on everybody's lips in the village. The only ones against it were those who worked in Slovenia, because they wanted the money to be used for paving the dirt roads going into the hills. In the winter they found it hard to get there through the snow. People were even more insistent about laying a pipeline for running water. In the village we still drank the water from our wells. Emotions were running high that autumn; people flashed duplicitous smiles, and dismissed anyone who disagreed as clueless. The women listened and committed to memory who said what, and then rehashed it all whenever they ran into one another, like those ladies with my mom.

That same afternoon a man I'd never seen before came to our house. He had a mustache and wore jeans and cowboy boots. My sister and I were sitting on the stoop, and Mom talked with him for ten minutes, and then he gave her some money, and in return she gave him the key to our car. He got in, but she waved at him to wait, then ran into the workshop and came back with the monkey wrenches and drill. He turned the drill over in his hands. I couldn't hear everything they said, but he gave her back the drill and drove off in our car toward the hills. Mom put the tools back in the workshop, and as she passed between me and my sister, I asked whether the car was getting repairs, but she didn't answer.

My sister spent some time every day showing me how to read and how to write my name and *Mom* and *Dad* and *Sis*. I learned to read slowly; the opaque forms of words intrigued me because I could tell there were meanings inside them hiding from me. I allowed them the right to represent something other than themselves, and came to see written things with an additional, third face. I found out there were these invisible pockets I'd reach into each time I read something to myself or out loud. I began reading aloud everything I could: the labels on spices, advertisements, death notices, the ingredients on shampoo and detergents, license plates, and subtitles (at least the ones that stayed long enough on the TV screen). I'd interrupt the painful silence dominating the household by spelling: "*s-o-d-a*, soda," "*c-o-f-f-e-e*, coffee," "*l-y-e*, lye." Sometimes I'd even take a book off the shelf. What it was about didn't matter, I wanted to see what sort of words were written in it and if could I reach for them. I loved this new world, and now I looked differently at things that featured words—labels, books, stores, or tanker trucks—as if in their invisible pockets there were explanations and instructions, as if meaning and truth were waiting for me. I knew I would be able to hide in those pockets that were hanging from everything, and somehow I guessed I'd be able to fill them myself with promises. I could picture paradise as a vast expanse of reading corners in a perfectly white space with happy readers going into them to seek new memories and friendships, as people who are kind of lonely do, something I knew even though I was still small.

As for me, I longed for friendship, and maybe that's how I opened a pocket where it could be inscribed. I made two truly odd acquaintances, the kind that shape one's life. The first time I saw them was on one of those winter evenings that sometimes appear in late autumn, when things can no longer be clearly seen. I was watching Granny shoo the chickens into their coop for the night, like I always did. She was hunched and moving slowly, but she shooed the chickens into their coop with big, noisy energy. She called, "Bacawk-cawk! Chickicheechee! In you go! Bacawk! Chickichee! Consarn it, where're ya off to!" and clapped her gnarled, wrinkled hands. That evening I finally saw what the chickens were running from so skittishly. As soon as Granny

called "Bacawk!" out leaped a shadowy figure from the gloom between
the pigsty and the barn: it wasn't much bigger than a dog, and it wad-
dled on two feet, pushing itself along with one fist in the dirt. With the
other arm it kept tugging at its oversized coat, the sleeve flopping over
its hand and dragging across the ground. It swept the dirt along as it
moved. Around its feet, instead of boots, it had tied two of Granny's
white dishtowels embroidered with sayings: *Cooking the dinner was a
breeze—hubby says it's the bee's knees* and *Cook, bite your tongue so the
dinner doesn't burn.* On its head it wore an old-fashioned cap like the
one Dejan's granddad wore, and its face, as far as I could see, resem-
bled a good-natured hog. Its tiny eyes kept winking, first one, then the
other, and its runny nostrils opened and closed. The exterior of its snout
reminded me strangely of how I'd always pictured the interiors of the
noses of normal living beings.

As soon as it came prancing out of the dark, it loped after the
chickens and started kicking at them with its feet and flailing its arms,
and they scuttled off toward the coop. Another shadowy figure took off
after the ones darting in the opposite direction; this one had emerged
from the gloom between the corn crib and an old horse cart when
Granny called "Chickichee!" It was a little shorter and pudgier than
the one she'd called Bacawk, and it was wearing a chestnut-colored
cape with a hood over its head that rose to a tall point. Its head looked
a little top-heavy with two huge greenish webbed eyes, like the eyes on
a horsefly, and it was barefoot. One foot was nearly twice the size of
the other, and they were angled in opposite directions. But that didn't
seem to be much of a problem, because it padded cheerfully along
after each chicken that was eluding the coop. The two of them speed-
ily stowed all the chickens away, and Granny shut the coop gate. I
laughed and clapped loudly, and the two characters hugged each other
and bowed low like country fiddlers. The louder I clapped, the lower
they bowed, until their foreheads met the mud. They exchanged looks,
and Chickichee farted. I had to grab hold of my wiener to stop from

peeing my pants from laughter. Granny paid no attention to them or to me, she just turned to go back to the house, muttering, "Consarn them chickens." As soon as they heard that, Bacawk and Chickichee vanished, each into his own gloom. Granny added: "Come on in, let's fix us some cocoa."

I followed her, happy because I knew I'd see those two clowns again. That night I stayed at Granny's and could hardly wait till morning. When I got up, I gobbled a slice of bread with butter, salt, and an egg sunny-side up, and raced out of the house into the foggy farmyard. I went over to the fenced-in part and whispered, "Bacawk, Chickichee," but nothing happened. "Bacawk! Chickichee!" I said a little louder. I stepped into the farmyard through the gate in the chicken-wire fence, stood among the chickens, and crouched down to see where the two of them had jumped out from. From the gloom peered two squinty hog eyes and two horsefly eyes.

"Don't be frightened now, out you come!"

And the two of them stepped slowly and timidly out into the light. Chickichee wiggled his huge foot and stared down into the mud, and Bacawk tried without success to keep his balance and straighten the sleeves of his oversize coat.

"Why so shy now? Last night you two were madder than wet hens," I said, and Chickichee clapped and hopped onto Bacawk's back, and Bacawk set off running furiously in a circle. The chickens clucked in alarm and flapped into a frenzy with a cloud of feathers. Bacawk ran two or three rounds and then fell into the mud, and Chickichee tumbled after him. I laughed and clapped. Glancing around, Chickichee said: "Nobody but your granny calls us out, and she only does it while she's cooping up the chickens."

"Glad to be of help to her," added Bacawk, "but mostly we keep to the gloom." The way they talked was different from the way the people talked in the village, drawling out the short words and cutting off the longer ones. They rolled their *r*'s with tongue and throat, and yawned lazily through their *a*'s and *o*'s. They pronounced *nose* like *naoose*, and *home* like *haooom*. But I could follow them fine because they made the effort to be understandable. I could already see us putting together a whole fleet of boats and me teaching them to read.

"Much obliged," said Chickichee a little sadly. "Thanks for summoning us, we can't come out of the gloom unless somebody calls us."

Boy oh boy, did those words come back to haunt me.

9.

At first I thought everybody could see them, but they were just pretending not to, like when Mom told me I shouldn't stare at people with disabilities. Once she slammed the door right in Chickichee's face, so I went back to open it for him. Then he forgot to shut the door behind him, so she yelled at me for leaving it open. I started to explain why I'd opened the door. She crouched down and took me by the shoulder like she always did when she had a mind to tell me something that mattered. She said she'd seen I was in a world of my own. She asked if I was missing Dad, and whether I had left the door open so he could come in. I fibbed and said I just happened to forget. I was afraid she'd think I was strange and threaten me again with the folks who'd come and take me away.

So Mom didn't see them, and soon I realized my sister didn't see or hear them, either, because my two fiendish friends were constantly quibbling over who'd get to read and write with me. I warned them to keep it down and showed them where they were making mistakes with their reading, and then my sister would ask, a bit worried, who was I talking to. Maybe Granny was the only one who saw them, but she was so old she hardly ever watched *Numbers and Letters* anymore, so I could never tell exactly what she could see. When she did, she'd come up with such a cockeyed answer that she'd laugh at herself. It didn't bother me that only I could see them. I doubted their existence less than I doubted the existence of some of the people the grown-ups talked about. I could feel them, smell them. Theirs was the musty scent of rotting wood and wet leaves. In my world it was entirely possible that everybody had fiendish friends they never talked about that nobody else could see. They, too, would summon their friends from the gloom and converse with them in secret. (This is something I believe to this day, at least a little.)

We went everywhere together. Soon they learned how to behave in public, but often they squabbled. They knew they had to hide when guests came over, and in the evening, when I went to bed, they helped Granny bring the chickens in for the night. They'd be there again in the morning, waving to me while I ate breakfast. I'd wave back when Mom was turned away. They followed me to kindergarten and entertained me along the way. They'd run out into the road when they heard a car coming, and then at the last minute they'd leap into the muddy ditch. When an old codger walked by, Chickichee followed him and mimicked his walk. I hid my grin, and Bacawk picked up a rock and tossed it at the old man. The old coot turned and saw me standing there, laughing. He reckoned I'd thrown the rock. That made me mad, and I told them not to do that anymore.

"Sor-rry, don't be mad," they cawed like jackdaws, crestfallen.

They didn't come into church, or school, but sometimes when I was in class I'd see them from my desk as they stood on tiptoe, peering in through the window, elbowing each other. One time Bacawk pressed Chickichee's face so hard up against the pane that I could hear the glass cracking. I wagged a finger at them to stop, the way grown-ups do to mischievous children, and they responded with long faces and bowed heads. At first they obeyed me without a peep, and most of the time they were fun to be with.

They could never agree on anything. Chickichee said his favorite color was motley, so Bacawk rolled his eyes and said Chickichee was a buffle-brain and there was no such color. Bacawk was always throwing rocks, and Chickichee would tattle on him to me. Chickichee told me Bacawk once threw a rock at our neighbor Tonči's house—some people called our neighbor Laddie because he had a little dog named that— and almost broke a window. I told Bacawk he wouldn't be my friend anymore if he did that again. They said nasty things about people who weren't there and about each other. What's odd is that both of them seemed to be right. They often had fierce fights, which would end, as a rule, with Bacawk kicking Chickichee wildly and spitting on him while Chickichee lay howling on the ground. The first time I saw this was when I left a pail of water on the steps for them, because Bacawk told me they were thirsty. I went into the house and watched as the two of them, each on one side of the bucket, plunged their heads in. It was too small, so they collided, and neither of them could reach the water. Bacawk lost his patience and pushed his friend away from the bucket. Chickichee fell a few feet away, and meanwhile Bacawk gulped down two or three mouthfuls and dumped out the rest. Chickichee sat in the grass, legs crossed, head bowed. He reached up and pulled his hood down over his face. Bacawk stood firmly on both feet, planted a hand on the overturned bucket, and forced a laugh. He glanced toward the window and pointed to show me how pitiful Chickichee was. I went out and hollered: "What are you, crazy? Into the corner with you!"

Bacawk went all solemn, limped on his two legs and his fist over to the fence, and plopped down onto the ground.

I poured Chickichee a full bucket of water. He plunged his head so deep that only the tip of his hood poked above the rim. He asked if I was an angel, and I told him I wasn't. I was somehow pleased with myself, so I went over to Bacawk and explained that he mustn't treat Chickichee badly just because Chickichee was weaker. They made up and hugged and went off together toward Granny's house, as it was starting to get dark.

When I went back into the house, Mom wanted to know who I'd been talking to, and I said, "Nobody, just playing with friends," which was usually enough of an excuse for most silly things. And it was enough that evening, but I had the feeling that was going to be the last time. Mom knew I had no friends.

10.

The next morning my sister came into my room and saw that everything was topsy-turvy. My desk was upside down, and there was a flowerpot on the floor. I told her my friends had gotten into a fight.

"Who was here who made such a mess?" she called down to Mom, who was ironing.

"Mess?" shouted Mom back. "Not a soul's been here. Is this a joke?"

"See for yourself. Matija says his friends came over and made a mess of his room. A flowerpot's on the floor."

By the time Mom came up, I was on my hands and knees, doing what I could to clean and come up with a good story, but all I did was spread around the soil that had spilled from the flowerpot. I said the mess was made by some friends I'd invited in from the dark, and that they were naughty sometimes and often squabbled. I have no idea how I managed to speak so calmly when I was so furious. My sister looked at me, appalled. I can understand how I managed to forget everything else, but I can't for the life of me figure out how I succeeded in forgetting that look of hers. I can see it even now. Hers was a gaze of pure horror. Her face had gone pale, mouth agape, and her eyes were two wide saucers.

Later I heard Mom saying that I'd probably made up the story to avoid the blame, but my sister said she'd heard me talking every day with somebody who wasn't there and that I walked around the house at night. Mom came back to my room and helped me clean up. She told me I could tell her anything and she wouldn't be mad. She asked when one of my school friends might come over, maybe Damir or Silvija, and said that she'd make us sandwiches and crepes. I didn't respond.

I told Bacawk and Chickichee they were no longer welcome in the house. But this time there were no bowed heads or empty apologies.

"We'll see about that," said Bacawk menacingly, and Chickichee scowled over Bacawk's shoulder.

The next morning, while I was drinking my cocoa and Mom was filling jars with her homemade jam, we heard Granny's voice outside. Mom went out, and I could only hear bits of Granny's trembly nasal words, but I gathered that something had gotten into her coop that night and killed some of her chickens. When we went to take a look, the air in the coop was dry and hot, though the morning was foggy; bloody feathers were floating around and hanging on the fence. Granny went from one chicken to the next, stroking them and laying them in a wooden apple crate.

That evening, while we were sitting in Granny's kitchen drinking tea in silence, our old car pulled up to the gate, and out came the man in jeans with the mustache. Through the window I watched him load the box with the dead chickens into his trunk, and then he came in to give Granny money. Granny peeled off one bill, which she slipped into her apron pocket, and gave the rest to Mom.

I knew Bacawk and Chickichee were responsible for this. I could hardly wait for morning. I imagined how I'd hit and kick them until they hung their heads in shame. The next morning I told Mom I was going to Granny's before school because my teacher said I should bring in a seashell souvenir of hers because some kids'd never been to the seaside and had never seen a seashell. Of course, I never even said hi to Granny but went straight to the chicken coop. I threw my schoolbag into the grass.

"Bacawk! Chickichee!" I yelled. I had to repeat the summons several times before they stepped out of the gloom.

"What did you do to the chickens?" I asked, furious. "You were supposed to be taking care of them! Where were you?!"

The two of them exchanged looks. Chickichee grinned and hissed: "We were right here, nowheres else."

"Want more?" jeered Bacawk. "I'll off the rest of them, lickety-split. Bring them into your house, why don't you, if you love your chickens more than you love us."

Everything went black, and I flung myself on the smaller of the two. I slid across the mud, grabbed him, and tried to smash my whole fist into his huge green eye. My hand froze when I saw up close that, instead of a tongue, his mouth contained a bundle of fat pink mud-worms that suddenly burst out. I pushed him away and turned to Bacawk and kicked him in the head as hard as I could. I fell onto my back, and he rolled toward the old horse cart. He leaped up, grabbed me by the hand, and tore a patch of cloth the size of a handkerchief from my jacket. Two huge claws sprang through his coat from his elbows, and he jabbed them at my head. His second lunge only just missed me, but he did scratch my face from ear to chin. I stepped back and groped behind me for the chicken-wire gate. I couldn't find the latch.

"Consarn them chickens! Consarn them chickens!" I shouted. Bacawk and Chickichee always melted back into the gloom whenever Granny said that.

"You should never've summoned us," said Chickichee.

I finally managed to open the gate, slip through it, and close it, leaning against it with all my weight. We glared at each other through the chicken wire.

"What did you think? You could do as you please with us?" asked Chickichee. "Throw us out? Just you wait, you'll see hell. Just you wait, you'll see black earth. We'll show you."

"What do you want?" I asked, gasping for breath.

"What we want, you can't give us. We'll take it for ourselves," Bacawk said, leering. "First we'll kill all the other chickens, then we'll kill your granny. We'll stab her with a knife, right in the back. Your uncle and his wife—we'll chop off their heads while they're sleeping. Then we'll set your mother on fire. We'll pour gasoline all over her and burn her alive."

"Whatever you care about, we'll take it from you, and you we'll leave for last. You'll be alone in the house, and anybody who comes to visit, we'll kill them," Chickichee added, and clapped his hands together.

"I'll tell on you—don't even think about hurting anybody," I tried to shout, but all that came out was a desperate whisper of a croak.

"Who'll you tell?" asked Chickichee with a knowing smile. "Nobody believes a word you say, you've already lied to everybody."

"My daddy, he'll come and . . ." I couldn't go on, so with my ripped sleeve I wiped away my tears. They were mixed with blood.

"Your daddy ain't coming. You can't lie to us. Do you know where your daddy is? You don't. But we do."

I thought they'd torment me by saying nothing, but Chickichee could hardly wait to say it.

"Your daddy, he's being held by the will-o'-the-wisp folk up there in the forest, in the hills. Are you going to go get him?" he said. They staggered around in the mud, roaring with laughter.

"There ain't no will-o'-the-wisp folk. Or Mura maidens neither. I was down by the Mura at midnight, and there was no sign of them! They're not for real!" I said, though I wasn't entirely sure.

I arrived at school that day covered in mud, my jacket torn and my face smeared with tears, dirt, and blood. All the children went silent, and the teacher said, "Jesus," but then she remembered she didn't believe in such things, so she said, "Wowee." She took me to the washroom so I could splash my face and wipe off my pants, and she said I should bring Mom to school with me the next day.

I went back to class and, strange as this might seem, for a little while I forgot that Bacawk and Chickichee had threatened to kill everybody I loved. I sat with a boy we called Krunek and glued a collage onto cardboard. For a whole week Krunek hadn't said a word because he hadn't been able to pronounce *sixth* right. He'd said *sick* or something like that, and he said it like that a few times, so the other kids laughed at him. I told him how my dad was going to show those guys who came to kill the chickens a thing or two. Only at the end of the day did I realize I was actually describing Dejan Kunčec's father, not my own. He was the big burly one who dared to say, "Honest t' God." I needed somebody like that. For a moment, with all my heart, I tried to remember what my father's face looked like, and I couldn't.

As soon as I got home, I took down the box of photographs my sister had filed and labeled. I took them out and studied them carefully, but I didn't recognize anybody. In each photograph I saw a different man, never the same from one picture to the next. I held one closer and closer to my eyes to see it better. When my nose was touching it, everything blurred, and only then did I feel as if I were seeing him clearly. More and more the traces of his presence were disappearing in my mind.

Mom yelled at me that my pants were filthy and my jacket was torn, and Granny said I'd never stopped in to pick up the seashells. She was about to spank me, but then she noticed the scab on my face running from ear to mouth. I told her she'd have to go with me to kindergarten the next day, the teacher wanted to talk with her. She sighed and said I should go lock the door to the workshop, and then she'd make me some yogurt and an egg. I got up and looked out the window. It was already getting dark, but I could clearly see Bacawk and Chickichee waiting for me out there. Chickichee waved, and Bacawk was holding what looked like a rolled-up sock in each hand. Two little kittens. He held them by the paws, and when he was sure I was looking, he swung them around. Both kittens went limp. He tossed them into the garden that belonged to our neighbor Tonči. A shriek escaped me, and Mom glanced over, but they ducked behind the walnut tree. Mom said she would lock up, but I remembered they'd told me they'd kill her, so I mustered my courage and raced outside, locked the workshop, and came back into the house. That evening Mom didn't lower the blinds in my room all the way, and I woke up at one point and could see two shadows standing outside the window. I didn't see their eyes, but I knew they were watching me. I didn't dare get up to lower the blinds, so I prayed to the guardian angel more times than I could count, until I fell asleep, completely exhausted.

11.

The teacher tugged her dark-red sweater nervously, and with a lot of hemming and hawing and clearing her throat, she spoke with Mom about how I was a nice boy, but I'd been confused and disturbed lately. They talked as if I weren't there. All the other kids had already gone into the classroom, and from the hallway I could hear they were running riot, but this wasn't why she was so tense.

"Ma'am, I know this is a difficult time for you after . . . after you've been left alone with the children . . . I don't know what I'd do in your place . . . Really, it can't be easy—"

"A person grows accustomed," Mom interrupted her. Since the night I tried to throw Dejan into the river, she'd become much calmer. She wasn't crying anymore, but she also never laughed, even when saying something funny, and she didn't justify herself to anybody. "You can tell me, I see there's a problem with Matija."

"Well, you see, he's . . . I know he and Dejan Kunčec wandered off a few weeks ago . . ."

"They ran away from home. No point in beating around the bush. Everybody knows it by now."

"Well, that doesn't matter—they're children after all, as I always say. The problem's this: Matija is not socializing with the other kids anymore. He's alone most of the time."

"So what? Other kids keep to themselves. Might just be their stinky feet."

The teacher was thrown by this.

"Well . . . yesterday he came in all smeared with mud, bloody, in tears. Did you know that?"

"I did. On his way to school, he stopped by his granny's and slipped and fell into the mud by the pigsty. He was scared of coming home like that, so he went on to school instead. That's what I know."

"Something's going on with your boy. I've heard it said in the village that he threw a rock at an elderly gentleman, that he's been crying and yelling for no reason, that he talks to himself . . . Somebody just this morning said two little kittens were killed and thrown into your neighbor's garden . . . and then what happened with Dejan . . . Have you talked with him about his . . . dad?"

When I heard this I thought the teacher was going to ask Mom whether she'd confessed to me that they'd lied, that Dad would be back soon, that I hadn't killed him after all.

"Yep . . . but I figure he . . . he ain't made peace with that as of yet . . . He told me . . . Matija, why don't you be off to the classroom?"

"Yes, Matija, time to join the class . . ."

I didn't hear what else they said. The classroom was a terrible mess, which was a relief because nobody even looked at me.

I told Krunek that Dad and I had flown a plane. I told him Dad had been a helicopter pilot, but in Germany his friends at the airport let him fly a plane. I reckoned that adding "in Germany" was smart, because none of the kids had ever been there but me. That day Krunek began speaking again after a full two weeks of silence, and his first words were to Goran Brezovec and the others that I was lying because I'd said my father could carry a whole tree on his back, and then everybody laughed at me.

That evening we were eating our bread spread with pork lard for supper, and Mom said I'd be spending more time with my uncle now—he was probably the strongest person in the world after my dad. He'd take me to the soccer game on Sunday. And, she said, a man and a lady would be coming from Čakovec to ask me how school was going and if there was anything I was scared of. As soon as she said that, I knew exactly what I couldn't tell them. Whenever I said what I was really thinking, people looked as if they were frightened or angry. I decided to pretend that everything was fine.

From then on, I asked Mom to lower the blinds all the way to the windowsill at night, so I didn't see Bacawk and Chickichee, but I could hear them breathing and leaning against the glass clear as a bell.

The Miners played a good game, I could tell because the ref wasn't a jerk quite as often. The men and their sons stood on the embankment because it was too wet to sit in the grass. And I was there among them with my uncle, he with his beer, me with my soda. Dejan said hi, but nothing more. The men talked about the prospect of a water pipeline for the village, artificial fertilizer, and paving the roads, and they cussed a lot. They talked about a man whose name was Natz. From what I heard I gathered that Natz drank a lot, never shaved, lived with his old mother, and fought a lot—and well. One of Uncle's neighbors said a few days ago he and Natz had gotten drunk at a bar in the next village over and caused a ruckus.

"We sure did tie one on, like we never done before," he boasted. Their harmless banter with three Slovenes from across the Mura who happened to be sitting at the next table turned into shoving and fighting, and knives were even drawn. The fight turned into a proper pounding—bottles, chairs, and bodies flying—and at one point Natz pulled a knife from the shoulder of one of the Slovenes, examined it, and then put it right back in, as if into a human ikebana. An ambulance had to come from Čakovec. When they asked him why he'd done that, he answered, dead serious, that it wasn't his knife, so he put it back where he'd found it.

"Well, it weren't my knife," the men chorused, then laughed, clapped, and cussed. Uncle's neighbor said how Natz had been lurching out of the bar, drunk as a skunk, at the very moment the police pulled up. Staggering, he barely managed to find his old rust bucket Fićo and struggled, in vain, to unlock the door. The police came over, slowly, and one said he mustn't drive drunk. In his deep, sodden voice, Natz replied, intending to reassure them, "You just help me open her up, I'll do the rest myself." And they all laughed again, pounding their knees. I could see Uncle admired Natz. Having a friend like that would be nice, nobody would dare touch me. He'd be able to take on Bacawk and Chickichee with his knife and turn them into ikebanas. I sank into myself imagining this, and everything around me died away. When I heard "Honest t' God, honest t' God, damn-blasted old Natz," and right after that, "That ornery old son of a bitch!" I turned to see where this Natz fellow was. I thought I saw a fat man with a beard and curly hair walking slowly, arms loose and swinging, along the dirt road toward the grassy embankment. Somebody scored a goal, which I missed, and the ref was a vile old jerk. As the game wound down, the men cussed more, and the burning in my belly got worse because I knew I'd have to go home where the darkness of my horror was waiting for me. When we were passing the graveyard, we saw my mom and sister by Dad's grave. Uncle stopped the car, and Mom called to him to leave me at home and said she'd be back soon.

I pretended there was something I needed to talk about, and asked him about excavators, but when we reached my house, Uncle hurried me out of the car and left. Dusk had settled on the yard, erasing any sunshine or puffy white clouds, leaving only ghastly fiends. I stared at the ground, hurried to the door, and looked for the key. We usually left it under the mat or on the windowsill on the side of the house. I turned because I had a twitchy feeling on my back that somebody was watching. Nothing. The key wasn't where it was supposed to be, so I looked under the potted plant on the front step. I turned again and this time saw Bacawk behind me. He'd taken off his overcoat, and for the first time I could see his dark-brown body. He was made up of tube-like, curving bones and a row of ribs that extended into claws. There was a crunching and a crackling as this immense spiderlike creature reared over me. My jaw dropped, and I closed my eyes, hoping it would disappear by the time I opened them again. I keeled over backward onto my mom's potted plant. When I looked again I saw Chickichee popping up from behind the giant bug with a hoe and swinging it at me. It was clear he aimed to smash me on the head, and so, soundless with terror, I flung myself out of the way. He whacked me hard twice on the shoulder with the dull side of the hoe and once on the knee. On the next swing the hoe slipped from his grip. I leaped to my feet and lunged, pushing my way between them. I shoved Chickichee aside and felt a sharp stab in my back, just below my head. Everything went black from the pain, but I kept running. I ducked around the corner of the house and sprinted toward the neighbor's fence. For the first time in my life, I leaped over it—I have no idea how—and hid behind an old wooden outhouse the neighbors no longer used. It began to look as if dawn might be breaking, even though, in fact, dusk was just settling in. I was breathless and thought the whole world could hear me gasping for air, so I pressed one hand firmly over my mouth. I ran my other hand across the back of my neck and felt the swelling and dampness where I'd been stabbed. My hand was red with blood and dark with grime from the claw. Just when I thought the danger had passed and they'd gone away, Laddie, the neighbor's little dog, came trotting around the corner. At first he just looked at me and wagged his tail. I gestured to him to come over, so Bacawk and Chickichee wouldn't see his fanciful tail waving in the twilight. His fur was white, and they could easily have seen him. He stayed where he was, wagging his tail, and started barking. He wanted to play, I knew the bark. I made a face—as if that would have quieted him—and laid my finger across my lips. Laddie, of course, didn't understand. He barked again, louder. I threw myself onto him, hugged him close, pulled him to me behind the wooden outhouse, and lay on top of him.

"Hush, please, Laddie, please, hush, hush so they don't hear us," I whispered, and hugged him tighter, but he whined all the louder. His fur smelled of Turoš cheese. I felt his bark come from deep in his throat, and I pressed him there tighter. Laddie stopped wagging his tail; instead he began writhing and twisting around, trying to bite my hand or face. I mustered all my strength and pressed his neck as hard as I could till I felt something move under my fingers, something soft and slippery. I held his head and the upper part of his body so he wouldn't bite me, leaving only his belly and legs free to move. He thrashed a few times more. When I pulled away I saw he was lying still, not breathing. I peered from behind the outhouse and saw the porch light on by our front door. That must have been my mom and sister. Bacawk and Chickichee didn't like light. The light also went on at the neighbors' house, and Tonči and his wife came into the yard.

I thought of Dad just then. Not because I needed somebody to look after me, but because I knew I had the power to kill if I chose.

I couldn't explain what I'd done, and I could no longer pretend I was like other kids. Blood was oozing from the wound on my back, my shoulder and knee were bruised, and I was smeared head to toe, again, with mud. I went to vault over the fence, hoping that at least the neighbors wouldn't spot me.

"Matija, what are you doing?" asked my neighbor gently. "Playing? Does your mother know you're here?" Everybody knew I'd run off to the Mura that night.

"Just leaving, see ya, bye!" I sang out, and made a beeline for the gate.

"Hold it right there, Matija," Tonči said sharply. He was standing by the outhouse, staring at his dead dog. He came over, and I saw he was clenching his jaw because he didn't want to show how heartbroken he was. "I'm going with you. I'll have a word with your mother."

I said that Laddie had attacked me and tried to bite me, and I thought they'd believe me because my shoulder was bruised and there was the wound on my back that felt like a huge, slimy hollow with a scabby edge. Mom asked me coldly whether Laddie also knocked over the potted plant and smashed the flowerpot. Tonči started saying more to Mom about the two dead kittens he'd found in his yard. Mom asked whether he thought I did that, too, but he said nothing. Tonči started saying something more to Mom about Laddie, and she asked him whether he wanted money for the dog, and said she'd be going to the bank next week, but he just shrugged and left. The whole time my sister stayed in her room, listening to loud music. Mom dumped me into the bathtub, which was full of hot water, grabbed a washcloth, and scrubbed me without a word, pressing hard on the bruises on my knee and shoulder, the scab on my face, and the wound on my back. It stung, and I thought she was making the wound even worse, but I said nothing. She would have pressed harder if I'd said it hurt. That night I slept with her in bed and slept so well because I had no dreams at all. For that one night I was able to forget that soon everybody I loved would be dead because I didn't have the courage to rescue Dad from the will-o'-the-wisp folk.

12.

At kindergarten we were told to draw a picture of autumn and the many-colored leaves falling from trees. I drew a big spider standing on two back legs, a big horsefly with a hoe, and myself killing a little dog. I put that drawing in my bag before the teachers could see, and then drew trees and some children playing in the leaves. At home I wrote a message on the first drawing, about how everybody I loved would die, and I gave it all to my sister when she went to the cemetery. I asked her not to open it, just to leave it under the lantern. Mom and I waited for the people from social services. She dressed me up as if I were going to Mass and parted my hair with a comb. She started telling me what I was supposed to say, but then she stopped midway through a sentence. I sat at the table and watched her slice cake and brew coffee. There was something tense about her movements, something that worried me, so I came up with a new fantasy. I imagined that the spoon, fork, and knife were friends, each with a different secret power. The knife could cut through stone and fly up high, and sometimes it could make things disappear. The three utensils would laugh in the drawer, listening to people looking for whatever it was the knife had made disappear. The fork could speak with four different voices and in four languages. Sometimes the tines of the fork quarreled among themselves, but they didn't understand each other, and then the fork would hiccup. The knife and spoon thought the fork was confused. But the fork always knew what time it was and what the weather would be like the next day. The spoon was the most reticent, but it was brilliant at acting as a TV antenna. When it did, the knife and fork could watch, on its curved surface, shows from other countries that were sometimes broadcast on Ljubljana TV. But the spoon sometimes turned around, and then it was better if nobody looked. On that side everybody—even the knife and fork—could see themselves and what they were truly like. Most things and people, I thought at the time, were speechless after such a sight—lost and sad. I surely would be.

It was getting dark when the car pulled up at our house, and out stepped a woman a little older and plumper than Mom and a small man with combed, oily hair, in jeans and a blazer. He might have been the shortest grown-up I'd ever seen. He was wearing shoes with thick heels, but it was clear that he was only a bit taller than my sister. If I answered every question right, maybe they'd take me away, and then they would be my new parents. I liked that thought; maybe Bacawk and Chickichee would stop the killing then, or they'd kill the new parents, and that would keep my family here safe.

They sat at the kitchen table across from me and immediately lit cigarettes. Mom brought them an ashtray and asked if she should leave us alone. The woman nodded. This was a first for me, talking to strangers alone, and something prompted me to behave like I did with the teacher at school.

"How are you, Matej? We've been hearing about you for some time now. Do you know why we're here?" said the man. He spoke slowly, enunciating very clearly, and with a cloying condescension as if speaking to a very young child.

"My name's Matija."

"Sorry," coughed the man. "I have a son named Matej, and you remind me of him."

These people won't be my new parents, I thought. *Nobody needs two strange kids.*

"Matija, so. Do people call you by a nickname? What do your friends at school call you? Matko? Matek?"

"Nobody calls me nothing," I said.

"Your teacher says you've been withdrawn lately and you're not socializing with the other children. Why is that? Huh, Matija? Matija?" The lady thought I'd answer more readily if she showed she'd gotten my name right.

There was no good answer to her question. I couldn't just say, "Yes, the other kids don't want to play with me because I tried to throw my best friend in the river so I could exchange him for my dead dad, and they all think I'm some kind of monster."

"Well, I dunno," I muttered.

"We would like to hear from you about what's going on. You can tell us, I promise we won't breathe a word of what you say to anyone," said the woman.

"Not your mom, not your sister—nobody," added the man.

"Is there something you're scared of? Is there anyone threatening you or anyone who hurt you recently?" The woman went on, occasionally glancing at the notebook open in front of her. "Did somebody hurt your feelings? You know, not all pain is pain you feel on your body."

"Nobody's hurting me at school. And I ain't talking to anybody."

"And why is that, Matija?"

"It just is."

"Your mom told us you have bruises on your body, as if you banged yourself up somewhere, or as if somebody was hitting you."

"Nope."

"But I can see the scratch on your face. Where's that from?"

"I slipped and fell at Granny's, near the chickens."

"Matija, I have a feeling you're lying to us. I was like that when I was small. Two bigger boys from my street always pushed me around . . .

They hit me and shoved me and hurt my feelings, and I never told anybody about it because I was ashamed. And then I told my daddy, and he walloped them, and they never touched me again. Look, we are here to help you solve every single problem you have."

"Do you know where your daddy is?" said the woman.

"Up in heaven with the angels and my granddaddy."

"Do you miss your daddy? You must miss him. And how is it with your mommy and sister? They talk with you every day. Do they ask if you're okay?"

"Yep. They talk plenty with me."

"How would you describe your mom? What are three things you love about your mommy?"

"When she puts her hair up in a ponytail. And when we went to a fish restaurant and she asked if I'd like another Coke. And I love her because . . . she loves me a lot."

"Two of the things you mentioned happened before, while your daddy was still here. What's changed since then? Is your mommy still here for you, do you think?"

"Yep."

"Every day? Maybe one day you went to school dirty and hungry?"

"Yep, but . . ."

"Other kids don't come to school looking like that."

"But other kids . . ."

"Matija, your mommy loves you, I know she does, but maybe lately she hasn't been able to see to everything. Your house, your sister, you . . . Maybe she could use a little break, and we can see to it that you go live somewhere else for a bit with other kids. Maybe that's what your mommy wants. Hmm, Matija? Don't you think your mommy and sister might find it easier if you were staying somewhere else? Huh, Matija?"

"Leave me alone."

The man broke in loudly. "We've got to—"

"No, look," interrupted the woman. "Matija, listen to me . . . Tell me three things that aren't so good when you talk with your mom."

"I ain't talking with you."

The woman sighed and wrote something down in her notebook. She took another good look at me, as if gauging whether I was a 150-pound hog or a 220-pounder, and whispered something to the man.

"Fine, Matija, no need to be afraid of us. We just came to chat. Let's try it this way." And the man extended his hand, which I did not accept, and then he patted me on the shoulder. "You give a little thought to whether there's something or somebody you're afraid of, and if you tell us, I think the three of us can put our heads together and figure it out."

I imagined Bacawk and Chickichee knocking the man and woman to their knees and slashing them with knives. The man would be pleading desperately while trying to scoop his guts back into his belly through a big gash, while the woman would be trying to discuss something with him until her voice broke in her last shudder. They told me to go play in my room and asked Mom and my sister to come to the kitchen. The damned blinds were up again. I heard voices being raised a few times, but I couldn't tell whose they were. All I knew was that my sister wasn't saying anything.

". . . physical violence? You saying I beat my boy . . .?"

". . . now, now, we're on your side . . ."

". . . he has food on his plate, he's in good health . . ."

". . . never have heard of such a small child running away . . ."

". . . I ain't saying, but I also don't figure . . ."

". . . abuse . . ."

". . . and injures himself to attract . . ."

". . . you's saying I'm a no-good mother . . ."

They came out of the kitchen after a spell, and Mom, no longer making any effort to speak properly, said: "Now listen you here, I can't rightly say what I've a mind to do, but this treatment you speak of . . . I ain't got the money for such a thing. Understand? And if the village hears of this, that I'm taking him to . . ." Mom was interrupted by the sound of her own quavering voice.

The woman wrote something else down in her notebook and said to my mom and sister: "We'll be in touch," and for my sake she added, with her face stretched in a sour smile, "Bye bye, Matija. You be good now, okay?"

There was nothing I wanted more than to be like all the other kids, like Dejan Kunčec or even Goran Brezovec. I'd pretend there was nobody there when I saw Bacawk and Chickichee. But when they murdered Granny and killed Uncle and his wife, people would see for themselves that something weird really was going on. After the social workers left, Mom and my sister cried in Mom's bedroom, and I clenched my fists and told myself that no matter what I'd act like a normal kid.

When the house went still, I prayed, staring up at the ceiling, just so I wouldn't look at the windows, because Mom had forgotten to lower the blinds. After a while I heard a dog barking, and I knew they were near because that always betrayed their presence. When I think back, it's possible my terrified mind conjured those characters whenever there was barking, and that the two fiends were never there at all . . . but then so many other things wouldn't make sense. Glancing at the window, I spotted their shadows, still and mute. Bacawk was back in his overcoat.

I turned to the wall, figuring that they couldn't do anything to me if I didn't look at them. I was rigid with terror, clenching my teeth, shutting my eyes, and clinging to the sides of the bed. When I'd prayed my third shaky prayer and said amen, I turned again toward the windows and opened my eyes. Something was standing right by my bed. I heard breathing, and for a moment I thought maybe Mom had heard me tossing and turning and had come to tuck me in. I sat up quickly and switched my bedside light on. There was Bacawk. I screamed, and he smirked and covered my mouth with his coat sleeve. He was huge, at least twice the size he'd been when I'd first seen the two jolly fellows by the chicken coop. He leaned on me, pressing my shoulder, so

I couldn't budge. Everything stank of pus. He opened his coat, and a feeler swam out with a long, slender barb. I writhed and twisted, but couldn't do anything except pull my mouth back from Bacawk's hand and say, breathlessly, "Honest t' God, honest t' God. Damn-blasted Natz!" As soon as I said that, I heard a deep, powerful sputtering under the bed. That made Bacawk stop, the malicious smirk vanished from his face, and his feeler withdrew. A fat, hairy arm with greasy fingers and grimy nails grabbed Bacawk and, with a single powerful yank, pulled him under the bed. At that moment everything went quiet; the only sound was Mom coming down the hall toward my room. It was too late for me to turn out the light and pretend nothing had happened.

"Everything's fine, Mom, you can go back to bed," I said confidently. She peered sleepily through the door. It seemed like she had half a mind to ask something, but she could see I was smiling, so back she went to bed. I slept until morning curled up like a crescent moon, because I'd wet my bed in terror. *Things are finally taking a turn for the better,* I thought.

13.

I saw them the next morning as soon as I left the house. Natz—big, fat, ornery Natz—was holding the two of them upside down by the feet, heads dangling. He was so tall that their hands weren't even touching the ground. Natz was not a talkative man, I knew, maybe he had never mastered human language. He nodded toward what he had in his hands. Chickichee whimpered, saying look at how this big guy was torturing him, and this was all my fault. I told him: "You deserve it. You wanted to kill my mom and sister and Uncle and Granny! Just you wait and see."

That day at school we sang again about the girl who was headstrong and persnickety. I was happy and quiet, but I was waiting impatiently for a moment to show that I was just like everybody else, that I was better. I kept circling around Dejan.

The day was almost over when I noticed it was snowing. I said so out loud, and everybody ran to the windows. Since I got there first, the others pressed in around me, and that was the first contact with them I remember as nice, even though they smelled of straw, unwashed hair, and feet. I wanted for us to all stay squashed together like that, all twenty of us. After a minute the teacher said we should go do our coloring, so we all trooped back to our desks. Just then Bacawk and Chickichee popped up from below the window. We eyed each other, separated only by the windowpane and hatred. They were barely able to peer over the ledge, so nobody but me could see them. I saw fear and a plea lurking in their eyes. I thought back on everything I'd been through. I remembered my dad, Laddie, my mother crying, and sleeping curved like a crescent moon. I hesitated momentarily and then whispered, so nobody else could hear, "Honest t' God, honest t' God, damn-blasted old Natz."

Natz dragged them from the window to the playground, so I could see what he was doing. He grabbed their heads and smacked them hard a few times onto the pavement. Then he dropped Bacawk, who slid limply to the ground and lay there, still, and he grabbed Chickichee by both feet and pulled his arms as if he had a good mind to rip him in half. That strange silence of falling snow was interrupted only by Chickichee's plea for help. I relished it. A thin white layer was already coating the ground.

Natz had turned his back on Bacawk, who scrambled to his feet somehow and limped toward a pile of rocks. He didn't look as if he were capable of lifting anything, much less a rock the size of Natz's head, but I covered my eyes when I realized, to my horror, that this rock was going to hit Natz from behind. He fell, first to his knees and then flat onto his face. His huge frame lay like an island amid a snow-white sea. Chickichee flew several feet to the side and then clambered up. Everything in my head was creaking and shuddering, but I managed to hear the teacher tell me that we'd looked at the snow long enough now and I should go back to my coloring.

Bacawk picked up another stone, this one a little smaller, and went over to Natz, who had managed to roll onto his back. Bacawk dropped to his knees, and twice he smashed the rock down on Natz's huge head. Blood spurted after the first blow, and the second blow made a big dent in Natz's skull. It was no longer round, but more of a half globe. His face had split in two. Chickichee crawled over to them. They were quite far from me, but I remember that there was no longer any trace of fear or pleading in his eyes. Just unchecked evil. He pushed Bacawk aside and plunged both hands into the opening in Natz's head. He worked in three fingers of each hand, and with a grimace he widened the crack. Bacawk came over and tore at the growing hole between Natz's right eye and his mouth. Chickichee grabbed Natz's hair, already soaked in thick blood, and jerked several times in the opposite direction with all his strength. Once the hole was opened wide, both of them scooped out the contents of Natz's head, a mush of blood and white tubelike worms, which were the only moving parts left of him. They slurped them into their mouths and greedily gulped them down. Steam rose out of Natz's head. After the third bite, Bacawk froze. Clearly he had the collywobbles, and he bent over and puked a powerful jet of gray-pink vomit. Chickichee paid no attention; instead he reached for all of it— the parts that were Natz's and what had just erupted from Bacawk's gut.

I couldn't tear myself away from the sight, I was thoroughly mesmerized. As background noise, like the falling of snowflakes, I heard the children behind me tell the teacher I was shaking and my pant leg was wet. Again. It was as if by wetting myself these last few days I'd been creating a safe space in those places where I felt the most desperate. And I kept staring helplessly at the scene while a knot, in time with the pounding of my heart, was rising from my stomach to my throat.

The teacher took me by the shoulder and turned me, as if positioning a petrified doll. The children didn't laugh, they just stared in horror, as if I disgusted them and they saw me as less than human.

An older teacher brought a dark-green blanket, and they wrapped me in it before I sat in his car. He dropped me off at the house, and I hid the blanket behind the fence. Before I went in, I looked around once more, in case I caught sight of them. If I had, if they'd come after me, I would have felt defeated. Beneath the horror and disgust, there was something oddly comforting about Natz's dead body being devoured by the two repulsive fiends. The body gave in without a fight. *If'n I'm gone, maybe they'll disappear too,* I thought. *Everybody will be better off.*

I came into the house and saw my mom, sister, uncle, and his aunt all sitting around the kitchen table. Nobody asked why my pants were wet. Uncle was smoking a cigarette, and they were all drinking something strong.

"Come in," said Mom plainly. "An ambulance had to come for Granny."

"Did they stab her?" I asked so softly that probably nobody heard.

"She had a stroke. A palsy come over her. It's like a stab to the head. We'll all go visit her tomorrow, after the plows clear away the snow that falls tonight. There'll be more than three feet by morning if this keeps up."

Through the window I could see Bacawk and Chickichee perched on the fence like huge birds, waiting for nightfall. I was sure I'd go that night to the forest to find Dad, even if I never returned. If I didn't, by next Sunday, or maybe even the next day, they'd all be dead.

14.

When snow falls, I knew even at the age of five, everything gets quieter. Sound doesn't travel well through the flakes, and those take their time, preferring to breathe in the silence, wondering whether it'll be cold enough for them to survive another few days before the afternoon sun finally nudges them down into the darkness of the earth. Still, through the quiet, I could hear myself being summoned to the forest.

Mom had put a large flowerpot on my windowsill, and there was no way I'd be able to lift it. That night I waited for my mom and sister to get ready for bed, and then went to the bathroom even though I didn't need to. I had to get my boots from the front hall. Mom was sitting on her bed, reading an old issue of *Neue Post*, which reported on what the members of the European royal families were doing and where they went skiing.

"Not asleep yet? It's late, you'll have trouble getting up tomorrow," she remarked when she saw my shadow in the hallway. I went in to her. If only I could tell her what was really the matter with Granny! And that I might never come home again.

"Had to pee. Mom, I've got to tell you something."

She put down the magazine and lifted the covers, and I crawled under.

"I know I'm strange. I figure this won't make a whole lotta sense, but I've seen some things."

"Well, well, my boy sure is talking like a grown-up," she said to herself. "You're right, I can't know what you've seen. I just want you to be healthy and happy. I can see you're scared of something and you don't dare tell me what."

I wanted to say I'd already told her several times what was wrong, but she hadn't liked what I'd said. I had half a mind to ask her if she wanted them to take me away. I was angry she didn't answer my real question, though I hadn't actually asked it.

"You don't hate me? You don't think I'm a . . . monster? I know I ain't like the other kids—"

"Look," she interrupted me, "you're all I care about, not the other kids. You be just as you are, but as healthy and happy as you can be. Promise me that."

I wriggled out from under the covers and told her, from the doorway, doing my level best to keep my voice steady: "Don't worry now, everything will be fine."

I faked peeing, flushed, and called out, "G'night" once more from the hallway. After that I went calmly to the front door and unlocked it, and took my jacket and boots back to my room. My corduroys and warm shirt with long sleeves were, luckily, on the floor. I wrapped an undershirt around my ears. I'd seen Bedouins on TV do that.

After Mom's light went out, in total darkness I took off my pajamas, slow and quiet, got dressed, pulled my boots on, and retied the shirt around my head to cover that top part of my ears that always felt the cold worst. After each step in the dark, I stopped and froze like a statue. I heard Mom breathing deeply and synchronized my steps to her breathing, opened the front door, and walked outside.

There was no moonlight like there'd been that night at the river. I stood for a time on the steps by the front door, and when I could see beyond the tip of my nose and the falling snowflakes, I set out. I needed to cross the street to the intersection where the chapel stood, and then go straight past the graveyard along the bumpy old road through the fields toward the hills. My sister and I had walked along this path a few times on our way to gather chestnuts. It had seemed to take us forever to reach the forest, and I remember my feet hurt. Now my feet were light, and I knew no pain would stop me. Before I passed the chapel and crossed the intersection, I heard a car coming down the main road, so I crouched by a neighbor's fence. Past the graveyard I could see farther than before, but still no more than a few feet ahead. The perfect silence was interrupted: "My, my, where're you off to?"

Chickichee. I turned and strode toward the voice. I couldn't see them, but they seemed to be standing by the graveyard entrance. I could still picture what they'd done to Natz, and my breathing quickened, but it never occurred to me to run away. They'd catch me before I reached the nearest house. That's why I said, "If'n you mean to do like you done today to Natz, do it now. I'm on my way to the forest."

The two shadows didn't move, nor did they make a sound.

"I am off to fetch my dad from the will-o'-the-wisp folk, and when we come back, better that you two are gone. He'll beat you straight into the dark mother earth."

Having said that, I turned my back to them and set off. I braced for something to hit me on the head, and then everything would go black and I'd sleep forever. They'd find me in the morning lying in the middle of a big dark splat in the snow near the graveyard, with no face, all my flesh ripped off to the bone. But all I could hear was the squelching of their steps behind mine.

I knew I was headed generally in the right direction because my right foot sank deeper into the snow than my left foot, which meant I was walking on the very edge of the road. Once in a while I'd look back at the village and see lights on in a few houses, a good bit away. The streetlights, I remember, went out in winter while I was still up, around ten.

Cold has a smell, a particular one, like something burning. I wondered how I'd be able to keep going, because I could see almost nothing by then. Soon enough came the answer. From afar I began hearing shrieks, long, painful shrieks, the kind people make when they're falling from a very high place. I soon saw the first lights flicker on the edge of the forest. For the next while I no longer heard Bacawk and Chickichee behind me. By that point the thought of returning home had vanished from my mind. I was less frightened of what I'd see in the forest, where they were surely awaiting me, than of going back.

My uncle once told me that if I was afraid of something, it was a good idea to count it out or measure it. Like counting out the seconds between a lightning flash and the clap of thunder. The only thing I could count now were my steps and breaths. The rest belonged to the dark. The moisture in my nose and lungs was thick, my feet squeaked and wobbled, I no longer felt anything below the knee. I began feeling very tired, my eyes teared up with the cold, my tears stuck to my lashes like colorful soap bubbles. After a long blink I could no longer see flickering lights, only the dark shadows of the trees. Among them there was nothing but a foreboding sense that somebody was waiting for me in there. I reached the first tree and stopped for a spell, glanced behind me once, and pressed on. I continued over the uneven ground, guessing at the angle of the slope, which meant I was going uphill. I stopped and looked up. There were fewer flakes now, but the wind was picking up. My head felt heavy because my shoulders were in knots, and my legs felt like glass, about to shatter any minute now under my weight. The sky was only slightly lighter than the bare treetops. Those weren't branches, they were cracks in the sky.

I yelled, called to him so many times, but nothing. No echo, no answer. Then, finally, something inside me shifted. I looked up at the sky, into the abyss, actually, maybe darker even than the ground. Once you've gazed into the abyss, you carry it inside you for the rest of your life. I peered back into the forest, where the lights of the will-o'-the-wisp folk I was sure I'd seen earlier had now vanished, and that glimpse of darkness and nothingness, so much worse than anything else they could have shown me, took root deep inside, nestled into the back of my mind like a rat. I turned, trying to see where I'd come from, but from the first nest skittered out a few smaller rats who made new nests of their own, one in my heart, one in my belly, one in each of my knees. There was no way to fend them off. These ratlike things live inside me to this day.

Hard to say whether I truly came to understand something in the dark and nothingness. It would be better to say I gave in to it, recognized it, embraced it. Perception-wise there were no insights, I no longer had the strength for a fight. This was the first time I said out loud that Dad was gone for good. Still, I was no coward. If there is a hero in me somewhere, it's that small boy. Never again did I have as much courage, never as much as when I was most frightened, when everything I'd known turned out to be wrong.

A piece of me stayed forever in that forest. That part of me goes on searching for him in the place where it lost his tracks. Sometimes it feels as if that darkness is where I belong, though I did survive that night. There are times even now when I hear the dark place calling to me, to come back to the forest floor, soft with fallen leaves and branches soaked in damp and rot. I go there in my dreams. You, of all people, know that because you were with me when I'd wake up some spring nights terrified and stare into the darkness, trying to discern a shadowy outline. I don't go there of my own free will, just as things rarely happen in dreams the way the dreamer would like them to happen.

Since I didn't know where I was, I kept going uphill, and this decision may have saved my life. After an indeterminate time I came to the top of a hill, where the trees were sparser, and again I spotted several lights far away. This was an upside-down world I was seeing, the world of the will-o'-the-wisp folk. I needed to leave the village to be able to truly see it.

My eyelids were drooping, and for each step downhill, as I headed toward the lights, I needed all the strength I could muster. The snow had stopped falling.

I had somehow made my way back to the road leading toward the village, but my hands, feet, and head were so damned heavy that they pinned me to the snow. Suddenly I was hot, terribly hot, and I longed to strip off my clothes because I feared my belly might boil. But I was too weak. So I just lay there and looked up at the sky. It was no longer quite so dark, the day must have begun to dawn, because I couldn't have been there long without freezing to death. I was found at daybreak by a man from one of the houses on the road to the vineyards. He was driving to work and almost drove right by me, because he thought I was a dead fox.

So it was dawn when I acknowledged that Dad was really, truly gone, and that night I became absolutely certain that it was all my fault. That I had a terrible power, and that all I had to do was wish for a person's death and they would die. I realized that everything in the world dies, and there was no way to deny death. The thought that etched itself into me that day—the image of his cold, white body, which, because of a flash of hatred, was lying motionless, buried deep underground— filled me with a chill, and that feeling has been the only constant in my life. Except, perhaps, the face in the mirror, but that, too, has changed over time. Only the chill has remained the same all these years.

15.

I recall regaining consciousness a few times at the hospital, opening my eyes, and then sinking back to sleep.

Each waking was to another world. Once, out of the corner of my eye, I saw my sister sitting by my bed doing her homework. Another time the room was empty. The third time my uncle was there with a friend from work, talking about the water pipeline and municipal funds. They didn't even notice I'd opened my eyes. I don't know how many days passed before I was finally able to keep my eyes open for more than a moment. The room was empty, though, and just when I'd almost drifted back to sleep again, Granny came in. I wanted to say hi, but I was too weak. She was in slippers and a bathrobe, with a kerchief tied around her hair, just like at home. She limped and held her right arm close to her body, the hand crooked inward. She couldn't close her mouth all the way—her lips were a little skewed, as if pulled by an invisible thread. She talked slowly, wearily, and told me I'd come down with a bad case of pneumonia, and they'd cut off two of my toes because they'd frozen. I wanted to tell her how happy I was that Bacawk and Chickichee hadn't killed her, and that now we were rid of them for good. I wanted to ask whether I could take my dead toes home with me, but nothing came out of my mouth. Granny pulled a chair up with her good arm and sat down, then she took out her rosary and began praying. Her monotone lulled me back to sleep.

The next morning I woke up, and there were three kids playing cards. A dark-haired kid noticed me watching them and said: "He woke up. I'll get the nurse."

The nurse brought me a tray with food. I wanted to sit up, but my head was spinning. When I saw a tube sticking out of my wiener, I had a moment of collywobbles.

The boy was named Sandi, and he had trouble breathing. He said he'd been at the hospital for a hundred years. The other, smaller boy was Viktor; he'd had his tonsils removed and had trouble speaking. The girl was Biljana, and she didn't know why she was there exactly. Every night she'd start shaking and choking, and Sandi would go running for the nurse.

Later that day Mom came. She brought me two juices with straws and an orange. More than anything I wanted to tell her how sorry I was that I'd killed Dad, but I couldn't, I just cried. Only Sandi was in the room then, and he pretended not to watch.

A little later the lady who'd come to our house came and asked me if somebody was hitting me. I realized I'd better do my best to seem normal, so I told her I was silly to have sleepwalked to the forest and that I didn't remember a thing. She wanted me to draw something, so I drew a hedgehog and a bear and a snowman on skis. She wasn't particularly pleased with this, so I drew myself, Mom, my sister, and my uncle playing around a swimming pool and climbing onto a playground slide. I even wrote *MATIJA* by the sun, and then *MY NAME IS MATIJA I BE FIVE*. She asked me whether my sister ever scared me, and I lied and said she didn't. Before she left she said I'd be talking once a week with a nice lady in Čakovec, and I could tell her everything that bothered me. I knew exactly what to say to her. Just like at school. I'd lie that everything was fine and that I was happy and had tons of friends. When you're very small, you're one person. Later you pretend you're at least

181

two, and then three, and so it goes until you get big. I was many kids, but there was only a small piece of childhood left inside me.

I had a good time at the hospital, especially after they took the tube out of my wiener. We played cards and told jokes. Sometimes I thought about how I might bring Dad's body back to our house. I'd dig him up and embalm him. My sister had read to me about that from the book *1000 Whys and 1000 Becauses*. It was what the pharaohs of Egypt did—they smeared the body all over with chemicals and oils so it wouldn't smell bad or rot. I could embalm Dad, put marbles in for his eyes, and dress him up, and he'd live with us in the house. Of course, this would have to be a secret, but at least we'd be whole in the evening, in front of the TV. He'd be with us at dinner, even if he weren't eating. That mattered less, somehow. Maybe we'd have to tie a kerchief around his head to hold his jaw in place, so his mouth wouldn't drop open and flies wouldn't fly in. That's how they did my granddad up when he died.

On the third day, when they changed the dressing, I saw where they'd cut off my little toe and the one next to it. My feet were swollen and bluish, almost black in some places. They hurt and itched at the same time. The nurse told me they'd thrown the toes away. She said I could go home in two days. This was good news, but I'd hoped somebody from my class would visit while I was still in the hospital. I'd show them where they'd cut off my toes, and how I was playing cards with my new friends, and then they'd all love me again. But nobody from school came.

I wasn't afraid of going home. Bacawk and Chickichee could peer in the window every night, as far as I was concerned, and I'd still sleep peacefully. I had more courage than them. After all, I'd gone into the forest, and the two of them had hightailed it out of there. The only thing they would get from me now was scorn.

On the next-to-last day, Mom came to visit with the parish priest. He brought me a big bar of chocolate with puffed rice. At first we talked a little, awkwardly, and then Mom went off to look for a doctor, and the Father and I were left alone. At first I was a bit sheepish because I thought he'd come to tell me he'd noticed I was bored at Mass and knew I was counting people.

"How are you, Matija? Is your foot hurting you?"

"No it ain't, Father."

"I hear you'll be coming home in two days. Are you glad?"

"I am glad, but . . ."

"The things you tell me are heard only by you, me, and God, our dear Father. I won't tell anyone. I think you want to tell me what you were doing out there that night in the snow. Am I right?"

"Well, I don't know as I'll tell you that. I would like to ask you something, though. What's it like while a person is dying?"

"Why? Did you feel you were close to dying?"

I didn't say anything, and we sat in silence for a time.

"When we die, we join our Holy Father in heaven," he finally said, plainly.

"Well, that part I know, my granny told me, but what's it like there?"

"Well . . ." The priest drew in a breath and gave this some thought. "Imagine how things were when they were the very best, when you felt the safest, when all the people you love—your friends and everybody—were together. Can you remember that? Try to close your eyes and think."

I squinted and couldn't see any sort of clear picture, but a cozy warmth stirred in my belly. Like I was waving at people who weren't worried and weren't sitting at the kitchen table staring into space on a sunny day.

"I think I know. When you want something to never end."

"Yes, exactly right. Happiness and satisfaction without end. That's what it's like when we are one with our Holy Father."

The priest went on saying something else about invisible people who work for God, and how our parents and grannies and granddads when they die are always with us and looking after us, but I began thinking about something while he was talking.

"Father, where do the people go who killed somebody?"

"If they don't repent, if they don't seek God's forgiveness, then to hell. Why?"

I burst into tears. When I was able to breathe again, I whispered: "Can you give me forgiveness? Forgiveness from God?"

"Why, son?"

"Because I killed my dad."

He looked at me, shocked, but quickly recovered. "No, Matija, no. Who told you that?"

"Nobody, it's just I know, 'cause I—"

"Matija, listen to me now . . ."

"I glared at him and thought I hated him when he wouldn't say nothing about the treasure, and afterward I never saw him again!"

"Matija, your father was sick, and that's why God took him. You had nothing to do with it. You have to be good now, do what your mother says, and believe that your dad and your Holy Father are look-ing after you, and they won't let anything happen to you. You will do a lot of good in this world, and maybe some bad things, too. And when the time comes, Saint Peter puts all your bad and your good things on a scale, and when the good ones tip the scale, then the door of heaven will open, and you'll be with your dad again, and with all the others, as a being of light."

"But Father . . . will I know him when I get to heaven?"

"I'm sure of it. Your soul and your dad's soul know each other from before. What do you remember first when you think about him?"

"I can't see his face no more. But I think back to how we talked about the valley and about how we'd go searching for the hidden treasure."

"Then that's the way you'll know each other. And he's waiting for that. There are people who die a few times during their life. You're one of them. But you should know that through God the resurrection also belongs to you. Don't ever forget that. That's why you can be without fear, because He will see to everything, but you must also do what you're told." And just as the priest was saying this, Mom came back into the room with a present wrapped in shiny paper.

We wished each other a merry Christmas and prayed, and after that Mom and the priest went home because the visiting hours were over.

Ever since then I've been on the lookout for people like myself, and I've written about their lives. I wanted to be part of their deaths and rebirths, I guess. And the whole time I was scared of what I'd see in them—people like myself. But I was even more afraid of my hatred and the vast power of killing. And I managed, somehow, to keep from hating anybody until the spring of 1991.

ANGER BOXES

1.

Over the next two and a half years, through the spring of 1991, the world changed completely. What sticks in my memory is the pervasive feeling of violence. The world is full of clocks and unspoken words, this I knew, but I'd begun to see how the things surrounding us acquire a sort of madness when we don't keep close tabs on them. They exist in all these different forms, and only when we look directly at them do they assume a defined shape. They do this for our sake because they know that otherwise we wouldn't know how to live. But this time the shift was something else. Nobody was watching us kids.

One spring day in 1990, I think it was a Sunday, there were national elections, and the Croatian Democratic Union Party won. The CDU opened a branch office in our village, and we were all proud that the party we thought of as ours had won in Zagreb, too. When the office was opened, only men were involved: a teacher, the doctor, the village head, Đura Brezovec—who now went to church with his wife every Sunday—Pišta, and several of the guest workers who had returned from Germany. Like my dad, they'd gone by bus to Germany to seek their fortunes. Since it was clear that even their children's children weren't going to find much fortune there, they'd come back to tell all the rest of us how we were supposed to live.

From the window of the fire station, we watched the dedication ceremony for the local party headquarters. They sang the Croatian anthem and placed their right hands over their hearts. I felt solemn in my chest because I heard they'd be making a new flag and a new country. I thought Croatia would become like Austria—Bad Radkersburg, for example. Only the returning guest workers knew all the words to the hymn, though, and I felt a little embarrassed for the rest of us. Then they sang to Mother Croatia, and the song said that all she had to do was call, and all the falcons would give their lives for her. They only knew the one stanza, so they sang it twice. Somebody began singing the opera aria "Arise, Arise," but all they knew was the refrain, so they quickly stopped.

Almost all the village men were at the ceremony, except those who worked in Slovenia. They knew they'd be out of work once there was no more Yugoslavia. My uncle was one of them. Several people from the village had already been laid off and were going to be replaced by Slovenes, so they'd come back to farm and find a job somewhere on this side of the Mura.

Uncle said people should be voting for independent candidates.

"If'n you ask me, I am all for them independents. They're independent, right? Their name even says so—independent."

As far as I could tell, he was not only the strongest but also the smartest man in the world. I remember that the Slovenes and the Croats often scuffled at soccer games and on the road. They blustered, scoffed, and called each other dumbasses. This stopped when the village decided they'd invest in artificial fertilizer for the farmers. Paving roads and installing running water would be put off for another year. This suited people, because for years funds in Yugoslavia had been set aside for the Belgrade–Bar highway—which people weren't happy about—and for building school auditoriums in Serbia or Macedonia, which drove folks mad.

A man I saw for the first time that day attended the dedication ceremony. He was fat—the buttons on his suit strained to close—and he combed his hair over his bald spot. He struggled to breathe and kept wiping the sweat off his upper lip with a handkerchief even though it was cold outside. Shouting as if he were angry, he spoke in an uninterrupted stream, which seemed to entrance everybody. He talked about how Međimurje was the Croatianest part of Croatia, how the people of Međimurje had stood up to the Hungarians, how Saint Jerome had invented the Croatian Glagolitic alphabet and been born right there in Štrigova. At this point Mr. Martijanec, the history and geography teacher, began to fidget and shake his head. He looked as if he wanted to say something but didn't know who to say it to. When the fat, sweaty man talked about how Međimurje lay at the heart of Croatia because only Catholics—like the Zrinjskis and other Croatian noble families—lived there, Martijanec winced again and said to Pišta that the Zrinjskis had been Protestants. Without taking his eyes off the fat man, Pišta replied indifferently: "So what? The Serbs are Orthodox."

At the end everybody applauded, sang again with their hands on their hearts, and then went to Imbra Perčić the electrician's vineyard to taste his wine. They sang there, and evidently somebody's aunt taught them to say, "All Serbs are motherfuckers." They got so drunk by midnight that Imbra declared them all full of shit and "fine with eating the hard work of others and guzzling human sweat," so they dispersed.

After that day, all over the village there was talk of things that didn't have to do directly with the villagers. We were being expected to read our own history backward, like reading a book from the last page to the first.

We were instructed in what to think about everything that had, supposedly, been going on under the communists. Apparently they'd stolen from and tortured us, and we'd always had to keep our mouths shut. We were also told how we were supposed to remember. Some of the memories, which had seemed genuine as recently as the day before, had to pack up and take the bus—like Dejan and me did that time—and leave our little village forever. The most vociferous of the people speaking up at the time said that we, the people of Međimurje, were yokels and didn't care nearly enough about our country or our people.

The villagers' mouths were full of democracy, though mostly with their tongue firmly in cheek. When the teacher said we had to write two essays over vacation, she said, "Now there's democracy for you," and Mom said the same thing when we had to watch *Das Traumschiff* instead of *Dirty Harry* on TV. Anything might suddenly be democracy, and at one point even Zvonko Horvat became known as Democracy.

Zvonko Horvat was an older man who lived down the street, near Granny's. He was one of those people who was always talking about how the folks of Međimurje were yokels and ought to try to make their homeland proud. He'd worked his whole life in Germany. Somehow he gave the impression of having seen the world, knowing about everything, but all he'd really done was work in a mine, and it wasn't clear what he could have seen a few hundred feet below soggy German dirt. With an air of desperation, he called on the local people to muster the will to get things started. He was all for us producing wine in Međimurje and exporting it to Germany. As nobody contradicted him, I made it to adulthood assuming Germans had only lousy wine and were waiting eagerly for ours to arrive. Zvonko reminded everybody around him of their place, and didn't hide his great admiration for the people of Dalmatia and Slavonia—whom he'd served with in the Yugoslav People's Army—or his regret that we weren't more like them. He seemed to perceive their bluntness as charming honesty.

"A man from Dalmatia, now he'll tell you how he's doing, but not a fellow from Međimurje—polite to your face, maybe, but behind your back he'll be smearing you with mud."

Zvonko was rarely interrupted, not just because he talked without pausing for breath, but because sometimes he offered such bizarre comparisons that nobody could follow them.

"This Mesić fella, and Kostić, or whatever his name is. Each of them is out to be better than the other guy. See? That's how things was in the US of A. They flat-out refused to go to the Olympics when the games were held in Moscow. These things is all of a piece."

Or he'd get his hands on somebody at a soccer game and yell so everybody could hear: "What manner of people live here? See, Pišta? Are you all crazy? We were in Zagreb, see. A hundred thousand of us were in the square from all over Croatia, see, and they sang till the shivers went up and down my back! But aside from us, not a soul was there from Međimurje. Why're we so crazy? Tuđman, he said this is our time to show what real live patriotism is, but what do our contrary old geezers here do? Nothing. And hey, we drive one place, we drive another, we wave our Croatian flag out the car window. And when we did that in Zagreb and in Zagorje, the folks—they clapped! People on the streets, see, they clapped. Then you cross the Drava, and not a peep. People turn their heads and look away. They turn their backs on you!"

"Enough already with all that talk," someone grumbled about him. "He spent a good twenty-five years in Krautland while things here were the worst they've ever been, and now here he comes preaching at us to say how we're supposed to conduct ourselves. Damn-blast Zvonko and his democracy. If'n he don't want to be here, why didn't he stay up there with the Krauts?"

Once, at a soccer game, after his third beer, he started really grating on people's nerves, even more than the jerk ref did. Imbra Perčić, downing his fourth drink, finally said: "I ain't partial to your behavior, Zvonko. Off you went to Germany to work, you earned your pension up there, sure enough, but we're hardworking folks, too. And now you come out here like you have the wisdom of the world. Go easy, why dontcha, put on the brakes."

Zvonko, not used to being criticized, was caught off guard. The best thing he could come up with was: "Then why dontcha go to Serbia, Imbra, if you think things are so great there?"

"Well, well, got your goat, did I, Zvonko? Will you look at him all upset. What an asshole," Imbra remarked, also visibly agitated, to the person standing next to him, "and he says this to me, who's never so much as set foot in Serbia. It was Tetovo, y'know, Macedonia, where I served in the army."

Zvonko, for his part, complained to an indifferent Pišta: "Folks around these parts won't even think about lending a hand, know what I mean. Now, I've done me a thing or two in my lifetime, know what I mean. Seen the world. In Germany when you work, you work. Know what I mean, Pišta?"

Imbra shot back: "Cut the crap. I care about my folks, too, which is exactly why we need to keep an eye out so those Krauts of yours don't screw us over like everybody else—the Hungarians, the Serbs—always have."

Zvonko lunged at Imbra to throttle him—he could no longer bear being contradicted—but he slipped and fell flat on his back. He winced with pain, and the whole thing might have turned out pretty badly if somebody hadn't laughed and said: "Now there's democracy for you."

The next day while walking down the street, Imbra said, "Well, lookee here, there goes Democracy," and everybody laughed again, and from that day till his death by hanging, Zvonko Horvat was known as Democracy.

They told us at school that we shouldn't greet each other with the commie "hail" anymore but instead say the new Croatian greeting, "Good day," and that our teachers were now just "Teacher," not "Comrade Teacher," like we'd been told to call them before. I knew something big had changed when the priest came to our school play, sat in the front row with the principal, and then later went to the teachers' lounge for coffee and cake. I was happy they'd finally made their peace. Everybody said Croatia had to start being its own country. In the spring of 1991, a month or so before the suicides began, a Serbian singer named Bebi Dol won a contest. She was competing to represent

Yugoslavia at Eurovision, but we were convinced that a Croatian singer we'd never heard of before, Tedi Spalato, was way better. He dressed in robes like a friar and sang a song in which he prayed to God for a girl-friend. Some joked that it was good to see a priest interested in women: "It's refreshing, honest t' God, to see that not all priests are pansies."

Others were a little more serious, saying they were happy to rub Serbs' noses in the fact that we were Catholics.

"Damn-blasted Serbs."

"They're shooting at police."

"And putting up barricades."

"Enough already with the bad-mouthing."

Even the kids in school began talking about Serbs, Croatia, democracy, and especially Franjo Tuđman. There was a sternness about him. He spoke with his sizable mouth practically shut, his upper lip would twist, and when he talked about how we had to love Croatia, he lost control of his voice and he'd do this yodelly thing. He wore big square glasses with thick frames and had wavy hair. His hair first swelled up, then flattened down, then swelled up again. I wanted to love him, but I just couldn't. He didn't have a dog to protect him from a bomb, like Tito'd had, and he hadn't sent the Germans packing, either. And besides, I was worried he might do something buffle-brained. All those democracy honchos looked like they had no idea what it was they were supposed to be doing. The Special Police officer reporting to the president on TV fumbled halfway through and forgot what he was supposed to say. When Tuđman went to the United States, the president there didn't receive him. We saw on TV that they stayed at an ordinary hotel and took taxis, like tourists in suits, and the passersby stared at them like they were nutcases. We missed out on the pomp and circumstance, the red carpet and brass band, and all the soldiers wearing white gloves. I was afraid nobody would want to recognize us and take us seriously. That would be bad, because we'd begun taking ourselves very seriously indeed.

The new story had appeal. I was happy to believe we were descendants of the Tomislav royal line, a much different and finer people than the uncouth Bosnians or Serbs. Closer to the Germans and Americans than to the Russians and Turks or any other such sorry folks. A brave and noble people.

I wanted us to eat sandwiches on triangular slices of bread like in the US of A, and have a hundred different kinds of salami and chocolate like in Bad Radkersburg, and drink Coca-Cola from a can. I wanted to wear Bermuda shorts, bright-colored T-shirts, and white high-tops like the kids in California wore. I was sick and tired of stories about the partisans, wartime couriers, bombers, clowns, and persnickety girls; about how the Adriatic Sea connected us to the whole world; and about how Tito was kind to children and loved to hunt. I wanted to be the BMX Bandit and Karate Kid. I began to imagine being capable of great things, and that when I did something in front of everybody, they would all leap spontaneously to their feet and applaud, first slowly, then louder like they do in the American movies, when an old veteran stands up from his wheelchair and salutes with a tear in his eye. I believed this was possible, that people in the village would change, and that I wouldn't always be met with discouragements like "All right already," "No, no, no," or "Come now, come now, come now."

"All right already" is what people said when somebody who'd been taking dancing lessons came to a wedding and danced differently than the other folks who'd been stitching a two-step across the floor. Somebody would say, "All right already," and everybody would know that what came next was "Cut the crap." When somebody on Vujčovo Hill knew how to ski proper-like and started zigzagging left and right instead of going down straight like everybody else, somebody would mutter, "All right already" . . . and everybody knew that next came "Knock it off." It was the same when somebody said, "Come now, come now, come now" . . . They all knew that next was "Get over it."

It had been over two years since I'd gone to the forest and nearly died of exposure. And for half a year after that, I went once a week to talk to the lady at the Čakovec medical center, and told her stories about my good friends, about how we had camaraderie and played with Legos. There wasn't actually much of that. Mom once told me to invite kids over to have soda, sandwiches, and cake for my birthday, but nobody would come, and once she was supposed to take Granny for a checkup in Čakovec, but she didn't have anybody to leave me with because none of the parents wanted me around. I had to lie to the lady at the medical center so she wouldn't send me to the big woman and little man with the dumb questions. I drew pictures for her: people, animals, dogs, trees, tanks and planes, imaginary beings, the earth and the sky. She didn't know I was drawing the sites of my hidden remorse because I couldn't make the world better for me and others.

I left some drawings and messages on Dad's grave, though I wasn't sure he really read them. Somebody was probably taking them. I corresponded with my buddies from the hospital for a bit. Eventually I stopped writing Viktor and Sandi because I got bored. But Biljana stopped writing me. She didn't usually write much about her sickness, but she said once that they were moving her to Zagreb and that she'd ridden in an ambulance. She wrote me about the pony they'd promised her when she got better and the pop band Novi fosili. She included stickers of singers and actors, the kind that came with chewing gum. I stuck them on one side of my bed to remind me of her. I prayed to God she stopped writing to me because she got bored and not for some other reason.

The children in my class hadn't forgotten what I'd tried to do to Dejan Kunčec; word got out about it, maybe he told them himself. I'd have given my eyeteeth to be like the others, but I knew even then that I'd lost that chance a long time ago. On the other hand, I was unappealing enough that they left me alone. I sat by myself. At least that's how it looked to everybody else. Bacawk and Chickichee were still around, lurking in my peripheral vision. I was strong enough by then to ignore them, and I'd become good at that. Now and then, at lunch break, one or the other would dart out from under the table and wing a gob of phlegm into my soup or spit into my mashed potatoes. I went right on eating just to spite them, though this did turn my stomach. Sometimes they watched me through the window at night, but I was no longer afraid.

And besides, things weren't like they used to be at home. When summer came there was no trip to the seashore. We ate the same food for days: dishes made from offal and buckwheat groats. The water pump kept breaking, and the roof leaked during summer downpours. This at least gave me some amusement, scampering around the attic with pails and bowls, thinking about how I could become a consultant for households with leaky roofs. The only truly upsetting part was having to wear a Yassa tracksuit with foot straps, which I was ashamed of. I wanted one of those bright-colored tracksuits that made a slithery sound, like the other kids wore. Mom was looking for a job, but all she could get was part-time work on the weekends. She'd help out in the kitchen and as a waitress for weddings at the Međimurska hiža, and sometimes bring home leftovers.

My uncle and his wife still helped us out, but less and less. He was worried he'd lose his job in Slovenia, so he was saving for a tractor. One day he brought me a blue soccer jersey and cleats and told me a junior soccer league, the Pioneers, would be starting at the Miners Croatian Soccer Club. I was excited, but anxious because he said each boy would be asked to show what he could do with a soccer ball. I didn't have one. I felt a little better when Franjo, my only friend, said that he was going to try out for soccer, too. He was in fourth grade and lived a few houses down from me toward the Mura.

The very fact that his parents had named him Franjo suggested they didn't care much for him. It was the kind of name that made you think of granddads, and his last name was Klanz. So of course everybody called him Franz Klanz. His parents were pretty old and drank a lot, which I knew because they didn't mow their grass often. I also knew they were poor, because they had a black-and-white TV set with no remote, and for Christmas they just had a scrawny little tree on the table with colored bulbs that blinked nervously, and—this was the biggest giveaway—they used a wooden outhouse behind their house. The outhouse must've clogged up for a while, so they did their business outside, in the garden and the bushes. They had a dog they tied to a scraggly tree on such a short leash that it could hardly move. Its head would poke out from one side of the tree, its rump from the other. Sometimes it had to sleep half standing and half lying in its own shit because it had no way to kick dirt over it. Every time Franz's dad walked by the dog, he'd deliver a kick to its muzzle. The dog was overjoyed when someone tossed it a scrap of something from the kitchen window, along with cusses and reminders that it was a mongrel and ought to be grateful to be getting anything at all and they were so kind. Franz's mom always smelled of wine and onions, and talked like she was sleepy. In the morning she'd go to the store and come back with only bottles. Once, around nine at night, she came over to our house, and I heard her say that guests had stopped by, and she was wondering if, by any chance, she could borrow a bottle of wine or something a bit stronger. She took pains to be polite, talked loud and fast, and laughed at herself for not having wine to serve her guests. Mom gave her a bottle, and after she left, we watched her through the window. There was nobody at their house as far as we could tell. Mom told me she was a drunk, and I shouldn't be like that. I asked her how much a person has to drink to become a drunk, but she couldn't say. I reminded her that during the grape harvest everybody said they'd have a little to "make them abler" or to "give them cunning." Then she said drunks are people who can't stop drinking. I thought that could never happen to me because my cousin and I took Uncle's beer to Granny's bedroom and tried it one Christmas, and it was disgusting. It burned in my mouth, nose, and throat, and I couldn't imagine why anybody would want to drink it, no matter how cunning or able they'd be.

I often heard yelling from the Klanz house. At first I had the impression that Franz was a bit dense, but he talked a lot and fast, and he repeated words and sentences, so I started doing the same. His special talent was saying words backward. He was proud of this, because neither of us knew anybody who was as smooth at it as he was. We had every reason to believe he was the world champion at saying words backward. He was Znarf, or Ojnarf, Znalk, and I was, Ajitam Cečnelod. He explained that the secret was to picture the word and then flip it around. I liked him because his head was too big for his body, and I thought that as he got bigger his head would grow, too, and nobody would want to play with him. His eyebrows were always arched in the middle, which made his eyes look sad, but his mouth always stretched to the sides as if he were smiling. This made him look happy and sad at the same time. I saw no contradiction in this. Every day at home his eyes saw ugly things, but his mouth didn't.

We went to school and Mass together. He'd talk, and I'd be quiet and sit with my thoughts. When I was with him, in a strange way it was like I was by myself. When I was there without him, it seemed like I wasn't really there, or that I was somebody else. I didn't always listen to what he was saying, but I was glad for his company. He talked, and I looked at my toes in the grass, and that was enough that day for me to count myself among the happier beings.

2.

In early May 1991, about two weeks before the suicides began, the killing had already started in eastern Croatia, and people in the village spoke with a terrible satisfaction about the special forces and the massacre at Borovo. Franz and I were worried about our first soccer league meeting. For days he'd wondered if they'd choose him to be goalie. He asked if we should go alone or with his dad. I was scared of his dad, so I suggested we go alone. There hadn't been a junior league in our village before, but Goran Brezovec, son of the new village head, had reached junior soccer age, so a team was in the making. Within a few years, they said, there'd be a generation of strong young players. The coach was going to be Bogdan from Mursko Središće, who'd played for the Miners some years back and was famous for having slid into the best player from the neighboring village and breaking both of his legs. After that he drank for free at both bars in our village. When we got to the field, Bogdan was in a heated discussion with some men. His gaze was glassy, and his pudgy, ruddy, calloused face hinted that he often enjoyed his drinking privilege.

Franz and I didn't know where to stand, so we waited by the fence and eavesdropped on some grown-ups. A smallish man was saying what a little skeezicks his boy was, how he was as good as the older boys, how quick and nimble he was. I tried to figure out who he was pointing to, and it turned out he meant Krunek, who was maybe the clumsiest of them all. He was too tall, and when his feet struck the ground, they weren't in line with his knees and hips. He couldn't hang on to the ball; somebody would kick it out from beneath him every time. At one point he fell, and all three men stopped talking.

"Krunek, come here," yelled the little man. "Just wait till you see him do his push-ups. He does fifty like it's nothing. I've been coaching him myself. Yep, indeedy, that's my boy. Krunek, show us your push-ups."

"Now don't push yourself so hard, Krunek, don't tucker yourself out before the training starts," cautioned Coach Bogdan.

Krunek threw himself to the ground and began doing push-ups. He did the first four at the same pace, the fifth and sixth slower, and after the seventh his arms started wobbling. His shoulders sagged, and his head hung down, as if all he needed was to catch his breath for a minute and then he'd pump another forty in no time flat, but nothing happened. An awkward silence settled in, interrupted by Krunek's dad: "Well, what's wrong? Do it."

Krunek took a deep breath, shoulders sagging, and lowered himself one more time but couldn't push himself back up, and so he collapsed on the ground. His father hoisted him up and shook him, supposedly for getting mud on his shorts. The men went on talking soccer, and I began telling Franz about my dad.

I told him how my dad had played soccer in Germany and had been able to nail bicycle-kick goals, so his teammates had carried him on their shoulders and bought him a car that went over a hundred miles an hour, but he didn't dare drive it in Yugoslavia. I told Franz how Dad had flown a plane on the weekends because he was a pilot. Then a man named Zdravko Tenodi interrupted me.

"Hey, hey, what's this I'm hearing? Where was it now your daddy played?" He was frowning and cocking his head to the side, looking at me as though with intense interest. He smirked, spoke loudly, and jabbed the man beside him with his elbow.

"So, where did your daddy play?"

"Payern."

"Where?" Zdravko got even louder, attracting everybody's attention. "Palermo, was it?"

"No, Payern."

"Bayern, I s'pose. And when was it he played with them?"

"Before," I said, softer and softer.

"Before! Well, I'll be damned! Now that you mention it, I do seem to recall him playing." Zdravko winked at somebody. "And you say he scored goals?"

"Yeah . . . a whole mess of 'em."

"My, my, a whole mess of goals, well, I'll be damned."

"He hit volleys. And bicycle kicks. And those goals to the top corner."

"Well, well, and who did he play with?"

"Rummenigge."

Now everybody was listening. With each answer, waves of laughter rolled through the group. My face was getting hot, and I started seeing red and yellow.

"Hey, Matija, let's go," said Franz, but I couldn't move.

"And what kind of car did he drive?" said Zdravko.

"It went over a hundred miles an hour."

"Whooeee, that's fast. So where's your daddy now?"

My throat tightened; I tasted metal and felt a tingling in my hands. I knew I couldn't wipe my eyes, because then they'd see I was crying. Somebody closer to me saw it anyway, and said: "Don't. See, he's getting a bit misty there around the eyes."

Somebody else quipped, "I'd like to know where his mom is," and they burst out in guffaws.

"Maybe somewhere having herself a little rub," said a third, jerking his hands bellyward twice. They laughed wildly and all started talking at once. I couldn't for the life of me see what my mother would be rubbing, or what that had to do with anything.

I wished they'd just go away, especially Zdravko Tenodi. Mladen Horvat, a slender younger man married to a woman named Milica, stepped out from the crowd. Until recently he'd been a first-string player for the Miners, and now he ran the bar at the team clubhouse and trained the goalies. All I knew about him was that he never drank, he didn't malign women or anyone else, and he was always kind to everybody. He stood behind me and Franz, rested his hands on our shoulders, and said: "Guys, you're outta line."

Most of them stopped, but somebody gibed: "Hey, Mladen, none of your beeswax, and besides, why shouldn't we be having a little fun? I'd sure like to take his mama for a roll in the hay, come to think of it . . . When'll she be stopping by to watch him play?"

Mladen took us to the clubhouse and retrieved two Cockta sodas from a crate behind the bar. He tried to cheer us up; he put his arms around our shoulders like we were friends, and said that grown-ups can sometimes be cruel to kids but we shouldn't take it personal, we'd see how they were when their wives were around. Through the window we saw Bogdan gathering the kids. I told Franz to go and that I'd wait for him. I gave him the cleats my uncle had given me, because Franz only had old cloth sneakers. Usually he talked a blue streak, but that day he was much quieter. All he said was: "If you ain't going, I ain't going."

I knew he wanted to be a goalie more than anything in the world. He was being more loyal to me than to himself. We watched the other kids practice for a while in silence, and then Pišta came into the bar.

"Honest t' God, the spuds'll be big as squashes this year."

"I ain't wild about how people are fertilizing. Is it a good idea to lay it on so thick?" said Mladen.

"Who cares? I haven't much farmland to speak of, just a couple of klafters. But I like how we fucked with the over-the-Mura folks: the damn-blasted Slovenes."

"But, Pišta, what's the point? I hear each farmer was given 30 percent more fertilizer for the same money. But it's too late in the season to fertilize the crops."

"Heh heh, just imagine how gorgeous the spuds'll be. It's all thanks to Miška Čurinof. He's heard he'll be losing his job over in Lendava next month . . ."

"Him, too? What'll they all do with no work? Drink all day?"

"We'll be farmers, I guess. And so what? We'll be off to war in no time anyway. It was Miška who made the fertilizer deal. He works at the warehouse. When they left him to his own devices, he decided to mix the artificial fertilizer with this other chemical—butanol, or whatever it's called. The foreman couldn't figure how it happened, exactly, but everything's piled on top of everything else there. So they couldn't sell it at full price. Damaged goods. Miška let Đura Brezovec know, and the village bought a huge load of the stuff. You must have seen it when they brought it in here."

Pišta snickered, finished his beer, and went home. Mladen told Franz he'd show him some goalie moves if he wanted. He gave us each another Cockta and asked whether we needed to pee. Franz nodded, and I was ready, too, so the three of us went out to the bushes behind the locker room. Mladen didn't watch where he was peeing; instead he watched me and Franz. Mladen's wiener was big and fat and stuck out of this little forest of hairs, while Franz's and mine were wimpy little pink things. He told us he had to go but that we could always let him know if somebody messed with us, and he'd be glad have us over to his house to practice our soccer skills sometime.

The practice wound down out on the field, Bogdan lit a cigarette and sat in the car, the kids and dads headed slowly home, and I asked Franz to wait a little longer. I didn't want to walk home with everybody else. We went along the road in the opposite direction for a bit, toward the river, where we sat on the embankment and watched the water. It wasn't dark yet, but some stars were already coming out.

I asked Franz what he thought stars would sound like if we could hear them and also what ants would sound like. The ants and the stars were both small to us, and just as far away. We agreed pretty quick about the ants, that they are always rushing—*sweet Jesus, will you look at them scurry*—all hurrying each other along with no time for explanations. They're far too busy to be sitting in libraries or on a terrace with a cup of coffee, but on rainy days they stay in their little houses underground and clean and do whatever they didn't have time for on the sunny days. When night falls, some of them try to see what's above the clouds using diamond periscopes, hoping to catch sight of their distant relatives, the flying ants, about whom legends abound. Meanwhile they say that camaraderie is what matters most, and they don't go to church, because they're communists. For the stars, Franz said, it seemed to him they look shyly down on Earth, hoping somebody will send up a kaleidoscope because they're bored staring at the same universe all the time where things change only when trucks loaded with candy pass on their way to another galaxy. The stars laugh only when they see a bird on a distant planet flying so high that it soars up beyond the breathable air and loses consciousness, then plummets like a pear down to the ground. Then they die laughing. The stars believe in God and go to church at least once a week. Or maybe, Franz said, the stars are silent. They don't say anything, or they talk so slowly that one word lasts thousands of years, and what we call silence is not truly silence but actually the sound they use to say the word for the time we live in. I asked him what the astral word was for the time we were living in, but Franz didn't answer. We stared into the water, and from the water Ajitam and Znarf stared back. I asked Franz if he thought there were two boys like us on the other side of the reflection looking at us and wondering the same things we were wondering. He thought about it and said he'd like it better if they were looking at this side without him in it. I wasn't sure what he meant by that exactly.

"What do you think it's like on the other side? Over on the other side, what's the world like there? What do you think, what kind of world is it, Matija?"

"You mean over on the other bank of the river?"

"Nope, on the other side of . . . that mirror. Of the river. The mirror of the river. Like we see ourselves in it, like on the other side of that," said Franz.

"I believe it's a world where everybody's good. They're kind to us there, Franz. You're the goalie, and I'm—"

"I heard there's a way through the Mura to an underground place where everybody's dead, and they walk around in the dark, looking for a way out."

"Naw, Franz. I thought my dad was down there . . . I was sure of it. But he ain't. I wish I'd never thought it. Ever since then, nothing's been like it was before."

"I figure it can be fixed, Matija, I think it can, it can for sure . . ." Every once in a while Franz said comforting things that surprised me and made me glad. Because through this crack I could see how, behind his walls, behind the curly hair and jaw, behind everything, there was a marvelous land with puffy white clouds, little houses with round windows, and horses cantering free. Because of this, I knew he'd be fine.

When I came home, I tossed my cleats in the corner. Mom asked me whether I'd signed up for soccer, and I said I hadn't and that they'd said bad things about Dad so I'd kicked the soccer ball at the coach's head.

I was the only kid in my class who didn't sign up.

Before I went to bed, Chickichee was waiting for me in the bathroom and insisted on telling me about how a long, long time ago, five centuries or more, our village had played a game with a neighboring village, and the goal was to leave the rotting corpse of a dog smack in the middle of the other village.

"Sweet Jesus, how they played—the game went all summer long. The carcass was already crawling with maggots. A boy named Miklauš from the next village wanted to put the carcass on our street, so he rode over on his horse, but our boys heard him. This kid by the name of Vajnč hit him in the spine with a hoe, and the horse spooked and galloped home. The next morning they found Miklauš dead on the horse's back, in the middle of their village, holding the dog's carcass. The mood soured for a spell, what with the boy being killed and all, but in time it settled down. And now when somebody teases somebody at school, others might say to the teaser: 'Watch out so's you don't get smacked with a hoe in the back,' and everybody laughs.'"

I pretended not to listen. I left the bathroom and shut the door behind me, leaving him with the stink.

The next day in gym class, the boys played soccer and the girls played dodgeball, as usual. Nobody would pass me the ball, so I got angry and took it, shoving Dejan. He fell and scraped his elbow. I reached to help him up, but he wouldn't take my hand. The teacher called me and asked why I'd done that. I didn't say anything, so for the rest of the hour I sat on a wooden bench and watched the others play. At one point, Goran called everybody over and they whispered. Nobody looked at me, but I could tell they were talking about me.

Later, when I was changing out of my school slippers and getting ready to put on my outdoor shoes, I found a clump of mud in one sneaker and something that smelled a lot like dogshit in the other. The teacher noticed, came over, and said: "Did you do this?"

I said nothing, but from my look she could tell I wasn't that crazy.

Although some kids had already put on their shoes and were leaving, she called us all back and said that this was no way to treat anybody, let alone a classmate. She asked several times who did it, but there was total silence. Everybody looked sheepish. She asked whether we thought this was acceptable.

Goran Brezovec spoke up, carefully picking and choosing his words to sound like somebody from the big city. "I do not feel this was acceptable, ma'am; friends don't do such things to each other. This is downright discourteous. I think if anyone saw something, they should say so. Today it was Matija, but tomorrow it might be someone else."

There was more talk about how we must be kind to one another, but I just wished no one could see me. In the washroom, cleaning shit and mud from my sneakers, I thought about how I'd like to be a ninja and throw shurikens at my enemies.

I was so angry that I started seeing red and yellow and realized this was a familiar place I'd nearly forgotten because I was scared I might hurt somebody. A mingling of sourness and heat, an ugly restlessness, the warm odor of my own body in my nostrils. I was afraid of this mood because I knew it could become huge, much vaster and darker than me. It was hatred. Twelve days later, people began dying.

There was already an aura of a death among us. Nobody'd died in a while, maybe even months. In the village, death was everybody's business. The most frequent question was not "How ya doing?" but "What'd he die of?" But the times were changing as far as death was concerned. It used to be that people died at home, in their beds, surrounded by family and a priest. My father, apparently, died alone in a white-and-green hospital, far from everybody. That was nobody's business but mine. After all, I killed him.

3.

The first to die was Mario Brezovec, only days after the Croatian referendum was held on the vote for independence. I remember there was something so damned warm about the young man. Folks in the village had never been particularly warm to each other, they were always bickering about something. If not about what they'd done, then about what they were going to do. With Mario, things were different. He was a socially acceptable object of adoration. He was incurably reckless but considerate of others, so he was forgiven every brash act. He was loved equally by young and old, and his escapades, when he was lousy and selfish and contrary and drunk, were told and retold as if he could do no wrong. His life was a public spectacle, and everybody approached him with a grin of approval and incredulity. Was there anyone else as charming? And when older women said Mario was an "unparalleled good-for-nothing," there was a tinge of Eros in their sentiment. Everybody knew he fucked girls whose boyfriends were off serving in the army; word was he'd gotten a married woman from Vratišinec pregnant and then beat up her husband. He was said to be a wily thief, though he never stole anything in the village.

"That Mario, if he don't slip a thing or two in his pocket while he's out at the Čakovec industrial farm, he'll reckon he's forgotten something. Honest t' God, what a scamp, that Mario."

With remarkable ease, he found himself caught up in the weirdest stories. Like the time, one Saturday morning, he'd gone in clogs and shorts to fetch a loaf of bread from the store, and they'd had to wheel him home Sunday night, drunk as dirt, with half a loaf of bread in his bag and all his money still in his pocket. The bread had been nibbled by the folks who'd treated him to drinks at the bar. Afterward he heard he'd ridden on a tractor with Pišta to go for a swim in Lendava. Pišta drove, and Mario stood on the hydraulic shaft holding on to the cab while clamping the bag of bread between his knees. They somehow borrowed swimming trunks along the way and were allowed onto the beach for free because the people in charge couldn't disguise their delight at the sight of a tractor parked alongside the sixty other cars in the parking lot.

The morning after Milica and Mladen Horvat's wedding, Mario woke up barefoot, still in his dress pants and an unbuttoned white shirt. He lifted his big, heavy head from the shoe that had served as his pillow. He coughed with his wheezy, smoke-filled lungs, rolled over, and saw he was lying in the middle of the soccer field. People walking by on their way to Sunday Mass grinned from the paved village path. Somebody called out: "Hey, Mario, how ya doing?"

Rolling over, Mario called out drunkenly, "Wake me when dinner's on the table."

The exact words he used to describe his adventures—without any intention to amuse—were parroted, and his turns of phrase became part of the public parlance. Everybody talked about how he'd once run over a drunk when driving his brother's car. The car jolted and bumped, but Mario went right on driving because he was drunk, too. Later on, he found a bloody hunk of flesh on the bumper of his Fiat 101, a piece of the bump he'd run over. More precisely, a piece of the rump. He said, "Hell, when I saw what it was, I threw that piece of ass as far as I could into the corn."

Later people always said, when somebody threw something really far, that they'd thrown it like a piece of ass into the corn. Nobody showed the slightest interest in the fate of the poor man who'd been run over. Mario's brother, Boris, was the one who went to the police.

The sexual energy around him seemed to know no age limit, and perhaps no gender limit, either. An older woman in the village named Mika Kukec was skilled at clearing foreign objects out of people's eyes with her tongue. Mario went to her when a speck of concrete got lodged in his eye at a construction site. Later he told the guys at the soccer game, "First she wiggled around with her tongue—that was nice, warm-like. Then she started licking my neck. Well, I reckoned she was still treating me, right? What do I know about witch doctors and their magic . . . When up pops my johnson."

Ultimately, even Mario's digestion became public knowledge. "Pišta, help, this is going to tear my guts to shreds," and "Mom just made some donuts, and I puked them all back up. It's the damn booze," and, charmed, people repeated whatever he said.

The only man in the village who was cool toward Mario was his brother, Boris, a year older and Mario's polar opposite. He was always serious and spoke with inexplicable contempt. At the same time, he strove to be liked by everybody. He'd talk about how he was always lending a helping hand, or how hard he worked. But while his younger brother managed without the slightest effort or intention, Boris was never forgiven for anything. One Christmastime, Mario collected twice as much money as God-fearing Boris when they and the other altar boys accompanied the priest on his visits to bless the villagers in their homes. When Mario smashed a beer bottle at a soccer game because of the jerk ref, he was met with howls of approval. When Boris did the same, they called him a fool because somebody was sure to cut themselves on the glass. When Boris talked about how he'd fucked, or puked, or taken a shit, they stared at him as if he were crazy. While Mario had worked occasionally as a mason after his classes at the commerce high school and barely scraped by, Boris was pathologically ambitious—he intended to make something of himself. As a kid, he knew he'd either go into the seminary or work at the gas station in Mursko Središće. Once he'd realized acne was not an insurmountable obstacle and that he had a taste for women, Boris chose the gas station, and in church he served only as sacristan. However, some part of his seminary dream stayed with him. He filled the cars with gas as if offering communion. Conceited and misunderstood. I occasionally seemed to see in his eyes the righteous conviction that nobody cared for him—he who had been so decent and fair to everybody his whole life—while his brother, Mario, who didn't give a shit, was the village sweetheart. Folks talked about Mario but never Boris, and that's all there was to it.

Franz spoke of Mario with admiration ten days or so after we didn't sign up for soccer. Every day we dribbled a beat-up leather ball around and talked about how Mladen Horvat was going to show us goalie moves, and then we'd play for the neighboring village's team and trounce the Miners the first chance we got.

"Mario said, 'Come on, Franz, come on, you'll play for us'—Mario said that, really, he came right over and invited me . . ." Franz kept repeating this, making it sound like Mario himself had invited Franz, and I kicked our ball harder and with greater and greater anger. I'd be alone again, now that Franz was playing with the older boys. It was going to be me and dumb old Bacawk and Chickichee for the rest of my life. Fantastic. He said they told him he was terrific at defense, and they weren't even playing games anymore, just shooting penalty kicks. Franz never lied, I knew that. He didn't understand that others couldn't tell when you were lying. They told him he could come every day, and Mario especially had praised him. The happier damned Franz was, the angrier I got.

"Matija, come down there with me today, hey, Matija, will you come? Come watch how I defend, hey, Matija . . ."

"I'll come, but just shut up," I said sourly.

"Maybe they'll ask you, too, maybe Mario will say how good you play, maybe he'll tell you to come . . ."

"Sure, sure, fine." This didn't sound likely to me.

As soon as I got to the field and sat on a damp tree stump, I regretted my anger and envy. Franz stood in the goal, and the guys kicked balls at him brutally hard, laughing and shouting about what a terrific job he was doing defending and that not a single ball could get past him. He glanced over at me with a proud smile that even his pain-filled eyes couldn't spoil. The blows followed one after another, and during every time-out he'd rub his ribs. When Franz started to lose steam, Mario piped up and reminded him he'd never seen a finer goalie in all his days.

I looked up to those guys. They were between eighteen and twenty, and we little kids hung on their every word with reverence. We listened when they gathered around a fence in the evening and talked about women, soccer, and which was better for wine: the local fox grapes or the imported varieties. We thought they knew what they were talking about because they smoked cigarettes, said, "Honest t' God," and swore, spitting to the side, ignoring us, talking shit about women, and laughing.

"What about Jadranka? I heard she's up for it."

"At first she held back, but I . . ."

"Smacked her?"

"Naw, just said, 'Bitch, why won't you, why won't you. Gimme head!' Y'shoulda seen how glad she was to go for it, how sweet she moaned."

When I listened to them talking, I wanted to be just like them when I grew up, but now all I wanted was for them to be gone. My legs shook with how fiercely I hated them, most of all Mario Brezovec. He went to the well of a nearby house now and then to slurp down big gulps of water from the bucket, and as time passed he went more and more, as if he couldn't get enough. I wanted him to die because he didn't feel bad about hurting my dumbass friend. After Franz was hit twice really hard in the head, I couldn't stand it anymore. I didn't dare say anything to the older boys, but I hollered to Franz: "Franz, let's go home!"

He replied, still happily taking the blows: "You go, I'll play a little longer with the guys."

Mićo, Goran Brezovec's older brother and Mario's cousin, spat to the side and called to me, "Hey, Dolenčec, you go home and tell that sister of yours to come to the field," at which point they all burst out laughing, except Mario Brezovec. He climbed groggily onto his bike and called over his shoulder to say he was going home.

I sat back down. Why my sister, I wondered. I was pulled away from my thoughts when a ball—I don't know who kicked it—hit Franz's head really hard, much harder than before. They all froze, silent, and Franz's hands flew to his mouth, and he fell to his knees. At first I thought the ball had knocked out his teeth, but I froze on the spot when I saw thick blood seeping from his mouth. As if a piece of him had fallen to the ground. Franz groaned softly, probably so he wouldn't bother anyone, and with one hand he picked up the piece of him from off the ground, putting the other hand into his bloody mouth as if groping to see whether something was missing in there. What was missing was a chunk of his tongue.

I didn't dare go over to him. It's hard to put into words, but at that moment I envied every single person in the whole world who wasn't there. The guys swarmed around him. Somebody told Franz to lie down, but he started gurgling and choking on the blood so they had him sit up. Mićo jumped onto his bicycle and went to find a car. After a few minutes—while Franz sat on the ground and bled like a pig, jamming somebody's sweaty shirt into his mouth, holding his tongue in his other hand—Tonči, my neighbor, showed up with his Fiat 101. He'd brought a plastic bag with ice in it, and they put Franz's tongue inside and gave it to him to hold until the ambulance came. Because of that scene, I nearly faint to this day—though I'd completely forgotten why—every time I see American kids in movies carrying goldfish in water in plastic bags.

More people from the village gathered on the grass. The boys who'd been kicking the ball at Franz said they'd kindly let the moron kid play soccer with them, and no good deed went unpunished. As they were packing up to go home, Mićo came flying back on his bike, white as a sheet, and said: "Mario's hanged himself."

"All right already, cut the crap. Come on, come on, come on," somebody snarled from the crowd.

"Mario's hanged himself. I was just at his house. Boris found him. He hanged himself in the bathroom. He's dead. The police've already come."

They headed for the village, but I stayed behind. I heard somebody say maybe Mario killed himself after he saw how Franz got hurt, what with Mario having such a soft heart and all, but then somebody else chimed in to say Mario had left before it happened.

When I got home, Mom had already heard about Mario but not that Franz was in the hospital. When I told her what'd happened, she didn't believe me. I asked my sister why people killed themselves, and she said they did it when they were really sad, when they had nothing to look forward to, and when they felt there was no way out. I sat down and drew Franz, bleeding from his mouth, and the guys standing around him, looking away. I started to draw Mario hanging himself. I drew the bathroom, and then I realized I wasn't so sure how people hanged themselves, by the hands or feet, so I didn't finish. All I could think was that I'd begun hating Mario that day, and then he died. I closed the door so nobody would hear me sobbing. For almost two years, I'd managed to keep myself in check.

"It ain't you who killed him," said Bacawk. "They only saw him around the village when he was happy. Nobody knew how bad he felt sometimes . . . The terrible sadness he felt, you can't even imagine. He'd be feeling real low, and all he could do was lie or sit there and stare into the darkness and long to go into the dark. Nobody knew it but his brother. He's the only one Mario told—that he wished he could die. And his brother never wanted to tell a soul about it, because he wanted Mario to be gone."

There was talk about how Mario would be buried. The priest was perplexed, he had to inquire at the bishopric. They told him no funeral for suicides, no rites. The older folks remembered they'd buried people who killed themselves by the graveyard wall in the olden days, or even just outside it, with no headstone. The thought of an unmarked grave was so awful that hardly anybody killed themselves. They first took Mario to Čakovec for an autopsy, or so we heard, to establish whether he really killed himself, if it was accidental, or if somebody forced him to do it. The next day he was laid out in the mortuary. I didn't go, but I heard they dressed him in a turtleneck so the wound from the noose wouldn't show. People, evidently, hanged themselves by the neck. I didn't understand how a person could die from that. It seemed to me I could hang like that for hours. The white coffin was carried by the boys who'd been kicking the ball at Franz. They did bury him in the graveyard, in the end, at the Brezovec family site. There were no rites, but after the burial the priest came and prayed for him.

The women on the street spoke in hushed tones about how terrible it was that somebody so young would take his own life, and some of them, even more hushed, asked why the family put out chrysanthemums, not carnations—after all, this was our Mario who died, and Mario's godfather had a German pension, so they didn't need to be so cheap. The men talked about Tuđman, the Serbs, the referendum, the potatoes, and the water pipeline. Somebody also said that he didn't know how they could possibly have put a red lantern on the grave instead of the white one they used for innocents. That's all wrong, and fuck it.

Aside from Mario's mother, who spoke and gestured as if she were very sleepy, the person most shaken by the suicide was Zdravko Tenodi.

He was the only one of the men to talk about Mario, about how he and Mario had been drinking buddies. He became strangely considerate and friendly. When he noticed me, he winked and asked me when I'd be coming to soccer. Whatever he meant by that, it made me furious because he was why I wasn't playing. I wanted to spit in his winking eye. I didn't know then, of course, that a few days later they'd be lowering him into the ground during a funeral with no rites, awkward for everybody.

4.

A few days later, Franz and I, as we'd done so many times before, were sitting across from each other at lunchtime. I can't remember what was more disgusting, my lunch of grits mixed with big chunks of gristle or Franz's tongue, which occasionally slipped out between his lips. It was bluish and bulgy, like my foot when they took off my toes. They'd given him strained tomatoes to suck up through a straw, and this wasn't going well because he had trouble breathing and kept trying to tell me something. I couldn't understand a word he was saying. He spluttered red globs of tomato into my white grits. For days there'd been rumors at school that Franz had to have leeches put in his mouth every day and that he might never speak right again. I was really sorry we had lost the world champion of backward talk. On the other hand, now maybe I could tell him about my astonishing deadly weapon. I told him what happened with Mario, that there was talk it had something to do with somebody's wife and that he killed himself for love.

Just as the last piece of grits slid down my throat, I heard a ruckus over where the cleaning staff and teachers were smoking by the open door. They looked upset, and the janitor kept shaking his head, saying he and Zdravko Tenodi went to school together and he couldn't understand how that man, so full of life, could kill himself. They said he worked at the ironworks in Mursko Središće and had a wife who worked in Čakovec and two kids. His daughter had married somebody from the next village over, and his son was in training to work in ceramics.

Two hours later, spluttery Franz and I walked home from school, and I managed to piece together bits of Zdravko Tenodi's life from the people leaning on their fences talking. He loved a party, was a little brusque, and was strict with his kids. He sometimes mocked other kids, they said, like the Dolenčec boy the other day at the soccer field, but that was just him having a bit of fun. He wore nicely tailored pants and was always clean-shaven. And how, how could a person like that take his life? He didn't owe nobody so much as a penny.

"He was behaving peculiar-like at Mario's funeral . . ."

"He and Mario were so close, though he was much older . . ."

"So they were friends, does that mean he'd . . ."

"And his family, and . . ."

It all merged for me into a single communal village voice, a dull baritone speaking in the monotonous drone of prayer. Mom was standing by our gate, pickax in hand, talking to Zvonko "Democracy" Horvat. He reported to my mother on a daily basis about world events, kicking off with "Why're they so crazy?" and "Poor folks," before rattling through his review of the newspaper articles he'd read about the cockeyed world. I figured she listened to him because he was lonely and old, or maybe because he reminded her of Dad. I pretended to listen to Franz and watched as he showed me how they sewed his tongue back on, but I was actually listening to Zvonko and Mom. Zvonko said maybe Zdravko's wife cheated on him, because she worked at the meat-processing plant in Čakovec and wore nail polish and makeup. And maybe Zdravko and Mario were "warm brothers," whatever that meant. They'd go to Zdravko's cottage and drink till morning, or so people said.

When we went inside, Mom told me I'd go every other day to Zvonko's to help him clean out his attic, and he'd give me some pocket money so I could buy one of those bright, slippery tracksuits. I asked Mom if he couldn't do it himself, without my help. She said sure he could, but he wanted to be kind to me, and didn't want it to look like he was giving us charity.

I tried to draw Zdravko, but I didn't know how he died (some said he hanged himself, others he drowned in the tub), so I drew him as a kid on his way to school. Over his head was a black cloud, and in it was a bike. I imagined him dragging the cloud along his whole life, and then one day the cloud finally came down and sucked him in. I put the bicycle in there so he could ride it to where he is now.

"You're right, he was a decent guy. He wasn't always mean to folks."

"And you know this because . . . ," I asked Bacawk.

He didn't answer, but went on to say there'd been something eating at Zdravko for a long time that pushed him to be cruel and make fun. When he was young, back in the old days, there was a house by the road leading out into the hills, near the graveyard. A widow lived there, and boys were taken to her so she could show them how to make children, how men do it with women.

"They put their wiener in her hole," explained Bacawk. "The two of us, we were there and we saw."

The story goes that Zdravko was nervous when his dad, a grim, taciturn man, brought him to the woman. An older boy was the first to go in, and then she called for Zdravko. He went in but came right out again to leave his shoes and socks outside. His father said: "I thought you was already done. No surprise that you ain't even able to do this right."

She told him to get undressed and sit on the bed. She checked to see if he'd trimmed his nails and if he had head lice, hummed a melody he didn't catch, took a warm wet washcloth and wiped his face, body, and balls. She took off her top, threw a leg across him, and straddled him:

"Well, let's see, how your little one jumps."

Zdravko froze the moment her breast brushed his shoulder and . . . sprayed out his milk.

I knew what Bacawk meant because the older boys talked about how stuff came out of your wiener when you squeezed it. She brought Zdravko back out, visibly ashamed. His father, without even looking at him, sent him to fetch a pound of sugar and some pork lard and told him to tell his mom it was for the village head. When Zdravko came back to the widow's house with the sugar and lard, he could hear his father yelling inside the bedroom. She was sighing and asking him to hush. After that, Zdravko Tenodi was cruel to anyone smaller and younger than him, and he steered clear of those who were bigger and stronger.

"And when he killed himself, what he was facing . . . was both stronger and much, much bigger than him. But he couldn't run away from it because this time it was inside."

The three of us pored over my failure of a drawing of Zdravko as a kid. This was the longest I'd seen them in two years. I hadn't forgotten what I'd been through because of them, but what they said was comforting. I couldn't understand why they were doing it, but I didn't care. They saw things I couldn't see. They were filling in the blanks. And proving that this wasn't my fault. But I wasn't certain whether they were helping me or deepening my despair.

"Whenever I get mad at somebody—really, really angry—that person dies," I said.

"No. Mario ventured off into his own darkness, and Zdravko was gobbled up by his. We were there and we saw," said Bacawk.

The night he died, Zdravko couldn't sleep because his wife was out late again. He went out into the yard a few times for a drink of cold water from the well, and because he didn't want his son—who was lying on the sofa watching TV—to see his impatience. After the lights went out in the house, a car pulled up and his wife got out. She slipped her shoes off at the threshold, softly unlocked the door, and went in on tiptoe. She didn't turn on the light, she knew her way around in the dark; this was not the first time she'd snuck into the house in the middle of the night. She paused for a moment, trying to hear if her husband and son were sleeping. She went into the bathroom and washed up in the dark.

"She sat down and cleaned both her holes. She'd been poked all over."

She'd just put on her nightgown when she heard something . . . as if a pile of books in the living room had fallen down. She clenched her teeth, froze. Finally she let out her breath; after all she'd washed off the evidence. When she snuck back through the hallway, her shoulder brushed something—maybe a coat her husband was airing out. She lay in bed. She couldn't hear her husband breathing; he seemed quieter than usual. The next morning her son's scream from the hallway woke her. It had not been a coat but Zdravko brushing up against her. His eyes stared open at the ceiling, and there was a big stain, still wet, on the leg of his pajamas. He left her a note in his shoe: *No point in sneaking around in secret anymore. I'll be watching.* She stuffed it into her pocket and ran out to find a neighbor to take Zdravko's body down.

"He knew by her smell she'd been with another man. He couldn't stand it, after so many years. So that's the reason he did it."

At the second quiet funeral that week, there was no mention of flowers or lanterns. The men talked about how Mesić and Kostić were breaking up Yugoslavia right before their very eyes and how Mario and Zdravko were decent fellows, and the women talked about how they were faring with their tomatoes and lettuce. The loudest was Trezika Kunčec, an elderly woman who had recently begun declaring in a big, pushy voice what she was cooking and doing all day.

Zdravko's wife was dressed in black, leaning on her son, wiping away tears, and blowing her nose. She wasn't wearing makeup or nail polish. A week later (after a few more strange things happened), she came to see my mother and brought sugar and some coffee wrapped in white paper. The two completely different widows smoked cigarettes, drank coffee, and talked softly for a long time. The next year, she moved to Čakovec.

I added an explanation to my failed drawing and took it to the graveyard. My sister had asked me a few times to give her my draw-ings, saying she wanted to leave them at the big church in Čakovec. I declined; someone seemed to be collecting them after I left them on the grave, and that was enough for me. In a few days I learned where they were going: with that strange old lady, Trezika Kunčec.

Bacawk and Chickichee told me it wasn't my fault, but I found this hard to accept. Nothing had changed, other than my hatred coming back and people dying. I couldn't tell exactly when I crossed the line with my anger. I was having trouble spending time with Franz, he was leery of soccer balls now, and his stuttering, ugly tongue made me feel sick to my stomach. So when I came home from school, I'd disappear into the attic, where I tried to pour all my anger into an old carved dark wood box about the size of a woman's makeup case; inside it was a red velvet pillow. I thought I'd be less of a danger to my mother and sister once I'd poured everything I had into the box. The little pillow was just the right size to muffle my shouting, and it was dusty enough that my throat quickly went dry and raspy, and I had to stop. I yelled that I hoped everybody would die, that I pooped on everything, and that I was full of hatred. I figured if even a little part of me felt like that—even a part I couldn't control—it would be enough to kill somebody, so it had to be shut up inside the box. After that, I'd mash the pillow into the box with every ounce of my strength, using both hands; I'd mash it in until my hands began to shake something terrible, and until I had only enough strength left to slam the box shut fast. The anger would drain out into the black earth overnight, or at least that's how I imagined it in my mind. That was the rightful place for the anger, in a box and in the earth, not in people.

That Sunday I really paid attention to the sermon, probably for the first time. The priest talked about how we don't have the right to take our own life, because it was given to us by someone else, and we must never lose hope. He said we must pray for our brethren who had died so tragically, and not be selfish but make an effort to help Croatia and Croats. I was the only one who knew that none of this had anything to do with Mario, or Zdravko, or the village.

5.

"Worraps!"

"Klim!"

"Egattoc!"

"Oknovz Ycracomed!"

Now I was no slower than Franz, and the game developed new rules. I'd say a word backward, and Franz had to point to the thing or pantomime it. When I said, "Klim," he spread his legs and arms and gestured like he was milking himself. He was really fast, so I began reaching for longer, harder words.

"Lerrab gnub!" Franz immediately wrapped his arms around a huge invisible barrel, made an invisible plug with his fingers, and bunged the container. While he was grinning, I was plotting what to say next.

"Rotcart worrah!" He just rolled his eyes and settled importantly into the seat of the invisible tractor, glancing over his shoulder once in a while to check on the depth of the harrows. I was wild with envy. Nobody could hold a candle to him. And then I found a sticker out on the road, and on it were the words *1,4-butanediol* with a black *X* on an orange background.

"Loidenatub!" I said, and won. Franz squinted, then bugged his eyes wide, then shook his head. He mumbled something in protest, and I stuck the sticker in my pocket and, with hands raised, turned to walk to school, saying over and over, "Loidenatub. Loidenatub, my dear Franz."

When I heard between fourth and fifth period that Trezika Kunčec had been found hanged, I was relieved because I hardly knew her, so her death couldn't possibly be my fault. Several hours later I learned that right there on the dresser in her bedroom, next to where she'd tied her apron to the ceiling lamp and made it into a noose, lay three of my drawings. On one of them I'd written about how I didn't want people to die because of me, and my first and last name. I have no idea why I did that, when the person I had been writing to knew my name. Trezika had been behaving oddly for some time, spouting all sorts of nonsense to our neighbors—for instance, that I was her favorite boy in the village because I was growing up without a dad, and she thought I was lonely.

"He leaves what he draws and writes to his daddy and thinks his daddy will come back. I know nobody likes him. I feel sorry for the boy," she said.

She'd been taking my drawings from the grave and bringing them home when my mom and sister would miss one. They took the drawings so I wouldn't be seen as even weirder, while Trezika probably did it because she reckoned it was a good deed.

Franz and I were on our way home from school just as the police drove into the Kunčec yard. While spitting out and choking back spit, he tried to explain how they were giving him shots in his tongue with a needle as thick as a finger and how he hadn't been able to taste anything for days. I understood him only because he mimed it to me—what came from his mouth was just a mishmash of unformed sounds and sprayed spittle.

Medics and police swarmed in the yard, and bystanders gathered around the entrance to the basement apartment where Trezika had lived since her son married and, with his wife, moved into the house. Her son and his wife stood there, motionless; they didn't look sad or upset, but slightly sheepish. As if a bizarre dark family secret had been exposed by Trezika's death. One of her granddaughters, a high school student, sat on the front stoop wearing Walkman headphones, staring at the ground. I was happy because I was physically present, yet absent of responsibility. And then I heard my name. Trezika's neighbor Anika said the crazy old woman had told her she'd dreamed of me several nights in a row. I had wings and flew over the village wells dropping flowers into them, like a fairy-tale bee. That she'd said anything about her dreams was enough for the neighbors to spread rumors that Trezika was off her rocker.

"What kind of crazy is that? Who else goes around talking about their dreams?"

Anika wiped her tears while she talked with a chubby man in jeans and a leather jacket, not realizing that Franz and I were standing just a few feet from them. When I heard my name mentioned in her story, I tapped Franz in the belly to let him know he should follow me down our street. Then the chubby guy turned, noticed me, and nodded my way. When I put together his slanty smile, tufts of hair, and not-so-handsome face, I recognized Stankec, the policeman. He was holding a walkie-talkie and a notebook. He came over, said he remembered me—wow had I grown—and asked me if I'd been to see Trezika and had I given her any drawings. Though I knew Stankec was a nice man, I was scared shitless and said I'd never in my life so much as spoken to her. Franz was standing next to me, staring blankly at the medics loading the body into the ambulance. He was the only person there not interested in me. Everybody else was staring at the cop questioning the kid. I could hear them whispering:

"That boy is an odd one. I get the shivers whenever I see how he stares into space, silent."

"My oh my. There wasn't a soul Mario rubbed wrong, but Zdravko, now that's another story altogether—he went too far with that boy."

"Did he now?"

"When the kids were signing up for soccer that day. He mocked the boy—people say it was downright cruel. Picked on that boy and Franz Klanz, too."

"You're kidding me."

"I'm telling you. And now he's dead. And Trezika, too. You tell me. What are his drawings doing on the dresser at her place?"

"Oh pshaw! How could that boy be responsible for them killing themselves? Or did he tie them up and hang them all by himself? Come now."

"I ain't saying, but . . . he tried to push little Dejan Kunčec, Đura's boy, clear into the Mura two years back—we all remember that. And that ain't nothing. Are we supposed to keep quiet about it?"

The village was watching the same scene for the third time that week. The same mustachioed coroner smoking a cigarette, the same medics waiting for the same police—who now wore the Croatian coat of arms on their caps—to leave the house. The cops were taking pains to write down statements when a chubby boy rode up on a bike, went over to the medics, said, "Pardon me, sirs," and announced politely that Mladen Krajčić had killed himself.

"Would the law enforcement officers and the doctors see to him, too, now, seeing as they's here, so they don't have to come twice from Čakovec? It's not far, down the street a ways and by the chapel, to the right. His folks are waiting for you there, by the gate, you'll see."

In an indescribably brief instant, the roiling chaos dissolved into perfect silence. And I felt as if the air temperature had dropped several degrees. They had stopped staring at me and turned their attention to the boy, who, beginning to feel a little uncomfortable, got down off his bike and spit a few times.

There are people who, when they leave this world, don't leave a big void behind them. That's just the way it is, whether we want to admit it or not. As far as Mladen Krajčić was concerned, I'm pretty sure nobody would have cried for him had his not been the fourth suicide. Many folks in the Kunčec yard couldn't even place him.

"The fella across the street from the Bartols?"

"Naw, that would be Mladen Cucek. This guy was one of the Krajčićes. The fat one."

"Oh, Porky Mladen?"

"Naw, he ain't that fat."

The white ambulance, a police car, and Stankec's white Golf rolled off in the direction of the Krajčićes, and after them trekked all the others, everybody but Trezika's son and two grandsons. It was as if a wedding party had swung by to pick up the bride-to-be and was heading off to fetch the groom. I didn't follow, because I definitely had nothing whatsoever to do with Mladen Krajčić's death and I didn't want to be nearby, what with people already looking at me weird. I was sure I had nothing to do with it because anyone who looked at him could see Mladen was the perfect candidate for an early death. He was dull inside, in a constant state of disarray, and gave the sense he'd been dead his whole life but out of decency they'd held off burying him. He was a bachelor, around forty, short and on the heavy side, his figure built of three blockish chunks that looked as if they'd been piled one on top of the other without any particular skill. But aside from his odd shape, which he shared with everybody in his family, there was nothing remarkable about him. He was quiet and indifferent to things, nothing much excited or upset him. He might be noticed around the village. Might, but needn't be. His was the most absent kind of presence.

I remember he worked at a nearby gas station, that he occasionally had a wine spritzer with Boris Brezovec and a few school friends, but not much else. He never fixed a pot of *bograč* game stew on his birthday, nor roasted a suckling pig at New Year's. The other young men got asked if they were fucking anybody these days and when they'd be getting married, but not him.

I wouldn't have remembered him myself, especially considering what a good job I've done forgetting, but I remember how, out of the corner of my eye, I once saw a tic run across his otherwise expressionless face. I was sure it came from maybe the only thing he genuinely felt—that he was ashamed of himself. Maybe ashamed of his family. All the Krajčićes, men and women, old and young, were equally squat and square-headed, as if built when the creator was drunk. They had equally bland facial features, and only details, like the length of a person's hair or stubble, allowed others to tell them apart. They went everywhere together like a pack of domesticated animals. At every gathering, there they were, the squat Krajčićes, a footstool-shaped group in a community of humanoids. The only thing that set Mladen apart was that he wasn't always as damned cheerful as the rest of his clan. My uncle worked with Mladen's older brother, Pavel, and said everybody in that family was always laughing and ate vast amounts of food. Hunger, for them, was not a sensation but a lifestyle. Everything was arranged around meals; they knew of no other way to organize their everyday life. Food was the standard by which they lived, the occasion for, and topic of, most conversations. And being full meant being sleepy, which was a good enough reason to do nothing at all. They were a happy bunch because, despite their excessive appetite and the fact that most of them were diagnosed with high blood pressure by the age of thirty-five, they all lived to a ripe old age. They had their own theories about a healthy diet. After they gorged on sweets, they'd slice up salami and sprinkle salt over bread and butter. They believed the salt balanced out the sugar.

"Mom, people in the village are saying it's my fault that all those people killed themselves," I said after waiting for a few minutes at the kitchen table for somebody to ask me what was wrong or why I wasn't up in the attic.

"Well, what about it? Who?" She didn't look up from her plate, so I knew this wasn't news to her. "No point in paying any mind to what the people say in the village. Sometimes what they're saying ain't particularly swift."

I wanted to tell her that maybe those people were right and that sometimes I wished I weren't alive. Or at least that I were invisible. That wasn't such a big request, and it didn't involve anybody else. But I couldn't say that to her. We never spoke of the things that happened that fall. That meant a good part of me was missing for her.

"I might get a job in Varaždin, and if I do, we'll all move away from here. I used to work in Germany at a shoe and boot factory, and they're needing leatherworkers to make army boots and belts. Don't you worry about a thing."

Move away from the village and never come back. That thought so thrilled me that I forgot all about my anger box and went to my room.

I drew Trezika sitting alone in her basement. I drew the sheets of paper lying on her table, but when I tried to add details from my own drawings and messages, they looked like unrecognizable squiggles. I wasn't satisfied. I picked up my notebook and wrote, *I didn't know Terezija Kunčec, and I never even spoke with Mladen. This has nothing to do with me.* As soon as I wrote that, I felt better. But I was missing a real explanation. After a few minutes, it came up on me from behind, borne by the shrill, nasal voice of Bacawk.

Apparently they had spent a little time in every house in the village, because they knew all there was to know about Trezika. She was a woman, Bacawk said in a mournful tone, who'd been disappearing from her family's life, and she felt useless. They didn't answer her questions, sometimes walked right past her as if she weren't there. The fear of invisibility began jangling in her head, and sometimes she dreamed she was disappearing bit by bit. Her children and grandchildren wouldn't eat what she made for dinner. At first they were polite, and said they were planning to make French fries in their fryer. She'd bring five pounds of potatoes over, but through the window she'd see them opening up bags of presliced store-bought ones, the kind that came in clear plastic.

"Until, two days in a row, she threw green beans and tasty goulash to the hogs, and then she stopped cooking. Cooking just for herself was ridiculous."

And besides, she wasn't hungry; she'd eat her fill of cracklings and bread in the morning, drink milk in the afternoon, and that was enough. In the village, after the topic of death, the older women most often talked about what they were fixing for dinner, so Trezika started lying about that. The quieter the women she talked to became, the louder she was and the bigger the lies she told. Sometimes she felt as if she was starting to believe what she said, and she felt less embarrassed that nobody needed her. Later, in her basement, overcome by silence and loneliness, sometimes she'd even look for the fictive pot with beans in milk.

Aside from the invisibility, she was afraid her body would one day simply refuse to obey her, and instead do the opposite of what she wanted. Parts of her had already declared their independence, they'd fallen away from her. She'd get up in the morning, but half of Trezika would still be in bed. After several months, she stopped looking in the mirror altogether. Everybody she'd known had died, and it was as if she was seeing all of them in the mirror. The drawings and letters she found at the graveyard were her only solace.

"Because she saw she weren't the only one nobody cared for."

She wondered what her son would say when she did die, how her daughter-in-law would be sorry that Trezika was gone, how they'd all repent. Her grandchildren would cry and feel sorry they hadn't listened to her stories about the chicken-plucking bees, the corn-husking bees, and how children used to love sleeping in the hay in the barn. Sometimes in those warm-cold moments, she'd unwrap the kerchief from around her head and loop it around her neck, imagining the expression on her son's face when he found her dead. She'd tighten it like that, little by little testing her pain threshold, and only when her vision blurred would she look in the mirror. Nobody except Bacawk and Chickichee had noticed that in front of where she'd hanged herself in her bedroom stood a bureau with a large mirror. She hadn't meant to kill herself that day; she'd been sobered by the horror of seeing the awful funerals for Mario and Zdravko. She watched *Numbers and Letters* and was in such fine spirits that she made a noodle dish sprinkled with ground walnuts for herself, and then dug into the roast pork she'd cured, layered with bacon in an earthenware pot, a dish called *meso s tiblica*. The salt made her thirsty, so she drank down a whole pitcherful of water. Only then did the darkness overwhelm her. She wanted to see, once more before she went to bed, what she'd look like if they found her hanging from the ceiling lamp.

On the dresser were my drawings, and they were the last things she saw before the light went out in her eyes, when the chair under her feet tipped over. When she realized she was hanging, her face yawned into a surprised grimace, said Bacawk, and her legs flailed. She grabbed at the noose made of the torn apron and gasped, and her saliva sprayed the entire room. Swinging, she spun around her own axis.

"While she was watching herself in the mirror . . . she went limp. For a time, she jerked," explained Chickichee.

"When Mladen hanged himself, it didn't take long. He went limp right away," added Bacawk.

He said that when Mladen was in his mother's belly, she fell asleep one autumn day out in the fields amid the cornstalks and dreamed of water lilies and frozen puddles, and children such as these are condemned, from their very conception and ever after, to die by their own hand. Chickichee protested that was nonsense, so the two of them argued for a few minutes. But they did agree that Mladen hadn't been dwelling constantly on death. It was enough that several times in the course of his lifetime, just as every person does, he'd envisioned this scene quite clearly. The scene left him fearful and confused, but also gave him an odd sense of comfort and warmth at the prospect of an end to the desire and trouble a person embraces by living each new day. And then the moment came when the vision of his death took over . . . Usually people think a whole series of circumstances have to come together for a person to take their own life.

"But it's so easy. All it takes is being alone for a few minutes," mused Bacawk.

Chickichee said that when people die, first their sense of sight goes, then taste, then smell, and then touch. Hearing goes last. Mladen hanged himself with a rope noose in the barn, standing on the hog's slop trough. The last thing he heard was his family calling him to come and eat a meal of new potatoes, and he felt as if he could sense with his nose the soft and slightly oily smell of the thin potato skins. He also had just enough time to worry that the Krajčićes weren't particularly good masons, and that he might break the beam.

6.

The hours ticked by while I wrote and drew, glancing once in a while out the window. After Bacawk and Chickichee had said everything they had to say, they asked me why I'd never drawn them or even mentioned them in my writing. I told them I'd never forgive them for what they did to me when I was small and I didn't want to talk about them. To speak of them would give them greater access to reality than they now enjoyed.

Mom came into the room and asked why I was being so quiet and if I had done my homework. I said I had and quickly shut my notebook. She told me that if I had, I could go over to Zvonko "Democracy" Horvat's house. I didn't want to because he was always asking me things I didn't know how to respond to. She explained that he was lonely and maybe very sick, and he wanted to have company close by. Again she told me he'd buy me a tracksuit if I helped him out a little with his attic.

Democracy had made a bundle working in the mines. His wife, a little younger, had stayed in Germany, and he didn't often speak of her. There were rumors that he'd never gone out or spent anything while living there. Rumor had it that he left a huge amount of money in a German bank because he thought somebody would take it from him in Yugoslavia, but he was happier living in the village where he was born—alongside all the other poor people—than he would have been living in Germany as a wealthy man. Once he retired, he devoted himself to spending time with people, going to soccer games, and following a daily routine. Every morning he went to the store for fresh bread and a newspaper, and on the way back he'd stop and chat with whoever he ran into near the road; he'd lean on a gate, leaf through the newspaper, and make his observations, with special attention to reports about how somebody was oppressing somebody else.

"My oh my, will you look at that now, this Joža fella . . . poor people . . ."

And my mom was a receptive audience. She had a soft heart for the old man, a sort of tacit loyalty to all those who'd gone abroad to work. But in one respect, they were very different: Mom felt she'd made her peace with the way things were in Croatia, but Zvonko had not. Maybe he should have, because word got around the village that he had cancer. And it did look as if his complexion was a little sallow and he was hunched over.

Every house has its own particular odor, a mixture of the metabolisms of everything living inside it. At Zvonko's I smelled freshly mown grass, baked beans and smoked meat, the overheated TV, and a host of colder smells, which were, I think, from his memories. Like the sad smell of your favorite dish the next day in the fridge. He greeted me with a smile and invited me in. Something about it, like many of the homes of people who worked abroad, evoked a Bavarian mountain chalet. The carved wooden table and benches with red, white, and gold hues, the reproductions of landscapes framed as if they were originals. Needlepoints of little bunnies drinking water, and a metal plaque bearing the name of a minor German city. We sat on the sofa in the huge half-empty living room. There were Tops cookies, pretzel sticks, and Tok Cola on the table, and Zvonko poured me a soda. I felt a sudden sadness at the thought that this was the closest to a child's birthday party I'd been to since the night I tried to throw Dejan into the river. A Western film about two friends was playing on the vast TV screen.

"Those are Winnetou and Old Shatterhand. I always watched those movies when I was in Germany. They're blood brothers. They cut their hands with a knife, pressed them together, and mixed their blood. You and your friends probably play cowboys all the time."

"Actually, nope."

For a while we watched the movie. I could hear his breathing, labored, jagged. The Native Americans tied a man to a tree and left him to be eaten by ants. I understood this was interesting for Zvonko the way ninjas were for me, but ninjas were agile and stealthy and threw shurikens, while the cowboys were boring. Some of the Native Americans wore feathers and were bare to the waist, and the cowboys didn't have a single automatic weapon. I told Zvonko I'd like to see the attic. His blank look confirmed that the idea of cleaning the attic was just an excuse to get me there.

"Sure, let's go," he finally chirped.

The attic was tidy and clean. I spotted skis and goggles, a hockey stick, a miner's helmet, plastic chairs, a Ping-Pong table, paintbrushes so hard they could have doubled as weapons. A few piles of magazines about cars. He showed me his collection of beer cans, which he stored in a huge trunk. He told me he had over seventy different cans, not just from Germany but from the Netherlands and Switzerland, too. I asked why he collected them, but all he said was that he'd give them to me if I wanted them. I picked one up and peered in through the hole. The attic was dark, but within it there were these seventy even darker nooks. And inside each one of them, it seemed to me, was a person who'd betrayed Zvonko "Democracy" Horvat. He'd found the perfect receptacle in the beer cans, which contained the musty odor of when somebody disappoints you. These cans were his anger boxes. I shivered, told him I didn't want them, and lied that I had to go home. He said the pretzel sticks and cookies would be waiting for me, and he thought he had Haribo gummy bears somewhere. I wasn't sure I wanted them.

"Okay, see you soon, Uncle Zvonko."

"Listen, hang on. I could adjust my antenna. You'd have cartoons all day long. Should I adjust it? The *satelitempfänger*?"

I told him sure, and hurried off. It was still daylight, and I wasn't in the mood to go home, so was excited when I saw Franz on the road. When he saw me, he went off without a word to get our tattered soccer ball. We kicked it back and forth, and Franz gestured it was easier to swallow now, but still had to spit pink phlegm out every few minutes. I told him about the men from the movie who were blood brothers. Franz couldn't stop giggling, and pantomimed he must have at least ten thousand brothers among the mosquitos and horseflies.

Mladen Horvat drove by, stopped his red Yugo, and rolled down the window.

"What's up, boys?"

"Just kicking the ball around," I said, and stuttering Franz didn't want to hide that we'd been waiting for Mladen to start training us, so he leaned right up against the car door, tense as a slingshot.

"Nice, nice, any day now you'll be stars. How's the tongue, Franz? Can you talk yet?" asked Mladen, and Franz shook his head sadly.

"Don't you worry now, it'll come with time. I'm on my way home from work, and was thinking of kicking a ball around a little myself. You like to join me?" asked Mladen, brightly. Then he added, "But maybe your folks wouldn't like it. Matija, does your mother know where you are?"

"Don't worry, she thinks I'm at Democracy's place and expects me home in two hours or so."

"All right, then off we go. And we'll say you stopped by and we had wafer cookies and a little orange soda. If'n they ask. And if they don't, nobody's the wiser."

He told us he had to go to the store and that we should wait for him at the bend in the road on the way out of town. He had us ride in the trunk of the car because he said it would be fun, and he'd always wanted to ride in the trunk when he was a kid. The house where Mladen and

Milica lived was a five-minute drive toward the vineyards, on the village outskirts.

It was fun riding in the trunk, but by the end I was feeling queasy. Franz's mouth smelled bad, and I couldn't stop thinking about his half-dead tongue.

Milica was sitting on the terrace, smoking a cigarette. She was a gaunt woman with hollow cheeks. She barely greeted us. Mladen sent us to the garage to fetch a ball, and we could hear Milica asking him why he'd brought us. There was something angry and desperate in her voice. I thought Mladen was nice to agree to live with her, when she was so gangly and grumpy. When we came back from the garage, Mladen tossed Franz a pair of brand-new black-and-red goalie gloves, still in their package! Franz was nearly in tears, he was so happy, and didn't dare try them on until Mladen put them on his hands for him. We kicked the ball back and forth, and then Mladen put Franz through a few stretching exercises, and he told me to run around a nearby stand of trees to get myself into shape. I sprinted like crazy and reckoned he'd be pleased with how fast I'd been, but while still stretching Franz's legs, he said I ought to have gone slower, because now I was all tuckered out.

"I ain't tuckered, Mladen, I can go again."

"Naw, go indoors for a while—there are wafer cookies on the table—and tell Milica to mix you up some orange drink."

I went in and got some wafer cookies from the table, then sat out on the terrace. I'd never seen Franz so focused. Mladen told him that being a goalie wasn't just about standing in the goal, he'd have to follow the whole game, and run out to intercept the ball from the other team's players. He showed him how to throw himself under their feet, and he and Franz tumbled around. I scarfed down cookie after cookie. If they'd invited me, I'd have liked to try that tumble, too. Getting ready to go back, Mladen opened the trunk again. I told him that riding in the trunk had made me sick to my stomach, but he insisted. He explained

that next time Franz would come by himself, because they had to practice their goalie exercises, and I could come another time.

I saw things clearly then. I'd have to be as good as Franz if Mladen
was going to train me. I also wasn't consoled by the thought that he
was maybe feeling sorry for Franz because of his tongue and the fact
that his old man was a drunk, and because everybody in the village was
mean to him. No one was particularly nice to me, either, but who cared
about that. I needed my anger box, I could already hear the red velvet
pillow crinkling.

"I'm home," I called and raced straight up to the attic. It was already
getting dark. The box wasn't there. I flew into a panic.

"Where's the box?" I hollered. We'd been living for two years in a
hush, and suddenly my words resounded throughout the house. My
mom and sister came to the door of the kitchen, my sister holding a
half-eaten slice of bread with butter—a bite was still in her mouth. I
repeated as calmly as I could: "Where's the box?"

"What box? What's going on?" said Mom. They didn't realize the
danger they were in.

"The box, the wood box with a red cushion inside. Where is it?"

"I just put my makeup in it, that's all," said my sister. The alarm
from two years ago was back in her eyes.

"That's my box!" I shrieked and flew by them into the bathroom.

It was on the shelf over the sink. In one flip I emptied it. Eyeliner
pencils, cotton swabs, makeup, and nail scissors drummed on the bathroom floor tiles; the eye shadow completely fell apart. There was no
pillow inside.

"I threw the pillow out," I heard a voice say, unsure, from the
hallway.

I ran out of the house and only partly heard Mom say to pull myself
together or else.

I flung myself down onto my belly in the grass, and began yelling
into the dirt, but too much of it escaped out the sides. They stared at me

dumbly from the front stoop, I couldn't make them go away. I clenched my fists and ground my teeth and sank slowly into despair. The fury inside me hadn't waned, and the fear that they were going to die because of me ballooned. I stood up and punched our cherry tree with my bare hands. After the first two hits, gashes opened on my knuckles, so I kicked it. I don't know how much time passed before I dropped to the ground, exhausted.

"What's wrong, Matija?" asked Mom, softly. "Why are you hitting the tree?"

"I'm scared I'll do something to you," I said, and my sister turned around silently and went back into the house.

7.

There was no wake because they'd taken Trezika and Mladen to Čakovec for autopsies. Stankec and another officer stayed in the village until evening. The Krajčićes offered them homemade sausages and poppy-seed cake.

Events unfolding beyond the village had begun to accelerate and intensify, but very little news of what was going on in Eastern Slavonia and the rest of Yugoslavia made it to our village. Only the occasional snippet about shootings and barricades found its way into our small enclave of horror. There was no need to import fear—we had plenty of it to go around, and we submitted to it. We didn't know what to think about the people who had taken their own lives. It was mysterious because they were close to us, but they'd seen something we couldn't see. Now we were all watching each other, weighing every word, seeking the seeds of death. And we could sense other people watching us, which produced a false brightness and zest for life. We concealed, each in our own way, our suspicions and fears. When one person took their life, the disease was theirs alone. When four people took their lives, the whole village was afflicted. It looked as if the suicides would continue, though nobody could be certain there'd be more. I least of all.

I knew people were sad after Mario died, but after Zdravko, there was an awkward sense of relief that all this was somebody else's problem.

After Trezika and Mladen, it became clear that "somebody else" was a slippery concept that could, in fact, apply to any of us. The only ones who expressed their worry, though, were the older women; they were primed to lament all the droughts, wars, poverty, and illnesses. They started saying somebody had cursed the village. Might somebody, perhaps, be walking around at night from house to house, talking folks into killing themselves? The younger ones laughed at this, pretending scorn. I heard someone say that Mladen Krajčić had taken himself hostage, but nobody would pay the ransom. I heard someone else say that the parish priest would go bankrupt soon if people kept dying like this, because he wasn't paid if there were no funeral rites. They laughed sourly, and feigned goodwill covered the village like a blanket full of moth holes. Each unusual gesture only widened these spaces. One day, out of the blue, Rega Popičova bought twenty Animal Kingdom chocolate bars and handed them out to kids on their way home from school. Mom and I watched her from the window of the grocery store with the salesladies.

"What's this now?"

"She's giving out chocolates."

"Is she in her right mind? Sure, her son works up Germany-way, but I don't reckon they're rich. And those guest workers are tight with money after their years of working abroad."

"I should ask her if she's doing okay. It's not right for a person to go around doling out chocolates to other folks' kids."

"Don't you be doing that in front of the children."

There was talk that Miška Janek, a fifty-five-year-old man who'd recently lost his job at the Mercator superstore in Slovenia, had been behaving oddly. Zvonko "Democracy" Horvat was the first to notice.

"Something snapped in Miška when he saw people being buried with no funeral rites. He keeps saying that's how animals are buried, not people. Margeta says he ain't sleeping nights, he goes out and paces the yard. And then one morning there he is at Mass. And I wouldn't say he's particularly God-fearing—only ever used to be at Mass for Christmas and Easter."

Every day—morning and night—he went to Mass. He prayed loudly, unevenly, coming in late and then speeding up for the next phrase. He wasn't of a mind to blend in with the monotonous, unified praying of everybody else, he wanted to show both himself and them that he felt each word deeply. He thought God would hear his prayers and spare him. He was more and more fearful that he, too, would . . . succumb. Though he led a full life with his wife, Margeta, and his little girls, he became painfully aware of every second of loneliness and every possible instrument of death. His time on the toilet had become a prayer because he was terrified that madness might overcome him while he was sitting there and, before the rational part of him had the chance to call for help, he might stab himself in the neck with scissors. When afflicted by the ailment he so fiercely feared, though, people didn't call for help, but sank to their death in silence. On the Sunday after they buried Trezika and Mladen, Miška tried to convince everybody after Mass that the whole village should move to the parish hall so we could all tell the priest what we needed to. The whole village could sleep together, cook together like in the old days, maybe even go to the bathroom and shower together—then nobody'd be left alone, and nobody could kill themselves. It was pitiful to see a grown man so fearful that even his friends laughed at him, though it was clear they were mocking him so they could free themselves of doubt. Although he tried to hide his anxiety and speak calmly, he couldn't pull it off. His despair leached out of him, and he was convinced that only he grasped the vastness of the peril facing us all.

The priest told him that some things must be left up to the Almighty, but he, too, spent several evenings in a row strolling around the village, calling to people from their gates and chatting with them about worldly matters. Had he invoked the otherworldly, the inscrutable, he might have done harm.

On Monday morning, the local vet drove through the village in his car, a Wartburg, with a big speaker on the roof. He drove slowly and called folks to a meeting at the community center hall, where there'd be talk of the situation in the village and about what "a sound mind in a sound body" meant. Only those who weren't at work or out in the fields heard him. The farmers were still spreading fertilizer out there like crazy.

I was haunted by the presentiment that everybody in the village knew this was all my fault, but I didn't seem to be attracting more attention in the classroom than I had before. The teacher told us to tell our parents or teachers right away if we noticed anybody acting strange or feeling down. The children made jokes; this had to do with older and weaker people, not us kids. Some said they might commit suicide if they were kicked off the soccer team, others if they were suddenly much poorer, and others if they were to hit their head and not be able to move anymore. When somebody missed a goal in our physical education class, Goran Brezovec mocked: "What now? Kill yourself?"

They all listened to him and thought he knew everything because he was the biggest and his dad was the head of the village. He said if you stare too long at the Mura, you'll go crazy and kill yourself. You'll lose your mind because the water keeps changing shape and never looks the way it did before. He said soldiers on guard duty kill themselves because they're left all alone. A person starts talking to himself, and comes to find that he disagrees with his very own self.

The street felt a little empty that Monday evening when Mladen took just Franz in the trunk of his car. Now I started noticing all the other sounds around me, which Franz's mumbling usually masked. The street had a hollow ring to it, probably because of all the centuries of unspoken words. I didn't have anything to do, and I wasn't drawn to my anger box, so I did push-ups and imagined I was pushing the entire planet away. It didn't help much. I was soaked in sweat, but there was still too much rage in me. Late in the evening, when Mom and I were sitting in front of the TV watching *Traumschiff* and my sister was

playing records in her room, somebody knocked at the door. I was terrified, I thought the police had come for me or, worse yet, that somebody
else had died.

"Come over to the church. The priest has called us in. This awful
evil has been visited upon us, and nothing is helping. We'll be praying.
The bell ringer's there already," said our neighbor Julika, her voice calm
and quiet.

"What's wrong? Somebody's killed themselves again?" asked Mom.

"Nope, not yet. But Imbra Perčić is missing. He's gone off somewheres, and nobody can find him."

It was eleven thirty at night, and the streetlamps were already off.
Phantoms were moving toward the church in the dark. The pews were
full, people were praying the rosary. The chorused humming was broken
only by Miška, who was dramatically late or rushing. Every time he
came to the part "now and at the hour of our death," he would practically shout. At the end, the priest said there'd be confession every day,
and everybody should come: "With our purity, let us withstand the
temptation of this unknown evil, which has spread through our community, brothers and sisters . . ."

He, too, wanted to know what was happening in the village, but
he didn't have his own Bacawk and Chickichee, so he had to rely on
confession. We parted in silence at twelve thirty, and only Miška stayed
behind to urge the priest to call us together every night to pray.

We walked behind two old women. One of them said softly, more
to herself: "It's like we've come to the blackest darkness. I never thought
there'd be enough room in our little village for all of hell to fit."

"Hell can fit inside one single person," said the other, and they
parted without a goodbye.

I wondered who hell would fit inside of next. I never would have
guessed it would be Milica Horvat, Mladen's wife.

8.

They buried Trezika at four in the afternoon and Mladen Krajčić at five so folks didn't have to go home in between. Instead they lingered by their garden gates. After the funerals, Mom sent me with a pail to fetch some milk. The street was still and empty at dusk, till Mladen Horvat's car turned off the main street onto ours. I took a deep breath and mustered the courage to ask politely when I could join them again for training. For days now the thought of his sunny yard by the vineyard with its one wooden goal had been keeping me alive. Even grumpy Milica couldn't ruin that beautiful picture for me. Franz wasn't in the trunk this time, but in the back seat, and when Mladen let him out, he looked like a dog that hadn't been let off its leash in a long time. He managed to bump into the front seat and the body of the car as he was climbing out. The streetlamps sometimes made things look different, but I felt sure his face was red, and he looked like he'd been crying.

"Now, now, wait a minute, what's wrong?" Mladen called after him.

I wondered whether Mladen had been teasing him about the stuttering—Franz was touchy about that. You had to pretend you understood every word, and it was a fairly complicated business. But something else was going on. Franz had a chocolate bar behind his back and walked straight past as if he hadn't seen me. I knew something bad must've happened, because he was completely silent—he made no sound at all. He stank as if he'd stepped in shit, and was walking strangely, knees pressed in. There was a black stain over his butt visible through the white soccer pants. I thought maybe he'd fallen on his ass or pooped his pants. I looked at Mladen, who was standing by his car grinning stupidly. He called to me loudly, now dead serious: "So would you like a Cockta soda and some wafer cookies again, eh, Dolenčec? Take care I don't go telling people what you did to him. Just you watch out."

He got in the car and drove away. I turned to Franz, but he was already gone. When I got to his house, I could hear they were beating him, and his mother was screaming something about what he'd done, but I couldn't hear his voice at all. Something had silenced him.

The next morning I hung around waiting for him before school. Law enforcement vehicles and an ambulance shot past me. By the first recess, word got out that Milica had killed herself, that she'd slit both wrists. Apparently she slit them lengthwise, not crossways like they do on TV. She'd been at nursing school so knew there'd be no way to save her if she did it like that. Nothing made sense now. Could my rage have possibly ricocheted off one person and killed another? Because Mladen was the one I was angry at. I couldn't have cared less about grumpy Milica.

"It's not your fault," I heard Chickichee whisper.

Mladen's wife killed herself because, Bacawk said, she couldn't bear life with Mladen anymore and couldn't see any way out. She couldn't have explained it to anyone, or said exactly what he'd been doing to her. They'd started dating when she was a senior in high school. Sundays she'd go with her friends to watch the Miners soccer games, and Mladen was the goalie. They all loved him in the village, almost as much as they loved Mario Brezovec, the drunk. He was polite and from a good family, and when Novi fosili gave a concert at the field, she noticed he had his eye on her. They married soon after she graduated. His father got a house ready for them. She was overjoyed, Bacawk explained, till she saw that behind Mladen's kind exterior lay something dark and twisted.

"She saw how he looked at her and how he treated her. As if he wished she were a boy, not a woman. He made her dress like one."

She lived in hope that he'd grow out of this over time. She tried to construct a happier image of her life in her head. Chickichee added that during her pregnancy she often dreamed that wild animals would come out of the forest and bow down to her child; she was like a forest princess, ruler of a world all her own, far from everything else. Sometimes she even retreated there when she was in public. But Mladen's sick gaze penetrated it more and more.

She lived with her revulsion, comforted that at least nobody else knew what Mladen was like. But she came undone when she saw how Mladen eyed his nephews, nine-year-old twins. She watched how he touched them, how he wrestled with them and tickled them, how he took them into his arms when they were playing so that he could rub up against them for a minute. He went to the bathroom to pee with them. At weddings he danced with the little boys; he'd go with them to change into costumes and barge in after midnight, as if they were the uninvited guests that were customary in the village. People wept with laughter when Mladen, dressed up as a deep-sea diver, danced with little devils and altar boys. Milica quaked.

She never said a word to him because she didn't know how. In an act of quiet protest, she stopped eating.

"She'd fix dinner and then watch him eat, waiting for him to ask her why she wasn't eating, but he knew what she was after, so he said nothing."

She couldn't tell anyone what was troubling her, nobody would have believed her, she knew even her parents would turn against her. On the outside they looked like the perfect couple. They had a child, and spouses who barely exchanged even a glance in public were a normal sight in the village. Though he seemed absent, he took more and more control over her. He seemed to know everything she did when he wasn't home—maybe he dug through the garbage just to laugh in her face when she lied to him about how many cigarettes she'd smoked. He seemed able to predict her every sentence and clearly relished this ability. Even when he went to the bathroom, he'd leave the door open a crack so he could hear what she was saying to their child. He came into the bathroom when she was showering or washing her feet.

"'Did you think you could lock me out? You won't lock me out in my own home.' That's how he spoke to her and laughed at her. Then he'd splash her with freezing cold water and leave. And she'd sit on the edge of the tub and cry," said Bacawk.

He was so horrible that his presence was physically painful to her. She found a little relief when, alone with their child in the house, she'd smoke and stare into the distance, thinking about what life would be like if Mladen were killed in an accident on his way home from work, or if he came down with an incurable disease. She loved thinking about how a person with such a terrible secret had to carry some germ inside himself that would devour him from within, like rot. She only hoped this would happen while her child was still ignorant of the fact that Mladen wasn't a human being.

As for herself, she thought it was too late for a normal life like the ones Mladen read about in *Arena* or saw in movies. She kept going only because he seemed to want to hide it from the world. Until he began bringing boys home.

Bacawk said she almost fainted when she saw Franz and me climbing out of the trunk of Mladen's car, and she complained as much as she dared, but it was as if nobody heard her. The next time, he brought only Franz. She saw them from behind the house, near the garage. Mladen was explaining how a goalie had to be flexible and that Franz had a muscle in his back that wasn't loose enough yet. He told him to bend over, this might hurt, but that's what he deserved for not stretching every day and getting all the exercise he needed. Mladen pushed him over a tin barrel that stank of stagnant water, cussing at him. Franz couldn't bend any farther at the waist, so he bent his knees. Mladen kicked him in the knee. Franz straightened his leg momentarily, huffed air painfully through his teeth, and bent his knee again. Mladen's comments became garbled, raging grunts, and Franz could no longer pull away. His white soccer shorts were down around his knees. He couldn't close his legs because Mladen's were there between them. In the dirty water, aside from the reflection of his face, Franz could see pollywogs wriggling restlessly whenever his pained gasp sprayed saliva with drops of blood.

"'Huh? What's that whining? You think you can punish me, you little cunt, huh? No sniveling! Want more? You'll get yours. What's with the groaning? No groaning. You piece of stinking shit. I'll shove yer shit straight back in.' That's how he talked, as if the kid had done something bad to him," said Bacawk, sadly.

Milica watched the scene all the way to the end, she saw him shove two fingers into the boy's mouth with one hand and grab him by the hair with the other; she watched him drop the boy to the ground like a beaten dog, how he panted and used his own sweaty T-shirt to wipe the shit off his dick.

The teacher was trying to sing a song about a chicken and an egg, and I could barely manage to keep from throwing up.

"Comrade Teacher . . . I mean Teacher, ma'am, I ain't feeling so hot. I'm sick. Please may I be excused?"

Angry that I'd interrupted her, she said I should take my things and go home.

When I got out into the fresh air, I felt better, but I couldn't erase the image Bacawk and Chickichee had etched in my mind with their whispers. They traipsed along with me, first on one side and then on the other. I was too weak in the knees to get away from them.

Milica was able to watch only because she'd already made up her mind. Mladen came in to get the chocolate, and she stood in his path, and for the first time she mustered all her courage and said: "And you think that's normal? God help me, you son of a bitch, you damn-blasted piece of shit, you think that's normal?"

Mladen laughed in her face, hissed, "Stop your squealing," and out he went.

"Fuck you, you asshole, you ain't coming near me again," she said, even though he couldn't hear her anymore. Later she fed the child, made dinner, and stared at Mladen while he ate. He looked a little tired; while he chewed, his only sound was an occasional coo at the child perched in its high chair.

"You were waiting for a boy to show up who wouldn't be able to tell anyone what you did to him," she said finally.

"What's eating you now?" he said, bored.

"Well, why not fuck me? I have nobody to tell, either," she hissed through her tears.

He jumped up from his seat, threw his plate, towered over her, and said: "Say that one more time, and I'll beat you down into the dark mother earth, I swear. Am I clear? I'm asking, am I clear?"

She stared at the table.

"Now you're quiet, you bitch. You're pushing me, pushing! I have had to put up with horrors, but enough's enough."

When the child and Mladen had fallen asleep, it was clear to her that she could never lie in that bed again. She sat motionless in the living room. All she could think about was stabbing Mladen in the heart with a butcher knife.

She'd already stood up to get the knife, but somehow she couldn't do it. She poured herself another glass of water because she was getting overheated at the thought of what she was contemplating. And the more she drank, the more she felt this was all her fault. And how much better it would be if she were gone. Better for her child, better for Franz.

Finally, almost with a smile, after she'd checked to make sure Mladen and the child were sound asleep, she lay in the bathtub, took nail scissors, and made two deep incisions in her flesh. She began to feel cold when she saw the blood gush out, but she was glad Mladen wasn't looking at her and couldn't hurt her anymore.

"But why didn't you say something if you were there? Why didn't you help her?" I turned and yelled at Bacawk. Milica was the only witness besides me and Franz, the only one who knew what Mladen was like. Nobody would understand what Franz was saying, and nobody would believe me.

"Why didn't you help her, you lousy rats?" I hollered. "And why didn't you help Trezika and Mladen and all the others?"

Chickichee said calmly, "Nobody sees us but you. They used to see us when they were small, while they were still scared of us. Later, out of fear, they don't see or hear us, even when we're around them all the time."

I walked past my house and to Franz's. His old man, a big fat bearded man with dirty hair and an unusually shrill voice, opened the door. He looked as if he'd just woken up. With unusual courtesy, he told me Franz wasn't feeling well but that he might be going to school the next day, if he wasn't running a fever. I asked whether I could see him, to give him his homework. From the door, the house smelled of feet and knitted sweaters that hadn't been washed in a while. He told me I'd see Franz at school and shut the door.

I came home and cried on the steps until my sister saw me and asked what was wrong. I said my head was feeling crummy and it wasn't anything too bad.

The next day they buried Milica. Mladen and all of Milica's family were tearstained, and everybody who'd gathered was disturbed. When I saw him, all in black, pushing the stroller with the child, I wasn't entirely sure whether Mladen really could be such a bad man. A person who cried as much as he was crying couldn't be all bad, I thought.

After the funeral, Mom and I stood with the folks who'd come, and I listened in. The men said it wasn't right that the police were interrogating poor Mladen like a criminal, and the women wondered how he'd manage now with the child, and why such bad things always seemed to happen to such nice people. Somebody said he was still young, and maybe, once time had passed, he'd find somebody else. Pišta said he'd heard there was somebody going around at night and talking people into killing themselves.

"Well, well, nothing makes a bit of sense anymore."

"In Slavonia, there's a war going on, people are shooting each other; meanwhile here we're doing the killing all by ourselves."

"There don't seem to be any way to make sense of how these people are connected."

"Everything is connected."

"Aw, Zvonko, don't you start with that muck. Nobody can know who's connected to whom."

"Maybe they were in a sect? And swore to do this?"

"Come now, please. What sect? Hush. We just buried Milica. Show some respect."

"Still, maybe somebody went around egging them on. There's talk that somebody's going around persuading people to kill themselves."

"Hush now, Democracy."

"What? What did you say?"

"Can it."

The fact that a reporter from *Medimurje*, the local paper, was at the funeral prevented the quarrel from spilling over into a knock-down, drag-out fistfight. And then somebody said that Franz Klanz had stolen Mladen's goalie gloves and a few other things, so the boy would be going to help him around the garden now that his wife was gone. Somebody suggested it was only right and proper for the boy to learn discipline, especially since his parents were such bums. Mladen would probably end up buying him school supplies, he was such a nice guy. I began feeling faint, and I told Mom I needed to go home.

I walked past Đura Brezovec, the village head, who was telling the reporter she mustn't write anything bad about the village, despite the five suicides in two weeks. He said there were decent, hardworking people living here. He was upset, clasping his hands, forcing a smile, and shaking his head as if trying to wriggle out of his shirt collar.

"See, people who aren't from these parts won't get it. They'll think we're all lunatics or something. See, people are afraid they'll lose their jobs, the ones who work over in Slovenia. But you could write, for instance, that municipal funds have been used to buy the very finest fertilizer on the market today. The economy and farming are our highest priorities. And we are in the midst of preparing for village games, so do come to those; we'll fix a big pot of bograč game stew, and the firemen'll perform their exercises. Bring along your camera then, you'll have plenty to take pictures of."

Nobody could make much sense of what the village games were about, but I reckoned they wanted to bring people together in one place and distract them from what was going on around us. They'd been looking for Imbra Perčić, the electrician, to set up the lighting for the event, but nobody knew where he'd gone. Bacawk and Chickichee told me that evening that Imbra was hanging from a branch only three hundred feet away from us, by the river, high up in a tree.

9.

The next morning I left the house fifteen minutes earlier, to be sure not to miss Franz. He wouldn't look at me, he just stared at the ground and tried to walk past. I blocked his way, he tried to go around, and I moved to block him again, and so it was several times until he shoved me away and mumbled something that sounded like "Evael em enola."

"I know you ain't stole no goalie gloves, Franz, I saw him give 'em to you."

He shrugged. That was the least painful part of it.

"You ain't going to Mladen's no more, Franz. We'll tell, we'll tell that policeman, Stankec, he's my friend, or the priest, we'll tell him what that jerk did to you."

Franz responded to each statement with silence and by spitting to the side.

"I'll help, Franz. You ain't alone." I knew I wouldn't be able to live with myself if I didn't pull him out of this, though I didn't know how to do that. I needed to figure out how to heal people, now that I was so adept at killing.

"We'll run away. We'll go to France. I have an aunt there, she's waiting for us. We'll go to a school for soccer players, where you do a little schoolwork and then play soccer all day."

He was touched by my sad lie, because he looked stiffly to the side, hoping the air would dry his eyes. We parted ways at school without him making a sound. I thought I'd never be able to penetrate his silence, till behind my back I heard him mumble, still clear enough, "Hey!" I turned, and Franz pointed at me and mimed a quick kick, as if passing me the ball. I could see on his face that he didn't believe we'd be able to run away. But he had a friend. Maybe that was enough.

At school the only thing the kids talked about was who'd seen the law enforcement officers and who'd heard our village was cursed. I was the only one who knew there was a new victim. His death was even less connected to me than Milica's, but I found a way to feel responsible for it.

Imbra Perčić was respected as an electrician, but he was known for giving people cruel nicknames and being rude to his customers. His whole life he'd managed to be domineering. He wasn't a member of the Communist Party, but he was the only electrician in the village, and in those last years of Yugoslavia, as I recall, this was a big deal. With something akin to joy, he'd leave people waiting for him for hours. Then he'd waltz into the house with his tools and adopt a tone of aggressive glee. After a few insulting jokes, mainly about the men of the household not being up to the task, he'd suddenly become serious and bend over the TV set or washing machine. That's when he'd stop answering questions. Oh, how he loved leaving them hanging, bouncing off the walls, and ricocheting back to smack the person who'd asked. After an uncomfortable pause, he'd respond with the sadism of a misunderstood master when anyone dared interrupt his spell.

"Might be the cathode needs replacing," the head of the household would say.

"The cathode? Oh, really. Cat-toad?" Imbra would look up, shooting a conspiratorial glance at the man's wife. "And where is this cathode? Show me, why don't you."

The head of the household would fall silent and long to be anywhere else. Imbra would then say in a conciliatory tone: "Oh, it ain't the cathode. We'll get to the bottom of this, don't you worry."

He was infinitely sure of himself, so much so that it bordered on arrogance. "You must be joking," he seemed to say. "How could you possibly be so dense?" The whole village rang with his inner song. At soccer games it wasn't so much that he was loud, but that he'd time his gibe, no matter how stale, for that moment that everything got quiet, so he'd receive bursts of laughter for it.

"What's up, ref? Having a bad day, are we?"

"Goalie! In from Switzerland? You're as full of holes as Swiss cheese."

He had a turn of phrase for anyone who happened not to be around just then, and with the phrases he maneuvered through a world ruled by asymmetry, turning it all to his benefit. For those who were a bit taller than him, he'd add Long to their name, Dry to those skinnier than him, and Porky for the ones who were fatter. He was a man of perfect proportions, and nobody seemed willing to dispute this.

Once, a few months before the suicides, he came to our house to fix the TV set. He brought me and my sister chocolate bars, a Braco one for me and a Seka one for her, and I didn't like the way he talked to my mom. He spoke to me as if I were slow and chided me for not knowing what a voltage tester and a Phillips screwdriver were. He said I'd never be a real man if I didn't learn how to fix things. I told him I was very good at breaking them, and he shot back that I should hold my tongue if I didn't have something more clever to say. By then I had better self-control, and I didn't hate him or wish him dead. But when Bacawk and Chickichee told me he'd hanged himself down by the river, I was no longer quite so confident. How much hatred did it take?

Bacawk and Chickichee said a huge fissure opened up inside Imbra when he began doubting his own worth some time back. And this oddly coincided with news that there was a young electrician named Čanadi living in a nearby village. Čanadi was cheaper, and we heard he was polite and didn't bullshit everybody the way Imbra did. Imbra's heart broke when he heard a few people in our village had called Čanadi and he did the job twice as fast while charging less than Imbra would have. And, as if fate had a sense of humor, now Imbra, the person responsible for cooking up all those nicknames, was christened with one himself. Folks began to refer to him as Imbra the Collector, because somebody said that they'd be setting aside the whole of their salary for Imbra to collect, even if there was nothing for him to repair, and that made everybody laugh.

Do you remember when we talked about how people sometimes catch their reflection in a store window and then adjust their expression, so they think they look just like the picture on their ID? They have no idea how much of their disappointment, disgust, and scorn they reveal on their face. They aren't aware of little gestures, sighs, and tics that say everything they don't in words. Our own collusion with the pretenses of others allows us to live in a more or less orderly world. But Imbra? Imbra now found himself trapped between a rock and hard place and saw no way out. He couldn't ignore them, all those people he no longer mattered to, yet he felt as if he could read their thoughts. Now he found out what being mocked and despised felt like.

Bacawk and Chickichee were sure that he'd still be alive if this had been all he was struggling with. But then the suicides began. He feared he'd lose control when it hit him, and in a panic he began praying to be spared, hiding it all the while from his wife, with whom he hadn't had a serious conversation in at least two decades. As is often the case with grown-ups who become religious when it suits them, so it was that Imbra the Collector began going to church. This was the only socially acceptable way of submerging his terror, at least briefly. He didn't want to look pitiful like Miška, so he ridiculed Miška along with the others. Meanwhile he prayed in earnest and did his level best, but the fissure simply couldn't be healed with prayer. He couldn't hide; he was certain that this horrendous thing would grow inside him, too, and there'd be no saving him. He wanted the bodies of those who'd killed themselves to be exhumed and buried outside the graveyard, because otherwise the whole village would be doomed. He heard there were women with children who'd left the village to stay with relatives for a while. And he wanted to go, too. He found consolation in the thought that there really was somebody who was going around talking people into doing it, and he imagined how he'd beat the living daylights out of the monster, punch them bloody, knock out their teeth, and carry them out into the middle of the village for all to see, and then finally turn them over to the police. He never, of course, breathed a word of any of this to anybody. Sometimes, in the evening hours, he felt as if darkness were coursing into him like a swarm of ants, through every orifice and pore, and he thought he'd go mad at the sound of their antennae in his belly. He paced around the house, saying he had a few more things to see to; he moved tiles that had been piled on the roof since before Tito died, hammered a board onto the sagging old door of the chicken coop. One evening he had nothing left to repair so he called to his wife that he was going out for a stroll.

"When his old lady asked why he wanted to go traipsing around and what would folks be thinking when they saw him poking around the village in the dark, he told her he was going to take a look at some property he was considering buying, so she quieted down and muttered something about how a person can take as good a look in the light of day."

He filled an empty Radenska mineral water bottle with water from the well and, sipping from it, he went out onto the street. Bacawk and Chickichee told me he hadn't planned where he was going, at first he thought he'd just go to the chapel and back, but since he didn't run into anyone, he decided to continue on to the parish hall. The whole way there, to his surprise, he was completely alone. This didn't bother him. He thought the village wouldn't be such a bad place if only it were completely empty one day a week. He didn't mind the village, not at all—it was the people he couldn't stand. He went by the soccer field and finally stopped at the Mura. He had nowhere to sit, so he climbed, naked except for his belt, up onto the first branch of a poplar. For a time as he sat there, he was happy, maybe for the first time in his life, because everything that had pressed him earthward, all of that, was down there below. He felt a chill and climbed onto another branch, scraping the soles of both feet against the bark as he went. He reckoned this was the last thing that would ever hurt him. He sat on a branch, took a deep breath, and closed his eyes for a moment. Then he fastened the belt around the branch he was sitting on and made a loop. He had to be careful not to fall as he leaned over to get his head through it. He looked once more across the river to the other bank, where the moon shone over the hamlet of Hotiza. He spread his arms wide and thrust himself free of his seat on the branch.

That's what Bacawk and Chickichee told me, and, though I wondered at the time if they were lying, there couldn't be any doubt when, several weeks later, Imbra Perčić the Collector was found. I heard about it from Mom long after we left the village behind. The only thing Bacawk and Chickichee got wrong was that he wasn't on the second branch of the tree, but was hanging at least thirty feet off the ground at the very top of the only poplar tree growing by the Mura. He was found after Slovenian territorial forces and the Yugoslav People's Army fought. The men from the village were combing the riverbanks for mines and biological weapons the army might have left behind. Pišta was the one who spotted Imbra's body hanging up there in the treetop, and said: "Well I'll be damned, a parachutist." It didn't strike them right away that there was no parachute. The body had already changed color, it looked like a half-rotten pear, and was, they said, buck naked. In the underbrush they found his clothes and the empty bottle of Radenska. Nobody could figure out how he'd climbed up there, he was no longer a young man. But so many strange things had been happening in our village that spring that nobody dared offer explanations by then.

Since they hadn't been able to find Imbra, the council wound up asking Čanadi to do the lighting for the village games. When they asked how much he'd charge, he said, "What do you mean? A portion of bograč game stew and a wine spritzer," so everybody had been calling Čanadi Mr. Decent, and Imbra Mr. Collector.

10.

The village games were oddly conceived. They weren't held on the first of May, nor were they the finale of the soccer season. Instead they were held midweek, I think on a Tuesday or a Wednesday. People said it was to celebrate the declaration of Croatian independence, but that was a pretty shaky pretext. Beyond the village there were tectonic plates shifting, Earth's pillars were rocking, but here we felt as if the last supports had long since fallen, and only by pure chance was the village still afloat.

Some fifteen mothers had left the village with their children, some to stay with relatives in nearby towns, others to Austria and Germany. Some of the wealthier retirees supposedly went off to a hot springs near Varaždin. The rest lived as best they could from one day to the next, relieved that the village wasn't being mentioned in the news anymore. That would have been a real disgrace. As if it weren't enough that folks from the neighboring villages used every opportunity to mock them. Not many people talked about Mario Brezovec and Zdravko Tenodi, but Trezika came up when one of the older women started acting strangely, and hardly anybody but me and his family remembered Mladen Krajčić. There was talk about Milica, who'd died the week before, but somebody said she had always been high-strung and that she'd stopped socializing after she had her baby, and maybe she'd started drinking too much when Mladen wasn't home, and he had barely been able to handle her.

I didn't feel like going to the village games, but Franz was finding it harder to bear the isolation. He was out on the street whenever possible, as if he couldn't stand to listen to the hypnotic rhythm of his own breath. After Milica's funeral, no one forced Franz to account for the supposed theft of the goalie's gloves, and I hoped that story would just fade away and he wouldn't have to go help Mladen around the house. If that bad thing happened only once, I hoped that maybe Franz could get past it. One day on our way to the soccer field, I told him about satellite antennas and how you could watch any TV show you liked; there were whole channels just for cartoons, and phones you could carry around with you that weren't attached to the wall. He stared at me, incredulous, the same way he looked at me when I told him how I was really feeling. About Laddie and my dad, Bacawk and Chickichee, and everybody who was waiting for me in hell. I needed to tell him everything that day, and we needed to take an oath of eternal silence and friendship. When we reached the field, I immediately spotted Goran Brezovec, Dejan Kunčec, and a few other boys wearing the new green soccer jerseys of the Miners soccer team. Their last names were on the backs.

"Well, well, lookee here, if it ain't Tom and Jerry," said one of them, catching sight of us.

"Fuck you," I yelled, and added, "Fuck all of you."

Never had that swear sounded quite as pitiful. I walked with big-headed Franz, who was still spitting around the bulky, bluish tongue inside his mouth. I would have given my eyeteeth to be wearing a green jersey with *Dolenčec* on the back. But the swear was meant to sound as if I was downright disinterested.

Everybody had gathered at the soccer field, even people from outlying villages. The hill people who lived above the vineyards at the edge of the forest, and who were quite strange, had also come down. Most hadn't had any schooling; they kept to themselves, lived off the land and the wine, died young, and seldom came into the village. There was talk that some of them had no idea about the Second World War because it had nothing to do with them. The men and women looked a lot alike, they dressed as if they hadn't been to Čakovec in twenty years, and now they swilled vast quantities of alcohol and laughed only when the hose burst during the firefighters' exercise and soaked the grass on the soccer field, or when somebody fell.

Everybody else perched on the embankment along the fence, going from the bar to the stands selling plastic toys, bouncy balls, and Croatian flags, then leaning against the soccer field fence, cold beer in hand, and listening to those speaking loudest about the Yugoslav People's Army barracks and the weapons that really ought to be retrieved from them. It all sounded as if this was happening somewhere far away, as if nothing would be encroaching on our village of hells. At first the hells knocked politely at the door, waiting patiently, as they'd waited in the gloom of people's farmyards. After that they pushed their way in, through cruelty and bickering. And now people, stripped of resistance, were just letting them into their homes. They opened the door for the hells without even waiting for a knock, let them in, and took them along wherever they went.

From time to time, people wandered over to watch a bizarre play starring Nevenka Brezovec, a high school student, Goran's older sister. She always got the lead in all the school performances because she was pretty and read with emotion, and her aunt worked on Radio Čakovec.

After the local firefighters showed they could handle any fire, the young soccer players filed in wearing their new jerseys given by the village and kicked balls around. Bogdan was behind the bar, and he didn't hear when they called his name to acknowledge him as coach. He was standing in for Mladen, the regular barman, who was home mourning his wife. After that the boys played two skirmishes for fifteen minutes each. After the first halftime, they were all so smeared with the mud left behind by the firefighters that nobody could tell who was on which side.

The soccer team played tug-of-war against the village hunters' association, which would have escalated into a drunken brawl if Đura Brezovec,
village head, hadn't announced that we should celebrate the independence of our beautiful homeland with dignity (at which point somebody
in the crowd heckled that he should've said "undependence"). Then the
national anthem was sung. The hill people stayed sitting but clapped
at the end. There was a suckling pig turning on a spit and black mead
being served. Black mead was so sweet that people gave it to kids, even
though it was alcoholic. Bograč game stew was cooking, and everything
smelled like a wedding.

Next on the program was Robi Šmujd, a sixth grader who played
"Bridge Over Troubled Water" on a synthesizer over a programmed
rhythm track, and then he accompanied the ladies' church choir for
"The Strapping Boys of Međimurje." They called him the Mozart of
Međimurje because by the age of four he could play "Frère Jacques"
on a melodeon, and his photograph had appeared in *Međimurje*, the
local paper.

After that, twins who were part of a dance group in Mursko Središće
danced to "Bad" by Michael Jackson, blasting it from a transistor radio.
The elementary school drama club performed, in Međimurje folk dress,
a selection of Marica Hrdalo gags from the sketch show *Gruntovčani*,
though people were so sick of those by then that they couldn't bear to
watch them anymore. After all the performances, Nevenka reminded
everybody of the bograč, the tombola raffle, and Jula Mlinarić's stand.
Jula was a widow who'd been asked to cook for the games, because
she'd won second place the year before in a Čakovec baking contest.
Her vanilla half-moons and Russian-hat cakes had beaten the creations
of seventeen women from other villages, all except one from Šenkovec,
but word had it that the woman who took the first prize was, in fact,
a professional chef. Jula was given a stand, and I watched her during
the performances as she earnestly served homemade mead, duck pâté,
fried crepes with mushrooms, boiled corn, and bishop's bread. However,

quite by coincidence, for some twenty minutes nobody had eaten anything at her stand. People would stop and chat with the dear woman who offered them food, but they would refuse. Some would say they'd be back in a bit, some that they couldn't possibly eat anything because they were still full from dinner. Some fifty feet away there was bograč stewing, and when she could see people eating it on plastic plates with slices of white bread from the supermarket, she couldn't hide her disappointment. She put on a brave face, saying hello, showing folks how delicious her dishes were by taking bites herself and washing them down with the mead. I watched all this while Franz was watching the game, and I felt I had to buy something from her. I was moving toward her when she suddenly froze, looked up at the sky, bent over, and vomited copiously onto the path. In one hand she was still holding a half-eaten piece of fried chicken, as if she intended to finish it.

Hot Ice, a party band that played weddings, distracted us from Jula. The field was crowded, high school kids smoked cigarettes behind the embankment, young couples were doing the two-step and waiting for the country polka to start, looking forward to dancing raucously and slapping each other on the butt, as if at a wedding. The hill people began shoving and fighting with guttural cries. Miška went from one group to the next, urging people to pray. When he realized some of them were making fun of him, he cried: "It's funny to you now, but just you wait till you get home and you're alone—you'll remember me then!"

He kept this up a little longer, then, discouraged, sat down near me and Franz, took out his rosary beads, and began praying while rocking rhythmically. He seemed indifferent to everything happening on the field but kept his eye out for the priest, and Pišta and Đura, who, with glasses of sauvignon, were going from group to group asking what they'd heard and what they knew.

"How're you doing, Joška? What about these suicides? Hear anything?" That was, roughly, the tenor of their investigation.

I realized this was why they'd held the games, to bring people together, get them drinking, and learn something. Drunken people declare their insights as if they're truths. At first, the always lively and savvy Zvonko "Democracy" Horvat trailed right behind them, but he gave up after half an hour. He leaned on the locker-room wall, muttering weakly, his face pale.

"All together like this, it isn't quite as glaring how really awful we all are . . ." This was the first and last thing I heard him say that sounded genuine, that broke through his know-it-all mask. He seemed to have made peace with something and no longer needed to prove anything. Grateful for his sincerity, I stood near him while Franz disappeared somewhere around the bar, where I'd seen his father trying to mooch a beer.

That evening, terminally ill Zvonko "Democracy" Horvat and I—knowing we were seeing the same things, though we hadn't exchanged a word—watched how everyone in the village, no matter how ordinary they might've seemed, flaunted how truly remote they were from each other, living in solitude and isolation. Behind the walls and fences, behind the identical facades and hedges, behind all that had been created to minimize difference, there were thousands of jarring images of pain and longing nobody else could've understood, and an enchantingly poignant music, silent to the alien ear.

We were all suffering, that much was clear. For a moment, standing next to Democracy, I was happy because I felt I wasn't really alone, we were all the same. Then Mladen showed up. He got out of his car in his mechanic's jumpsuit with a gentle smile. His teammates gathered around him with gravitas, and shook his hand solemnly, as if he'd just returned from a distant land. One of them thumped him on the shoulder and asked how he was doing. He shrugged and said, "Life goes on." The group settled by the bar, where Bogdan, already drunk, was insulting people and telling them they were clueless about soccer. They ordered a round, and Mladen pointed to Franz's old man and said they should give him a drink, too. Franz's dad made his way through the crowd to Mladen, flung one arm around him, and started talking, all the while holding Franz by the collar with his other hand. When I saw Franz was standing there like a statue, eyes fixed on the floor, and could tell nobody had any idea he was terrified, I ran over. When I pushed my way through the crowd, I heard Franz's father stammering: "My boy will be helping you out—hear me, Mladen. A child mustn't get away with something like that. Come over here, Franz."

"Well, that's fine, he doesn't need to start today, we can wait for tomorrow," Mladen answered, but Franz's dad interrupted him.

"No way, today he starts, enough of this idling around. Come, Franz, go with Mladen. You'll be done in a few hours' time."

Franz, frozen, stared at the ground and waited for Mladen to drag him away. I mustered every ounce of courage and declared: "Mladen, Franz didn't steal them goalie gloves." Mladen looked at me, and I thought I saw surprise in his eyes. But not fear. He knew I didn't have the guts to say what I wished I could say. And even if I had, nobody would've believed me.

"I stole them and gave them to Franz," I said louder, because nobody seemed to hear me. I stopped breathing from terror and shut my eyes. "I'll come and help you," was the last thing I managed to say. I'm not actually sure whether I said this out loud or not. When I opened my eyes, Mladen, beer in hand, was pushing half-dead Franz into the back seat of the car. Franz looked over at me just before the car door closed.

"Ajitam, tiaw rof em. Ll'ew nur yawa. Uoy n' em," I heard him say, surprisingly loud and clear.

"Uoy 'n em, Znarf, uoy 'n em!" I hollered after him, and two drunks at the bar laughed and whooped at me.

I somehow made my way over to Zvonko "Democracy" Horvat, crouched down beside him, and burst into sobs. Bacawk and Chickichee sat next to me and said I should calm down and wipe my eyes, people

270

shouldn't see me crying. I was sick and tired of them and that hellish village.

I asked Zvonko if I could come over to his place, watch TV—cowboy movies—look at his empty beer cans, whatever, just to push away the thoughts of Franz. Zvonko was jittery and weak, he didn't say a word all the way home, and once he got there he drank glass after glass of water. I took off my sneakers and curled up in misery on the sofa. I must have dozed off at some point; I'd become completely still and was staring blankly. I was alarmed by a loud thump from the next room, a sound that brought to mind a huge, fleshy insect, an insect the size of a horse, smashing into the side of the ceiling lamp.

I sat up on the sofa. Something inside me could already clearly imagine what I was about to see. The fear of what I'd see was less than the fear I'd be stuck forever on that sofa, turned to stone, so I stood up and went into the hallway. Zvonko was hanging from a noose tied to a wooden post on the attic stairs. At first I couldn't see the rope because the house was dark and the rope was thin, so it looked like Zvonko was floating. As if he still had the stamina to be polite, he twisted and jerked in silence, holding the noose with both hands. As if he'd changed his mind when he saw me. As if he'd realized that the only thing to outlive him would be the image of his helplessness etched inside me. I ran over and tried to hold him by the legs and lift him up. He was heavy and kicking wildly. I managed to get both feet several times, but then he'd flail and kick me away. He never made a sound, neither of us did, nor did any of Zvonko's memories as they watched the macabre dance. *Not again,* I thought. I had become an outright monster, even to those who were on my side.

I've always had dizzy spells when I find myself in hugely important situations. Maybe because I imagine those moments hundreds of times before they happen, invent a picture of what they'll be like, but then I always have to bind my fantasy to the reality. Zvonko's foot twitched, the big toe jerking upward, all the rest pointed firmly downward. I saw this because he had a sock and slipper on one foot but the other was bare. I looked up and saw his face was red and his tongue blue. His eyes were huge. It was strangely dazzling.

When he stopped flailing, I hoisted him up briefly, but he jerked backward for the last time. Since I didn't want to let him go, I lost my footing and hung briefly from his feet. I heard a crunch somewhere above me, and I thought I could feel it through my arms, too. It reminded me of when Granny nibbled a chicken foot from the soup and pulled it apart. His body was still, and I knew he was gone. My head was resting on his pelvis, and I felt moisture on my face. He'd peed, I realized. I took a few steps back and sat down in the corner without taking my eyes off him. He swayed back and forth and shuddered once more, but his face was dead and serene. He didn't stick out his tongue or bug out his eyes, at least no more than usual. He was utterly peaceful, and I thought he could see everybody who'd left our village during those days, and maybe he saw my dad. They were all together and could have a good laugh about this mess.

I don't know how much time passed before somebody found me, all I saw was dusk settling in. I was lucky, because usually nobody ever came to visit Zvonko. But Pišta stopped in to borrow an extension cord for the light over the bograč stewing station. He walked right in and from the door saw me sitting, back against the wall, wearing a frozen grimace, staring at the body. I think Pišta was never the same after that.

"Oh, oh, oh," he repeated, quavering, as if shooing evil spirits and monsters away. He grabbed me, tucked me under his arm like a puppy, and ran out.

Mom was motionless and mute in the stairwell when I appeared at the door with Stankec and his colleague. First they wanted to talk with Mom, so they said I should go and play. Bacawk and Chickichee were waiting for me in my room, as if they knew I'd lose my mind for good if I were left alone. They told me Zvonko had left everything in order, he'd written a farewell note and set out all of his documents on his desk, as well as money for the funeral expenses and the wake.

"He was very sick, the cancer ate him right up."

He became even more isolated, because he didn't want to tell anybody he only had a few months to live. People in the village knew he was doing poorly, but Democracy didn't want them looking at him with pity. He did his best to enjoy what time he had left. This didn't end up working, because he had the constant feeling he was late in getting somewhere. He'd heard earlier that those who get a terminal illness learn to live and experience their last weeks at full throttle. He didn't understand. This was the worst time of his life, not because he was afraid of death but because he didn't have the time to enjoy anything. When he went fishing, he'd pour brandy into the water, hoping to lure the fish to bite faster. While he'd been healthy, he used to grill slowly—he'd go to the woods to collect firewood, pop open a beer, and read the paper while the meat marinated. Now he used a hair dryer to blow air on the fire to make it burn as fast as possible, he ripped up the tongue-and-groove flooring from his summer kitchen because the boards were particularly dry, and he poured lighter fluid on the fire, which gave the meat that special bitter taste of the never-alive.

His thoughts were centered not on life but on his disease. Several times he dreamed he was shaking hands with his gall bladder. He tried to speak normally in his dream, but the gall bladder (he pictured it like a yellow sack with several big veins instead of hands) was vicious; it interrupted him and peppered him with questions he had no answers for. After several of these dreams, he realized his gall bladder reminded him of a strict teacher he'd had, the late Mr. Taradi. I didn't know how Bacawk and Chickichee were able to insinuate themselves into people's dreams, but I had no doubt they had.

When he'd imagined his death (as every person does sooner or later), he never thought he'd be done in by something from the inside, a pus-filled ulcer he couldn't even see, an inflamed wound that could burst and pour its poison into his gut. He never imagined he'd be devoured by something that was part of him, that he'd fed with food and alcohol. Death for him had always been a blow. A powerful pressure inside the head, a stuttering heart, a rupture, a fall from a great height. His grandmother had told him years before about a man who'd been walking through the village when a wall from a ruined house collapsed onto him. She told him they found bits of the man's brains all the way over on the other side of the street. The dogs licked them up, and the old women chased away the damn-blasted fleabags. That was etched in his memory, and all his life he thought that one day he, too, would take his place in such a picture. He couldn't bear a different sort of ending. He wanted to be the one calling the shots. If he had to die, he would die on his own terms. And he was afraid of loneliness; he thought death wouldn't dare encroach on his house if somebody was there with him, so that's why he'd wanted me around.

11.

When Stankec came into my room, he said nothing for a time, then he picked up a toy car from the floor and read what was written under the chassis. "An Audi 80," he declared. "A fine car. When them Krauts make a car, they do it right."

He was quiet a little longer, then he put his elbows on his knees as if he were about to stand and said, "Kid, you and I have known each other for a while, ain't we? You came to see us at the station with your pal—you were looking for your daddy, remember? What was your buddy's name?"

"Dejan. We ain't friends."

"Now why's that?"

"Why would he dare be my friend?" I said and choked back a sob. Everything hit me, and I remembered where Franz was. I started crying for the second time that day. Stankec laid his hand on my shoulder and said: "I'd like to know what was going on at Zvonko's. Your mom tells me you were going there . . . helping him around the house. You were the last to see him alive. He left a letter saying he was very sick and wouldn't be getting better, he put everything in order and left some money for the funeral. But it's a little strange that he's the sixth person to take their own life."

"The seventh."

"No, the sixth."

"Seventh."

"No, Matjaž . . . Mario Brezovec was first, Zdravko Tenodi second, Trezika third . . ." He pulled a notebook from his file. "Mladen Krajčić fourth, Milica Horvat fifth, and Zvonko Horvat sixth."

He called me Matija when he was serious and Matjaž when he was teasing.

"Imbra Perčić done hanged himself."

"No, son, he just took off for a spell. Maybe he was a bit shaken by all the people killing themselves, or because the Serbs are gearing up for war. But he's alive and well. I know Imbra, he trained as an electrician with my brother-in-law. He wouldn't take his own life—don't you worry, people like him like themselves way too much. He's off in Germany or Austria somewheres, sitting in a bar, drinking a beer, and talking about how he's the smartest and handsomest fella around."

"He hanged himself, 100 percent. Down by the Mura, from a poplar tree."

Now Stankec looked a bit worried, and I began thinking I'd finally found a person who would actually believe me. My hopes sank when he flashed a smile.

"Well, there ain't no poplars down along the Mura. Wherever did you get that, Matjaž? You have one of those—how do they put it—lively imaginations, but you shouldn't be fibbing. Maybe you're reading too much *Pixie and Dixie*, or watching too much *Tom and Jerry*. But tell me, when did you and Zvonko leave the soccer field together today? About what time was that? And, if you remember, did you meet anybody or stop in anywhere? Anything you remember."

"We ain't stopped in anywheres. Zvonko was kinda quiet. Here and there he was short of breath. We left about the time Mladen Horvat took Franz." And again I started sobbing. I couldn't breathe, but I went on. "There's something I have to tell you about Mladen and Franz . . ."

Stankec told me I could tell him everything that was troubling me, but first we had to deal with this matter of Zvonko "Democracy" Horvat. So I recounted everything. "And then Pišta came in to ask about the extension cord. He tucked me under his arm like a puppy and ran from the house like it was about to cave in."

"And that's all you know, Matija?" asked Stankec, looking me straight in the eye.

"No, I know all sorts of other things, I know everything, but nobody believes me."

"What do you know?"

"I know whose fault it is that people are taking their lives. I'm to blame—it's me. First people I didn't like were dying, but then the folks who'd been good to me started, too."

Stankec, oddly enough, didn't laugh. He didn't say I had a lively imagination, he just shut his notebook, put a pillow from the bed up against the wall, leaned back on it, and said, "Okay, go ahead and tell me," and waited for me to catch my breath.

"It all started when my dad and me were playing, and he told me that somewheres up in the hills there was this treasure . . ."

I told him about messing up the workshop and how my sister and mom were mad at me, and about Dejan Kunčec and how we went into Čakovec to the police station, and how I wanted to push Dejan into the river, but his father came and saved us, and how I began to be scared of things that other people didn't see, and how I understood that I was killing people with my rage. I told him about Dad and Laddie and why I went to the forest and almost froze to death. I told him why I'd been angry at Mario Brezovec and Zdravko Tenodi, and how my drawings killed Trezika Kunčec, and how my rage could ricochet, so it killed Milica Horvat, too. I told him what I thought Mladen had done to Franz and what he was probably doing that very moment. I admitted to him that I didn't have a single friend left, save Franz, and this hurt because everybody thought I was a monster. I don't know how long I talked. I remember my sister came to the door at one point and peered in, but Stankec just waved her away. When I finally finished, when I'd poured out all I had to say, I realized I wasn't sitting on the floor anymore but was standing and yelling, and my whole head was pounding. Stankec was still sitting there, leaning on the wall and watching me quietly. I gasped a few more times before he said: "I know everything you've said is the honest truth."

I felt the grip of a huge fist that had been clenching my back and constraining my every movement for the last two years gradually release. Everything that had controlled me, the world I'd been living in, the liminal world of the silent brothers Sleep and Death, the one that nobody else could see except as a speck in their peripheral vision at moments when a child's heart burns for no obvious reason up the throat and into the mind—it had all vanished, and I didn't care what would happen next.

"When I was small, I thought there was this man in a black coat who walked around the village and stole kids. I saw him so many times, and I was terrified of him, though I didn't know what he did with the kids or where he'd come from. Everybody told me he wasn't there and I'd just made him up. But two years later, they found the man in the black coat somewhere in Zagorje in the forest, and around his wine cellar were kids buried without their heads. He'd chopped off their heads with an ax and dried them in his attic. Matjaž, my friend, I'm dead certain you seen those things, but you gotta know they ain't your fault. You ain't to blame, because otherwise the kids in your class who put shit in your sneaker would be dead, right? Yet they're alive and well. Or our policewoman, Milena, woulda keeled over, because I remember like it was yesterday how you glared at her. It's hard to see it, but promise me you'll at least think about how this can't be the whole truth. Promise?"

"Okay," I said, with a genuine rush of relief. "I promise. But will you promise me something, too? Will you help Franz? Please, Stankec."

"I'll take a look into that, don't you worry. But I don't think Mladen would . . . Maybe you were upset that he played more with Franz than with you? Do you think?"

"Maybe so," I said.

"Let's go down to the soccer field. I have an idea. I have to find out where those medics have gotten to anyways."

Stankec told Mom we'd be back soon. He told his colleague he should go back to the station and write up the report, and that he'd hurry the medics and coroner along. They'd already loaded the body into the ambulance, dropped in at the village games, and were drinking wine spritzers.

When we returned to the soccer field, it was night, and the whole village looked as if it would be swallowed by darkness if someone ever switched off the lights. They all knew Zvonko killed himself, because his body was in the ambulance parked by the locker room. Still, nobody called a halt to the festivities. Or maybe that's why they kept going. Hot Ice was calling out the winners of the tombola raffle. The hill people were stretched out one on top of the other on the embankment, only one of them was on his feet, and he was dragging his half-dead wife along behind him, kicking her from time to time.

"Democracy hanged himself," Đura Brezovec kept saying, drunk and clearly dismayed. "This is definitely going to be in the papers, honest t' God. We'll be the laughingstock."

Stankec parked his car by the field while small dark-green shadows chased the ball. He left the car's headlights on and told me to come out in front of them. From the trunk he took a black cap with a brim and the Croatian coat of arms, the kind worn by the Special Police, and a big camouflage vest that reeked of motor oil and reached almost down to my knees. Goran Brezovec, Dejan Kunčec, and another five boys came running over. With quiet admiration, they watched Stankec and me. Acting like he didn't even notice them, he took his pistol from the holster, shook out five real bullets, and put them into my hand. When he was quite sure everybody was listening, when the Hot Ice guitar player stopped singing for a few seconds, he said: "Thanks for your help. You're our man in the field. I'll be calling on you again when we need you."

He whispered that I mustn't throw the bullets into a fire or smash them with a hammer, then turned off the headlights and went over to the bar to find the medics.

Suddenly it didn't matter anymore that I was the weirdest kid in the village. They all came up to me. I gave a few of them bullets, repeating Stankec's warnings about fire and hammers, and answered their questions. I said this was an ongoing investigation and I wasn't supposed to say much about it, but it had to do with a fella from across the Mura on the Slovenian side. I let Goran Brezovec try on the vest, but I didn't give the cap to anyone. They asked me if I wanted to play soccer. At first I said no, but the second time I gave in. They all wanted to pass to me. When I missed the goal, they thumped me on the shoulder anyway—the kids from my team and the ones from the other team. Everything was "Matija, look at this" and "Matija, did you hear how Zdenko's toenails were ripped off" and "Matija, come practice with us tomorrow." It seemed like they'd all forgotten who I was, and I truly believed that everything that had hurt me could just disappear. Maybe I could be a kid on the outside and a monster only on the inside. They wanted me to tell them what I'd drawn on the sheets of paper that had been at Trezika's, and what it was like when Franz bit off his tongue, and, finally, what Zvonko "Democracy" Horvat looked like when he hanged himself. I grimaced, stuck out my tongue, and bugged out my eyes. They were satisfied. Then somebody said, "Well, well, here comes Franz Klanz," and somebody else laughed. "Yep, I noticed something smelled bad."

I turned and saw him standing there quietly. The light was behind him so I couldn't see his face. He looked like a silhouette cut from black cardboard, as if his only purpose was to cast a shadow. Although he was my only friend, I wasn't happy to see him then. I wanted him gone just for that night, so I could be a part of something, even just a little. I'd thought for so long that this chance had been lost to me forever. *Go someplace else. I'll be along in a bit,* I thought. If only he'd allowed me that evening of that day, after I'd cried what I hoped were my last tears, I know I would've come back for him, I'd have done everything I could to keep him from being cast out—his apparent destiny from birth. But he showed up like that, in front of the kids in the green jerseys; he seemed to represent everything that was shameful and dirty in my life, though none of it was because of Franz himself. My memory of him is of utter pureness, and that's why it's so painful. I turned, shouted something about the game to the other kids, and then glanced back at him. He stood there, motionless. I went over and said he should go be with his dad, that I'd come over later, or we'd see each other the next day—I don't remember what. I didn't want anybody to see me talking to him, because, I thought, none of the cool stuff—the bullets, the cap, or the vest—would have sustained me after that. I saw his face, completely serious: this was a boy at his limit, his brow furrowed, his lips drawn downward. Franz didn't buy it. He began yelling in garbled fury. He leaned toward me, so close I felt his breath. He screamed—angry, wretched. I'm ashamed to confess that I pushed him away and probably said something like, "Come on, get lost" that only minutes before the other kids would have said to me. I turned my back on him. He fell silent. I couldn't see him, but I knew his mouth was agape and he was staring at me. And then I heard a loud gasp and a deep, burning growl, a sound that tore from the boy's throat, defying control, a wrenching bray to freeze the heart, but only if a person let it. Ever since, it seems to me, my hearing has been impaired. Now everybody was looking at him, and nobody was laughing. He kneeled on the ground, and, staring straight at me, scooped dirt with both hands into his mouth. Black earth full of the dark; only a very few know what that dirt was like. Once he'd filled his mouth so that his throat could make no sound, he got up, turned, and strode off into the darkness. I turned to the others and said something like, "What now? Kill yourself?" because that's what Goran was always saying during gym class, so I thought it was probably funny. And sure enough, everybody laughed, so I added, "Crazy Franz."

I thought he'd gone to his dad. The next day he'd still be pissed, but everything would turn out fine in the end. My happiness fused with the happiness of the village, and even though it did a shabby job of papering over the gruesome horror that had us in its grip, that night I loved every drunk who staggered by, I loved them all, maybe even Mladen. I wondered whether maybe I'd gotten it all wrong. Dejan Kunčec's dad drove me home, and Dejan and I burped in the back seat and giggled. That night Bacawk and Chickichee weren't around, and I fell asleep without fear. I knew I wouldn't remember my dreams in the morning.

12.

The next day I heard that my only friend had been floating in the cold river while I slept. The teacher came into the classroom, deeply shaken, and sighed. She blew her nose in her handkerchief and—halting after every sentence and staring into space as if she were reading to us from an invisible newspaper—said, "A child from our school drowned last night in the Mura. Franjo Klanz from class 4A. He was found by fishermen a few miles downstream. Near Mursko Središće. Now everybody, come with me."

At first I was calm. I was certain this wasn't true. In the crush of us leaving the classroom, Goran said, "Dolenčec told him to go kill himself yesterday at the soccer field." They lined us up in the cafeteria, and the principal was already there with his hands crossed and a law enforcement officer beside him. They asked if anybody knew anything about Franz. Somebody in the front row said that Franz had been at the soccer field, they'd seen him playing soccer, and then he played hide-and-go-seek with some other kids, and then he went home. A few others agreed, and nobody seemed bothered that it was a total lie. They felt better not remembering him as someone they didn't want around. I knew they all thought I'd sent him to his death, but I was sure he would walk in any moment, alive and well.

I felt a catch in my chest at the thought that maybe he'd run away and wouldn't come back. And then, even though I hadn't killed him, everybody would finally find out what I'd been hiding for so long inside me.

I crept out of school holding my bag and slippers, utterly shattered. The only thought that kept me going was that Franz would show up any minute now, that the body they'd found couldn't be his. A few people had gathered in front of the store: Pišta, the reporter from the *Medimurje*, Rumenige, Samanta, and some others. They were talking quietly, privately, and I slowed, hoping to hear what they were saying. Someone pointed at me, and they all turned. They didn't try to hide their stares. I stopped, ready to stare back at them forever, till I'd withstood all that they had to say about me. I wasn't alone. To my left was Bacawk, to my right, Chickichee.

Bacawk whispered, while I was standing like that, frozen, that Franz had gone from the soccer field to the river, that he was very sad. He stared into the dark water and saw our world mirrored without Znarf in it. That world was a good world, and that's why he went to take his place there. Not forever, just for a while. Just to rest his eyes for a moment.

"The boy wanted to be in a place where no one could see him. That's all he wanted. A place where no one could touch him."

He wanted to stretch out his hand, to touch, maybe for a moment, what was on the other side, and then he'd come back.

"Maybe the boy will return. You might have to wait a long time," finished Bacawk. I realized then that the two of them had been waiting for centuries for someone who would never come back.

"Look at how they're watching you," said Chickichee. "Like you murdered somebody. Like they're better than you. And believe you me, they ain't. They don't understand those who were here before them."

His voice faded into the distance with every step I took toward the silent group. The silence was broken only by a distant, low hum, which, when the wind picked up, became a rumbling, deep vibration.

"Don't go there!" hollered Bacawk.

My only thought was to endure my punishment and then vanish into oblivion.

"They want this to be your fault, but it ain't your fault that we're all cursed. There'll be no peace here till the end of the world, till fire blazes from the heavens and consumes everything, and the wind blows away all the ashes. That's what they used to tell us in the olden days," said Bacawk.

I stopped. So it was true. From the dark forests, a curse had been cast upon the village. And the curse did have to do with the murdered will-o'-the-wisp folk. But, Bacawk told me, the will-o'-the-wisp folk were not the cruel ogres from the north who'd ventured out of the forest and killed the good people of the village. They were peaceful, they'd been living in the forests since time immemorial, they'd been making colorful pots and worshipping forest gods in the likeness of animals. The ogres galloped in from the east on their horses, and when they came to the forests by the riverbank, they found a long-forgotten settlement, abandoned by a tall people who wore woolen tunics and metal armor. The ogres raised their camp near the riverbank. The forest dwellers taught the newcomers how to use floating two-boat mills. The ogres had only known mills run by beasts of burden. Close at hand was a trough for kneading clay, so they taught the ogres how to make bricks, durable housing, and kilns. They taught them to make candles, as the ogres had only known how to make torches. But the ogres were full of hatred. They fought out of habit. They despised all those who worshipped other gods and spoke other languages. Most of all, they hated the lights visible at night from the forest where the Candle Bearers dwelled, because they thought these came from invisible creatures inside the wax. The ogres barged into the homes and sacred places of the Candle Bearers.

They stole and destroyed. They beat and tormented. And in the end they killed most all of them. First the livestock, then the women and children, in front of the men they'd lined up at the edge of the forest. And finally they chopped off the men's heads.

The rumbling grew louder with each step as I moved toward the villagers, and each of Bacawk's words helped me see who they truly were.

A pile of corpses was buried in a big pit in the forest, and others were tossed into the river. It was the ogres who stayed. The children of the ogres' children embraced the belief in one God whose son had come down to Earth and taken all sins upon Himself. They atoned, repented, and were forgiven by God and their new ruler. And in return they were told that God had given them, and only them, that very land, with the mills on the river and the fertile black soil. And they were told that God made them good. They were made to believe that they had gone to battle for God against the evil forest dwellers. That the demons of their ogre ancestors could be reined in for perpetuity if they did as they were told. The bloodthirsty ogres threw the Candle Bearers' effigies to their pagan deities from the highest bluffs into the river, where they sleep to this day somewhere on the silty river bottom and summon those who survived. And the submerged church, and the monstrous people . . . all this was their legacy of blood, their legacy of violence. Papered over by a pathetic hope about boundless goodness. Bacawk took a deep breath.

"They can only survive by telling themselves something altogether different. That's why they see you as the evil one."

"So you are those who survived," I said finally, breathing hard. I covered my ears to block out the penetrating rumbling that made my whole body shake, but now it was resonating deep inside me.

"We are the last of the will-o'-the-wisp folk, the Candle Bearers, the forest dwellers. We're the ones waiting to be taken. That's why you see us, but the others don't. You're of our kind."

With a rumble, the first of a dozen or so tanks on their way from the Varaždin barracks toward Slovenia passed between me and the silent group. They were going to occupy the border between Austria and Italy. The group just stood there. They watched me while the green-gray behemoths thundered through. People came out of their houses, peered over their fences. They were used to fear. This was a moment of relief because they could now point to an enemy—now everybody could feel it, not just us villagers. Now nobody would care that we were killing ourselves.

13.

On my way home I managed to pass unnoticed. I became an unremark-
able detail in the picture everybody was staring at, spellbound, from
their front yards. The column of tanks had passed, but they'd left ruts
in the pavement on the main road. I heard that teachers in a neighboring village had tried to pull soldiers out of the tanks, shouting: "What's
gotten into you? Who are you going to shoot? Is there anyone here in
need of defending?"

There were rumors that some numbskull had thrown a beer bottle
at a tank, and it screeched to a stop and pointed its gun at the people.

My mother and sister were also at the fence. I didn't know whether
they were crying because of the tanks or because of me. I grabbed Mom
by the hand. "They said at school that Franz is dead. They think I made
him die. I ain't going back there, Mom, please say I don't have to!"

She told me, tenderly and firmly, looking away, "We're going to
Zagreb. We'll pack up and leave as soon as we can, as soon as they say
the road is clear. We ain't staying here. People're dying, there're tanks
on the roads. Things ain't as they should be. Everybody's gone plumb
crazy."

Granny wailed with all her strength, she yelled at Mom that there
was nowhere as safe for us as here. Even my big uncle cried. Mom just

stared at the ground, hunched her shoulders up high as if she wanted to plug her ears with them, and went into the house to pack our things.

"Anywheres is better than here," she said softly.

I sat down on the ground by the fence. The metal roar could still be heard in the distance, but I could also hear what the neighbors were saying.

"He said, 'Kill yourself.'"

"No way."

"He did, it's true, yesterday at the soccer field. They're all saying it."

"And he pushed him, I saw it. I'm sorry for the little Klanz boy. He was a decent sort, always said hello on the street."

I pushed my schoolbag away, lay on my belly behind the fence where nobody could see me, and thrust my teeth into the dirt, the cursed black earth. I gulped it down angrily, the way Franz had the night before. Time to go to the river. Franz would be waiting there for me. I wanted to hug him and sink with him into whatever place there was for those of us who were damned, into the deepest mud. That's where we belonged, in a grave with a greasy, dark bottom. And the spears of the marsh reeds would keep watch over us, and blind fish would guard the solemn quiet of the grave in that dark and ghastly peace, under the water lilies, waiting for winter and the ice. Coincidence could not be what had brought us there.

And I would've gone, too, if our neighbor Tonči hadn't found me and brought me into our house.

"Take him away from here. He can't stay," he said, and left without a goodbye.

The buses weren't running through the village that day, so we had to wait for the next morning. Mom made a few anxious phone calls, first to friends from Ljubljana, and then to a man in Varaždin. Finally she told my sister we were going to Zagreb. She didn't know where we'd stay or how we'd manage. My sister asked how she'd go to school there when she didn't know anybody.

Mom didn't let me out of her sight. When we got into bed around midnight, the bags were all packed in the hallway, and we could hear Miška calling my name from the road. He yelled for me to come for him, he was ready. He wouldn't stop, so Mom covered my ears with her hands. Soon after that everything went quiet, and in my head I only heard, as I had that whole day, Franz's voice.

In the early morning, before five, we stood at the bus stop a few feet from a group of workers. The pavement was rutted from the caterpillar treads on the tanks, and everything was covered with little black rocks. The stench of oil was still in the air. Aside from that, there was nothing to justify us feeling uncomfortable. At one moment someone from the half dark remarked: "That's right, take him away. We don't want him here no more."

"Oh, hush up, Vajnč, he's only a kid," said a woman's voice, a little softer.

"Well, fuck him—we were kids, too, but we knew what we were doing. I've had it with all of us being quiet."

"Fuck off, Vajnč. Can it."

Mom reached out to stop my sister when she started toward them. We went to the back of the bus, Mom and me on one seat, my sister on another. When we passed the graveyard, I closed my eyes, and for a moment I could picture Franz's funeral the next day. They'd also bury Zvonko "Democracy" Horvat, and people would stand on the street and talk about the tanks, the border crossings, and how they'd been doing such a great job laying down fertilizer. Franz's mom would be dead drunk and silent, and his old man, the idiot, would go on, loudly, so everybody could hear, about how Franz was a moron because he didn't tend to himself proper. And everybody, at least for that moment, would see him as a good man. When I opened my eyes, I caught sight of Bacawk and Chickichee. They were standing by the roadside at the very edge of the village. They didn't wave, they didn't call to me, they just stood there, silent, and watched me leave.

EPILOGUE

"How strange to see you. After all this time."

"I'm a little dizzy. This whole thing reconnected me to reality . . . you know, if you read it . . ."

"I did. What can I say?"

"No need to say anything, that's not why I—"

"Before, all I wanted was for you to stop lying. Now I'd give anything to think the things you wrote here were lies. Does anyone else know about this?"

"Nobody. Just you and Stjepan Hećimović."

"Who's Stjepan Hećimović?"

"A new friend. Long story. Actually a short story, but that's beside the point. I'm going to send it to the woman who's studying the case."

"Damn it, you have no idea how much I hated you when you sent me this. It was, like, what does he want now, after everything I've been through?"

"And now you feel differently?"

"I don't know. I still don't quite understand what this is. What we're doing, you and I, here after all this time, after all the shit."

"You saw my hell only from the outside, I didn't pull you in."

"Maybe you should have."

"Maybe I should have. But I didn't even know it was there. Look, to avoid confusion, let me say that I sent it to you because I wanted you to know. Even if knowing this makes no difference now. So you could finally hear what is perhaps the closest thing to the truth about me. And maybe you'll think a little better of me. Or worse—whatever. Simple."

"No, not simple. You know I shut that book a long time ago, and it wasn't easy for me to reopen it now, no matter what you thought. How long were we together? Was it really a year? How is that, for fuck's sake, even possible? How is it that something like that marks you forever? I needed to pull myself out of it . . ."

"Well, fine, that doesn't matter anymore."

"No, it does matter. You're here now because you're probably lost, because you don't know what else to do, so you're reaching for something you imagine still exists. And I can't do that, see?"

"I am lost here, but that is no different from any place I have been my whole life long. I've always been lost. With you, being lost was bearable."

"Oh, please. No, no. That's how it goes. There's no going back, Matija . . ."

"Okay. No way back."

"I'm . . ."

"Fine. I get it. I really do."

"Okay. Good. I'm glad we understand each other."

"Me too."

"Terrific. And what will you do now?"

"Don't ask things you don't want to know the answers to."

"But I want to hear."

"The only thing that people like me can do. Forget and wait and forget and wait. Damned scandalous in our times."

"Wait for what? Forget what?"

"Forget all those deaths. And everything that was forgotten, once and for all. And the new things that will be forgotten, you among them, you most of all. Because one thing is certain—what has been forgotten will come back of its own accord. There's no other way."

"If you say so. I know that look and your lively drivel. You jerk."

"You're Bleeding Heart, and I'm Jerk. But I am here absolutely of my own volition, not because I'm lost and being guided from some unknown place, like most of my life. And maybe you'll come back to me, too."

"Well, let's say that does happen. In and of itself, without my knowledge and without intervention. In a hundred years' time. What, in the meanwhile?"

"Not much, in the meanwhile. There's a river I need to visit. And a forest. And a few graves, one of them a child's. And many people dear to my heart. Do you think they've forgotten me?"

ABOUT THE AUTHOR

Photo © 2018 Mirko Cvjetko

Kristian Novak is a Croatian writer, linguist, and university professor. His novel *Dark Mother Earth* was awarded the Tportal Prize for Croatian Novel of the Year and was named one of the ten best Croatian novels in the last fifty years by *Večernji list*. The novel was successfully adapted for the stage, and a film adaptation is in the works. Novak is also the author of *The Hanged* and *Gypsy, Yet So Beautiful*, which was the recipient of the Gjalski Prize. *Dark Mother Earth* is his English-language debut.

ABOUT THE TRANSLATOR

Photo © 2005 Rahela Bursać

Ellen Elias-Bursac has been translating novels and nonfiction by Bosnian, Croatian, and Serbian writers for thirty years. She is the recipient of the 2006 ALTA National Translation Award, an American Association of Teachers of Slavic and East European Languages Award, and the Mary Zirin Prize for her book *Translating Evidence and Interpreting Testimony at a War Crimes Tribunal: Working in a Tug-of-War*. A contributing editor to the online literary journal *Asymptote*, Elias-Bursac spent more than six years at the ex-Yugoslav War Crimes Tribunal in The Hague as a translator/reviser in the English Translation Unit. Her translation of Daša Drndić's novel *Trieste* was short-listed for the Independent Foreign Fiction Prize in 2013.